NANO TRILOGY - II

ANCIENT WITCHOLOGY IN BATTLES

WAYNE E. CRISS

ISBN: 979-8-89216-036-0 (Paperback)
979-8-89216-037-7 (E-book)

Library of Congress Control Number: 2024918264

BookmarcAlliance
California, USA
www.bookmarcalliance.com

HOLLYWOOD BOOK REVIEWS
IN PARTNERSHIP WITH
BOOKMARC ALLIANCE

Nano Trilogy II
Ancient Witchology in Battles
by Wayne E. Criss

Nano Trilogy II

Ancient Witchology in Battles

by Wayne E. Criss

Author: Wayne E. Criss	**ISBN:** 979-8-89216-036-0
Genre: Science Fiction / Adventure	979-8-89216-037-7
Pages: 258	**Reviewed by:** Jack Chambers
Publisher: Bookmarc Alliance	

Nano Trilogy II

Ancient Witchology in Battles

Hollywood Book Reviews
EXCELLENT MERIT

by Wayne E. Criss

There has always been a fine line between science and the supernatural. While belief in the ancient practices of witchcraft and magic have slowed down considerably over the years, first in favor of religion and then in favor of the advancement of technology and scientific understanding, there are still those who believe in and practice the ancient rites and rituals of magical beliefs. Several cultures around the world have their own form of magic, and yet with the advancement of technology and the certainty that scientific theories and fiction such as nanotech will become a reality in the near future, there are some who are asking themselves if there can be a bridge between science and the supernatural after all.

In author Wayne E. Criss's *Nano Trilogy II: Ancient Witchology in Battles*, the four teen boys who began their crusade of vengeance against the industrialists and their nanotech killers who killed their fathers, begin to find the benefits of merging witchcraft and magic into their nanotech development. As the hunt for the Korrectorizer continues and the chaos that the villains group leaves in their wake around the world grows, the boys not only begin training and using witchcraft and trained animals in their fight, but build their own nanotech molecular systems to combat their enemy's tech as they seek to wage their brutal war across the globe.

One of the first things I really appreciated seeing in the author's extensive new mythos to his series was the inclusion of multiple cultures and belief systems in regards to magic and witchcraft. There are so many different trains of thought and ancient rites associated with different cultures that go far beyond the classic European witchcraft many know and love, and having that implemented into the narrative was great to see. The fusion of the supernatural with the science the author expertly wove into the fabric of this book was fantastically built. The way the author touches upon the fact that much of this sci-fi is not in actuality fiction, but a near future we are steadily heading towards, was mind-blowing and keeps the readers invested even more in the boy's battle against this nefarious group of killers. The rich dynamics these protagonists have amongst one another, from their shared mission and goals to the struggles to accept magic into their tech-heavy battles, and the shared grief they all have for their lost friends and family made the story really flow smoothly.

This is the perfect read for those who, as the author describes it, enjoy SAM books (science-adventure-mystery). The book also speaks to those who enjoy near sci-fi stories with supernatural elements, action, international and political intrigue, and suspense. The wealth of world-building the author fits into this novel and the fast-pace atmosphere the author is able to capture highlights the growing escalation the boys face in their fight and the adrenaline-fueled action which drives the reader deeper into this lore.

Thrilling, engaging, and mystifying, author Wayne E. Criss's *Nano Trilogy II: Ancient Witchology in Battles* is a must-read science, adventure and mystery novel that readers will not be able to put down. The twists in the narrative and the way the author makes both the supernatural and scientific elements of the growing world around these protagonists feel natural and alive on the pages will have readers hanging off the edge of their seats, eager to read the concluding chapter to this brand-new adventure series.

PACIFIC BOOK REVIEW
IN PARTNERSHIP WITH
BOOKMARC ALLIANCE

BOOK REVIEW

Nano Trilogy II
Ancient Witchology in Battles
by Wayne E. Criss

Nano Trilogy II

Ancient Witchology in Battles

by Wayne E. Criss

Author: Wayne E. Criss
Genre: Fiction / Mystery
Pages: 258
Publisher: Bookmarc Alliance

ISBN: 979-8-89216-036-0
979-8-89216-037-7

Reviewed by: Aaron Washington

Nano Trilogy II

Ancient Witchology in Battles

by Wayne E. Criss

Can witchcraft be a weapon? Do witches win physical wars? Black magic and voodooism have been existing since time immemorial. Not everyone believes in their influence, but the fact remains some people use it to their advantage. In *Nano Trilogy II Ancient Witchology in Battles*, the reader is entertained through a story whose main themes revolve around war, weapons of mass murders, brotherhood, and witchcraft.

The American Government Committee of Nanotechnology needs sharp minds, dedicated individuals and reliable manpower to operate. A call is made to recruit people from the International Witches Conclave in the hope that their input will help in the organization's mission. The musketeers, together with others, train with the different witch factions while on the other hand boys develop nanotech molecular systems to help in the fight. The boys use their intelligence in cyber hacking, trained wild animals, herbs and magic from the witches to fight their battles.

Nano Trilogy II Ancient Witchology in Battles is an out-of-this-world book. The author introduces a concept not many writers think of; witchcraft. Going to battle requires strength, intelligence, and weapons, but who even thinks of witchcraft? I like the inimitable method Wayne E. Criss took with the plot. The reader is enchanted throughout the book. You learn about the different forms of witchcraft in different parts of the world, and how similar some cultures are despite their visible differences. I enjoyed the entire plot, but my main favorite parts of the book are in the chapters that had stories about Gypsy witchcraft, Shamanism witchcraft, Irish witchcraft and the entire structure of voodooism.

While reading this book, it is interesting to note that just like how science is fascinating, witchcraft is intriguing too. It can be seen as a special science which has a major impact on humans across the world. Wayne E. Criss is an exceptional writer and storyteller as he never loses the reader - even when narrating about technical subjects. The plot gets to be more thrilling with each new development, and soon readers pick favorites. The boys were my favorite in the book, as their resilience and persistence got them to reach their targets - most of the time. I commend Wayne E. Ciss for being engaging, and giving his characters matchless traits. The characters of Chief Byianswa, Princess Luminitsa, Quetzalcoatl Totec Tlamacazqui, and Queen Cleopatra were well crafted. The musketeers were also wonderful, and in my opinion, among the most interesting characters.

I recommend *Nano Trilogy II Ancient Witchology in Battles* to readers that enjoy a good storyline. From the book, you get lessons on loyalty, the dark world, cyber wars, technology and war. No character in this book is bland. Everyone brings something different and the suspense from time to time - keeping you insatiable for more.

THIS BOOK IS NOT SCIENCE FICTION
IT IS SCIENCE NEAR REAL

This is a SAM novel
Science – Adventure – Mystery

A special thank you to Dr. Nur Bilge Criss, my wife and Professor of History and International Relations, who has been a leader by my side for many years. Her continuous flow and re-adjustment of ideas has allowed me to blend my scientific training and knowledge with social understanding. Just as our living world on this planet has become an amalgamation of science and humanities, we will continue to blend science and humanity into fascinating near real stories.

CONTENTS

PROLOGUE

Nearing midnight, the Voodoo Priest (Houn'gan/Hungan) sang and danced around the huge red blazing fire at the center of Table-Top Mountain just outside Cape Town, South Africa.

There was a large group of black Africans watching him cast a black spell on the person who had paid for and orchestrated the death of Kef's father and all members of his mining crew in the Saatfordam Diamond Mines a couple years ago. In front of the fire and the watchers was a small altar which had three vials on it. They separately contained a person's hair, fingernails/toenails, and one tooth. There was one lit black candle, and a white African doll with gray hair that had been placed on the altar. The air was filled with lightning and thunder. Drum beats grew louder and faster. Ritual words entered the air and traveled upward and outward. The Hungan was singing to the Voodoo Gods, Ogun/Storm and Guede/Death, in an ancient dialect of Zulu. He was asking these black gods to strike.

At midnight the drums, dancing, and singing suddenly stopped. The Hungan's assistant opened the three vials and placed the contents from each on top of the doll on the altar. The Hungan was now naked and sweating profusely. The pupils of his eyes were turned into his head. His assistant handed to him a red and black rooster. He placed the head of the rooster into his mouth, and bit it off, sprayed the rooster's blood all over the waiting family members, and threw the body of the rooster onto the fire. He picked up the doll, also bit off the head, and then threw the body of the doll into the fire. The Hunan opened his mouth to the gods and gave a sky piercing scream, his head turned and faced backwards, and he collapsed onto the soil. There he remained unconscious until sunrise.

The following evening at the Sun-Down Restaurant on Kaapstad Bay, four high school boys, African, Chinese, Turk, and American, were eating an octopus/squid/shrimp dinner, drinking Pepsi colas, and celebrating. The African boy was translating and reading loudly from the evening *Johannesburg Gazette* which was published in Swahili and Zulu.

"The front-page headlines are—Voodoo strikes Saatfordam family—"

It says, "Shortly after midnight last night Mr. Heinrich Saatfordam, Founder and President of the Saatfordam Diamond Mines, jumped/fell from the roof of his four-story mansion in Diamond Valley just outside of Johannesburg. He died instantly. He was found by his wife and family servants. His neck was broken, and he was bleeding from every orifice of his body. Family members said that at the time of his death the sky was filled with thunder and lighting, but there were no clouds."

"This is obviously the result of a very powerful shaman from somewhere, declared the police. Voodoo deaths like this have rarely been seen during the past few years in South Africa. A famous witchcraft professor at Johannesburg University, not to be named, declares that such an extreme mutilation has never been observed in South Africa, ever. Someone imported a super shaman."

The African boy looked at his buddies and said. "What do you think?"

The American boy broke in and looking at the reader burst out. "Wow! You were right. Witchcraft can be a very powerful weapon. I am surprised, shocked, and ready to learn more."

The Chinese boy added, "During the years I lived in China I used to read about witchcraft killings in many places in Southern Asia and northern China. What I remember is that the killings varied from region to region. So apparently each type of witchcraft, or shaman, has his own methods which bring his specific results."

The Turkish boy asked. "Do you think that this could be an effective strategy in our fight against these nanotech killers?"

The American boy responded, "We have been battling the Korrectorizer and his Committee of International Conservative Industrialists for the past five years. What have we accomplished? More than five hundred people have been killed, each in a macabre fashion. And that includes our fathers and friends. Previously working with the International Commission in Washington in an attempt to identify and eliminate this group has failed. This clandestine organization is now using even more sophisticated nanotechnology molecular systems to eliminate scientists and entrepreneurs of high technology. Everyone has run out of ideas. We should definitely consider different types of witchcraft as possible counter-attack weapons."

MAYBE IT WAS TIME TO STOP ATTACKING THE PAST USING THE FUTURE
AND IT WAS NOW TIME TO ATTACK THE FUTURE USING THE PAST.

MAJOR CHARACTERS

FOUR MUSKETEERS

Jamie O'Reilly [Ey'tuka] – Boston – American
Li Jiang [Tsu'tye] – Nanking/Los Angeles – Chinese
Kefentse Legoase [Na'via]–Cape Town—African
Aykut Turan [Mo'ata] – Istanbul-Turk

O'REILLY FAMILY

Jonathan O'Reilly–lawyer and president of Celtic Inc – Boston
Jackson O'Reilly – lawyer and vice president of Celtic Inc – Boston
Dagda Murphy – founder and president of ISAAT

LEADERS OF THE WITCHES

Ms. Banthnaid O'Keeffe – High Priestess of Irish Witchcraft and current President of the World Witches Conclave

Queen Cleopatra – Voodoo Queen of Africa and the Caribbean

Princess Luminitsa – 115-year old Princess Witch of European Gypsies

Priest Wu Xian – High Shaman or WU Master of Shamanism of China

Chief Byianswa – Chief Shaman of the native Indians of middle/north North America

Quetzalcoatl Totec Tlamacazqui – High Priest of the Aztecs and followers in Mexico, Central and South America

OTHERS

Dr. William Stronger – Chairman and Professor of the Department of Nanotechnology, MIT, Boston

Dr. Albert Langdon – nanotech scientist – London – ETT

Dr. Edward Kline – nanotech scientist – New York City – ETI

Dr. James Walters – nanotech scientist – Ottawa

Mr. Charles Somersham – businessman – London – ETI

Mr. Gregory McCorland – businessman – Edinburgh and London – ETI

Mr. Quaid Gang Hu (Tiger) – businessman – Hong Kong and Shanghai – ETI

Ali Abdel Aal – businessman – Cairo and Alexandria – ETI

Dr Frans Gunter – nanotech scientist – Munich

Dr. Mario Kemps – nanotech scientist – Buenos Aires

Mr. Fsustino Mariniti – billionaire businessman – Rome and Milan – ETI

Dr. Anneka Andersson – nanotech scientist – Stockholm – ETI

Mr. Jackson White – businessman – London – ETI

ETI – Equus Transport International

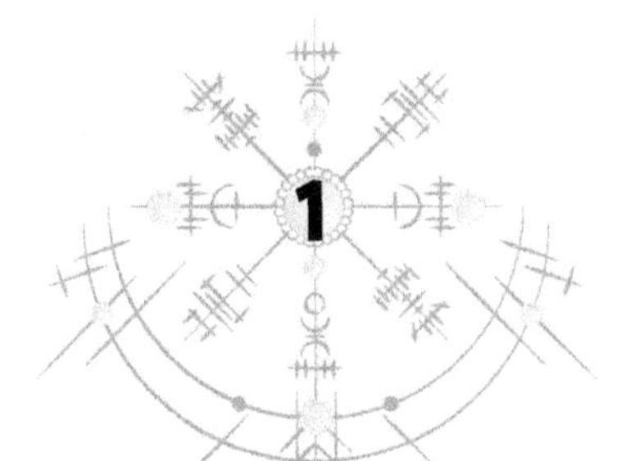

CAN WITCHCRAFT BE A WEAPON?

Witches, witchcraft, and magic have been in this world of hominoids since the beginning of social communications, when mankind was forced to live with other mankind. It is thought that witchcraft history began about 40,000 years ago, while high technology has only been here for the past one hundred years. Is it any wonder that witchcraft could defeat technology at any given point in time?

Witchcraft has evolved differently in various places on earth. But all "witches" continue to use many forms of highly developed mental and physical skills, connections to the past, and energy-controlled features. Modern day witchcraft is still very active in classical Europe, Central and East Asia, Christian Africa, Caribbean, North, Central, and South America.

And there are many names for the various forms of witchcraft such as magic, sorcery, black magic, occultism, necromancy, voodooism, shape shifter, hoodoo, illusionist, makutu, demonology, diablerie, shamanism, sortilege, spell casting, and hypnosis.

All witchcraft has a form of spiritual communications derived from the four elements of nature: fire, water, earth, and air. So obtained, this psychic energy provides control in a wide variety of ways to create white or black witchcraft.

Some of the practitioners of witchcraft function as a wiccan (group as in a religion); others perform a hedge witch (practice alone). Both have varying degrees of success. Most successes are for positive events. But the results can lead to negative events for targeted humans and has been so used throughout history.

Two months after the witchcraft 'demonstration' in South Africa, the Four Musketeers returned to their homes and initiated their own unique conference computer system, specially encrypted, using their own modified version of the Avatar language. In conference they always used their assigned Avatar names.

Ey'tuka (Jamie in Boston) entered the encrypted thirteen letter-number code and called up his buddies, "Ey'tuka is present. Who else is present?"

In response he heard:

"Tsu'teye (Li from Nanking) is present"

"Na'via (Kef from Cape Town) is present."

"Mo'ata (Aykut from Istanbul) is present."

Ey'tuka continued. "Thank you for responding so quickly. And we want to thank Na'via for showing us the power of the past. I was very impressed and I certainly think that we should explore this area as a possible weapon for counterattacking the nano-weapon killers."

"I agree," responded Mo'ata. "There are many types of this power as proven throughout history. We should at least explore what is possible today."

Tsu'teye added, "Yes. Not only is it a great idea, but it probably is an approach that Korrectorizer's Committee of World Conservative Industrialists would not think about."

"I was surprised by my mother's choice of shaman and the methods he used in his spell," replied Na'via. "But I did not begin to understand the power in such ancient rituals and magic languages. It would take us a lifetime to learn and successfully employ such skills in warfare. So? So!"

With an emotional voice, Mo'ata said, "They killed my father and my beautiful dog. I want revenge now, not in many years from now. I do not know of another super weapon system that is available today, except the nano-tech weapons, which we also do not know how to use. In the witch's spell that was used the shaman did not know the target, did not see the target, did not go near the target, yet the target was destroyed."

"It seems to me that witchcraft could be a more powerful weapon than the nano-tech weapons that we have been seeing," added Ey'tuka. "I know it has certain advantages over nanotechnology. Why? Because psychic components are part of the shaman's spells; and such are not part of nanotechnology. I bet that there are many advantages as well as limitations that we do not yet begin to understand. We need to learn a lot, and fast."

Ey'tuka continued, "I performed an online research about magic and magic users and what I understand is that there are many different types of magic today. Most can be used for good or bad. Apparently, the modern ideas of magic began few hundred years ago by the Celts who were Indo-Europeans. They were a very spiritual people and had many gods and goddesses. Druids were the priests who follow pantheism, which means one creative life source. They schematized nature into seasons and selected holy days based on the movement of the sun; and they believed in souls for all life forms and reincarnation of those souls. In fact, they consider magic, religion, and science as one complete associated existence. A person can observe life from any or all of these philosophical or psychological thought processes. So, there is much for us to learn to understand how magic might help us."

Mo'ata replied, "Then let us study about witches and witchcraft and learn the advantages versus the disadvantages of different types of magic."

"Mo'ata is right," said Ey'tuka. "If everyone is in agreement, let us each choose a witchcraft and learn about its type of magic. And then we can again talk about using it. Is everyone in agreement?"

And the response was a calm yes from each boy growing to a man. When they began this 'war' five years ago it was sort of a challenging and fun thing to do. But now each had lost his father, family members, and friends through very macabre killings. Besides, they might just be on a 'to kill' list of their 'enemy'. Their world had rapidly changed. It had become a scary place to live. But they would not be intimidated. And indeed, vengeance was an element in the forefront of their minds. The real question is how do a bunch of boys challenge a world wide organization which has almost unlimited access to scientific knowledge and monetary support.

Tsu'tey spoke up, **"Remember the words of Sun Tzu in his 'Art of War':**

-If you know the enemy and know yourself,
You need not fear the result of 100 battles;
-If you know yourself but not the enemy,
For every victory gained there will be one defeat;
-If you neither know the enemy nor yourself,
You will lose every battle."

"During these past six years we neither knew the enemy nor ourselves. And yes, we lost all battles 6 deaths in 2028, 6 deaths in 2029, 24 deaths in 2030, 24 deaths in 2031, 350 deaths in 2032, and 5 deaths in 2033."

"I got these numbers from my Uncle Dadga," said Ey'tuka. "And yes. I think that we did not know our enemy. And I know we did not know ourselves. We lost every battle. We must immediately change our approach and start winning some battles. Now, at least, we have some ideas about nanotechnical molecular weapon systems."

"Recently, Uncle sent to me a current list of suspects who may be producing or using these systems in causing international homicides. How did he obtain this?"

"The US government has created a new Division of High Technology. Within this division there is a standing Committee of Nanotechnology Control. My Uncle's company was again awarded the contract to form the vanguard to fight these specific killers. So, we will continue to have access to the American government's intelligence apparatus in the nanotechnology field."

"Therefore, if you want to continue to fight Korrectorizer and his Conservatives, I do. We at least now partially know and will continue to learn about the enemy. And we can also continue to learn directly from my Uncle's ISAAT as his people pursue our common enemy."

Tsu'teye commented, "I like those ideas very much. This is our last year in high school before we have to get serious about choosing a university and a profession. So, we have only two summers that we can devote to learning witchcraft and black spells. Let us each read, study, and choose a type of witchcraft, identify a shaman and learn from him. And see what happens. I will look in China, Japan, and Southeast Asia."

Na'via said, "I will do the same in Africa and with black magic in the Caribbean area."

"I have always wanted to learn about the Romanian gypsies and their lifestyle," Mo'ata responded. "We have a large colony here in Istanbul in the Belgrade Forest out near the Black Sea."

And Ey'tuka added, "I have visited my family in Ireland three times. One time I even met a real Celtic witch. And I know my Irish Aunts would love to teach me about Celtic gods and goddesses."

"Are we all in agreement to pursue a new line of attack on our fathers' killers?"

There were four yeah! There were zero nays!

"We will call it the new witchology. And I will also find out about the annual meeting of the World Witches Enclave and ask for their help," finished Ey'tuka. "I spoke to my Uncle Dagda about what witches could do and what they could not do. He told me they help their people in need. And yes, they can do things that normal people cannot do. So-lets-go—

2

THE REAL FIRST TEAM I

FIVE GENTLEMEN WERE SITTING in a large office on the twelfth floor of the O'Reilly Building on Plymouth Avenue in downtown Boston. The building housed the law firm of O'Reilly, O'Reilly, O'Reilly and Associates and the O'Reilly family's Fortune 500 firm of CELT IMPORT/EXPORT. Each was reclining in a comfortable arm chair in the conversation corner of the huge redwood paneled office. Their coffee cups were empty as they had been in a deep discussion of what was becoming a major world-wide problem. Suddenly they became engrossed in new information on just that problem. They were watching Russian television channel SS3 in English.

'Yesterday, Dr, Boris Kukryniskyk, President and CEO of Russian Chip International-Moscow Technology, was found dead, at home, and in his own bed. He had died of internal bleeding, but there were no puncture wounds on the body. This morning we obtained a copy of the autopsy report. It said that he had no blood vessels coming from his heart and his major arteries were missing. They had apparently dissolved. His chest, abdominal cavities, and his neck were filled with blood. How could such a thing happen? We talked with an American surgeon, Dr. James Decater, from the Karjinsky Medical School and Hospital Center, who declared that it had to be another nano-tech assassination...

A major investigation into the reasons and cause of the macabre death of this famous Russian Scientist, who received the Nobel Prize in Physics seven years ago, will certainly be carried out by Russian and international health authorities. This is the fifth such macabre death this year, each at a different place in the world. It is becoming obvious that no top high-tech scientist is immune...

Mr. Johathan O'Reilly was the oldest brother of three fraternal triplets, average size, thick dark hair, brown eyes but light skin, beginning to gray a little, in his late fifties, just retired from eight years in the Oval Office in Washington, DC. He was sitting in his favorite leather arm chair, first looking out the window down to the Charles River, then turning to look around the room. He gave the other four men a heavy frown, the ex-President said, "And all of this happened on my watch. What did I do or not do to allow this new world-wide disease to start and get out of control?"

His brother Jackson, ex-US Attorney General, looking very much like his brother, said, "Do not blame yourself. All of us in this room were involved. Today we know many things that we did not know then."

This was to be more than a friendly get together among friends. It was a time to try to resolve a problem which grew out of their recent past inadequate efforts.

And he looked at Dr. William Stronger.

Chairman and Professor of the Department of Nanotechnology at the Massachusetts Institute of Technology, Boston, middle aged African American with light skin and dark green eyes, walked with a limp, courtesy of the American military, and life-long close friend, answered, "There is no doubt in my mind that this is a new molecular version which illustrates the growing sophistication of these nanotech molecular weapon systems."

And he looked over to Dagda.

Brother of the O'Reilly's mother and therefore uncle to the two O'Reilly brothers in the room, grand uncle of Jamie, having lived the past 5-6 years heading the American legal investigative efforts to combat this nanotechnology, Mr. Dagda Murphy commented, "Yes.

Looking back to the death of Theodore O'Reilly, Jamie's father, 6 years ago, today there are indeed new and more sophisticated nanotech molecular systems. There are obviously now several clandestine scientists around the world who are researching weapons applications. They remind me of the armorers of ancient times:

'Get Your Weapons Here – Not for Hunting—Only for Killing'."

Mr. Dagda Murphy was big, bald, with wrinkled forehead, brown eyes, long arms and broad shoulders, and still maintained his military commando body. Over the years he had established and built the famous international security company, ISAAT (International Security Assistance and Anti-Terrorist Corporation). This Irish-American Corp. led the past five-year battle in an attempt to identify the sources and the uses of nanotech weapons around the world, both for cures and deaths. He was now also leading the new current battle through the American government's new Division of High Technology, standing Committee on Nanotechnology Control.

Mr. Murphy spoke up, "Over the years we have seen a continuous increase in the sophistication of nanotechnology systems used by the international conservative industrialists as they attempt to kill off internationally famous scientists and entrepreneurs of high technology. Several years ago, it began with simple stoppages of the functioning of the heart, throat, areas of the brain, eyes, and lungs. And then it progressed to digesting/dissolving the membranes of internal organs such as intestine, stomach, and liver. Next they used nano-systems which digested lungs, bones, and even brains. So, I am not surprised that they can now target specific blood vessels anywhere in the body."

"Dr. Stronger, can you explain how this rapid increase in sophistication occurred?" Asked the past President.

In response Dr. Stronger replied, "I will ask my associate, Dr. Timothy Greason, to help me for a more complete answer."

{Dr. Greason is Dr. Stronger's right arm in the high nanotech research laboratory at MIT. Dr. Greason was recently awarded the prestigious Watson-Crick Award as he was chosen for his research discoveries using gene control of MoAB (monoclonal-antibodies) to develop nano-tech system targeting methodology. This allows the biological active portion of the nanotech molecule to have a homing capacity to hit any cell, tissue, or organ in the body.}

"It is the common role of the scientific advancement," Dr. Greason replied. "Introduce a unique idea into the scientific community. If it is a great idea, excellent scientists will grab on to it and immediately develop, cultivate, expand, and profit from its potential—for curing and/or for killing. And yes, possibly there will be a 'mis-use' of that potential. Big money supporters can also speed the developmental processes in their direction."

"Let me read from my current summary thinking about this Nanotech System which is simply a group of molecules designed to target selected vital tissues or organs in the body and effect their activity in a plus or minus way. You will see the progression sequence."

1) "One molecule – one active nanotech molecule for one target organ in one person—injected into the spinal cord, travels up into the brain, binds to a specific area of the brain that controls a vital organ, and turns it off (e.g. heart, lungs, throat, kidneys,...)
2) Two molecules – one active nanotech molecule plus a MoAb molecule (homing component) for a small group/family of people—enters the body via the lungs or blood, not body digested, binds to and acts directly on one body organ target, and turns it off...
3) Several molecules bound together – one active nanotech molecule, a MoAb molecule, digestion blocker molecule, delayed action molecule, etc. for a large group of people—enters the body via the stomach or blood, binds to and acts directly on one body organ target, and turns it off...PLUS

"All nanotech systems are self-destructive and disappear after action!"

Mr. Jackson O'Reilly, recent past Attorney General as well as recent past Chairman of the Presidential Commission to investigate the nanotechnology associated with MUSD (Medical Unexplainable Sudden Deaths), asked, "Will this progress continue and how?"

Mr. Murphy quickly jumped in, "And please, could you give your opinion concerning the possible international distribution of these nano-systems? I assume that they are produced at more than one location and dispersed to other locations for use as a killing agent; especially if these weapons contain more than one component."

Dr. Stronger responded. "If you will remember from the massacre, several years ago, at the Ciragan Palace in Istanbul, the investigation of those killings identified 'something' in the frosting on the cake eaten by more than 300 participants of the conference. Remember the deaths were caused by the dissolving/digestion of body bones. At that time Dagda sent an uneaten piece of this cake to our laboratories at MIT. Dr. Greason's research team analyzed it. They found a nanotech system present, extracted it, analyzed the atomic and molecular structure, and determined that it contained four linked individual molecules. We now understand how this system works and can duplicate similar ones. We are currently trying to design and produce a nanotech blocker for all such systems."

"And to answer your distribution question. That is a simple capitalistic phenomenon. You need a Nanotech System Hit Team composed of:

1) Nanotech and MoAb scientists—design and create a nanotech (weapon) system for a select body organ and the total number of people targets,
2) Laboratory Technician – mass produce nanotech system for curing or killing,
3) Distributor – buys/markets/delivers nanotech system to selected user/assassin,
4) Decision-Maker – selects or determines the human and body organ targets and arranges for the assassin,
5) Assassin – individuals who introduce nanotech system into the body of human target"

"Why do I use assassin and not killer? In my opinion this is a very expensive-sophisticated system, not a high school kid suddenly obtaining a gun to kill off his classmates."

Mr. Murphy let out a loud moan. "Is that all?"

Everyone was quiet for a couple of minutes. Heavy thoughts circulated through five well educated, intellectual heads. But no one could manage a question or even provide a potential direction to travel.

"And to answer the earlier question of Mr. O'Reilly," said Dr. Stronger. "Yes. The multi-component nanotech systems present many additional problems. The various components could be constructed in different laboratories, transported to various other laboratories for assembly, and then transported again, or perhaps even designed for a final last-minute re-assembly at the killing location. So, there is no 'weapon' until the last minute. You cannot be arrested, charged, or convicted of pre-meditated murder if you are carrying unassembled gun parts or an empty gun."

"Today, outsourcing in product manufacturing is common. Some American automobiles have as much as 80-90% of their component parts made outside of the USA. The assembly plants may be in the USA. I suspect that 'manufacturing nanotechnology' with these more sophisticated nano-weapons will also be using this concept. It certainly makes identification of nano-system 'manufacturers' very difficult to accomplish and almost impossible to stop. Can you imagine a four or five-component nanotech weapon, each component produced in a different country, and the final target for the weapon is in yet another country? The final human target could be anywhere."

"Impossible to stop? No! Yes? Ideas!"

"There are certain chemicals and biologicals which are necessary to manufacture all nanotechnical systems and similar molecules. These can be identified and purchasing of such atoms and molecules can be internationally monitored, and quantities of purchase and shipping/transit can be recorded. Suspect laboratories can be 'listed' and regularly checked for 'manufactured' nanotech systems, for cure or kill. A Mono-Tech-List of laboratories can be established. And most of the select professional correspondence, financial accounts, and life styles of the scientists and associates in these laboratories can be continuously monitored. But it will require solid international political cooperation. And that will probably be very difficult."

"And one last comment. Sophistication? A couple hundred years ago in the American Wild West 'cowboys' carried a 'six-shooter', made by one person and which killed with one piece of lead, smoking gun. Today, only a super educated/trained/skilled person can produce a killing weapon made of 2-3 molecules that can be used to selectively hit an intra-body tissue/organ and activate/inhibit-cure/kill that targeted person and then disappear—no smoking gun.—Sophistication!

Ex-Mr. President spoke up, "Remember near the end of my second term we hurried to pass several laws to allow high technology products, especially nanotechnology products, to be considered in the same legal vein as terrorist weapon systems, or at least as dangerous as toxic chemicals, powerful drugs, and radioactive materials. These new laws allowed for the monitoring and regulation of certain precursors and products of nanotech systems. The laws required that all of these 'regulated' substances be recorded and sent to a specific government authority."

"As of now we are one of very few countries that has passed and implemented such legal efforts. Most countries, including both high and low technology countries, have not confronted this growing problem. They simply believe that their people are not involved in such sciences or activities. However, we have solid data which spells 'otherwise'.

"From Mr. Murphy I know that the Committee of Nanotechnology Control has had excellent success in focusing on the personal lifestyle and families of potential manufacturers of nanotech molecular systems. Monitoring the professional activities, American and international bank accounts, annual scientific and IRS reports, investments, international travels, both professional and personal friends, general lifestyle, and specific expenses such extra financial burdens of children's higher education or older parent's medical bills, have all helped to identify possible 'suspects', at least for the scientist nanotech designer. Others?"

"If you will allow" said Mr. Murphy. "I have a previous list of 'suspects' or 'candidates' with me. Let me bring you up to date."

"Three years ago, we had seven top candidates that we thought were involved in the macabre deaths related to nanotechnology. Examples: Dr. Kukrynisky-Moscow, Dr. Gunter-Munich, Dr. Kemps-Buenos Aires, Dr. Walters-Ottawa, Dr. Langdon-London, Dr. Andersson-Stockholm, Mr. Mariniti-Rome, and the three Chinese brothers, Drs. Jung, Cho, and Chi Jiang from Berlin, Nanking, and Los Angeles, respectively. All three Chinese brothers are dead. And you just heard this morning that Dr. Kukrynisky is dead. Not one of these doctors was under arrest or being charged with any type of illegal nanotech activities. Our executive and judicial powers did not prove adequate. Today, these latter four men are no longer in the world. They are dead. But that is not our 'fault'. We did not 'catch and punish'."

"Our investigation of Dr. Gunter, Dr. Kemps, and Dr. Walters is ongoing; all new evidence shows more and more their positive involvement. Dr. Kemps was investigated, but lack of cooperation by Argentina authorities has kept our data collection small."

"So, we have five nanotech scientists who have manufacturing capacities who are being continuously monitored, and if adequate funding is allowed, we will add seven more such candidates. Please notice. Our candidates are all scientists, and one businessman. We do not have any distributors, decision-makers, or assassins on our list."

Ex-Mr. President frowned, "Thank you very much everyone. I wish to meet as a small group of five 'interested citizens of nanotechnology' every few months, We can meet here in my office on a Friday afternoon. All of us routinely work here in Boston, so this makes for a reasonably 'nice' late afternoon Boston tea party. Does this work for everyone?"

All were in agreement. But there appeared to be a couple more questions before they could leave.

Mr. Murphy spoke up, "What about Jamie and his Four Musketeers? How can they play a role in these overall efforts? Or should they? They are still children. What do you think the risk would be?"

"Remember, in the proximate past they contributed to the understanding of this nanotech problem more than the entire American government!" responded Ex-Mr. President.

"And they even provided us with the first sample of a nanotech killer system from Istanbul that caused more than 300 very macabre deaths."

"In my humble opinion, each of these four children lost their father. They are very mature young men who have revenge in their minds. You will not be able to stop them from their pursuits. So, turn them loose. Stay in touch with them. Help them where they need help. And they will give you bread for your seeds."

And Mr. Murphy had another question. "What is your opinion about this sudden killing of Dr. Kukrynisky. Why now? Is it possible that he might have been a member of Korrectorizer's Committee of World Conservative Industrialists; and that there was a split in the decision making for the next one or more nanotech targets?"

Ex-Mr. President responded, "I thought the same thing as I listened to the television a while ago. It certainly was an unnecessary mode of killing, unless HE (Korrectorizer) wanted to show just who was the Boss. Or do you think that there are several involved in making those decisions, and Dr. Kukrynisky lost the vote?"

Mr. Murphy countered, "All of our collected data and information sources say that there is only one Korrectorizer and a committee of approximately nine or ten people, each using pseudo-names and representing certain international groups such as petrochemicals, steel, metals, chemistries, hoofed-meats industries, fertilizer/pesticide based agriculture crops, silicon based chips, cyber security systems, transportation, and the international gold consortium. Most of these industrial and commercial groups are in danger of immediate, financially difficult changes because of high technology, so they are highly motivated in supporting the status quo attitude."

"And with that level of potential financial backing, many laboratories could be supported which would perform nanotechnological research, for curing or killing," Dr. Stronger added.

"If someone approached me, offered me a few billion dollars to design and construct a certain type of nanotech system, for curing or killing, it would require some hard thinking to say no, no, no."

"Are our military weapons manufacturers considered guilty of mass murder in the numerous wars that our country has been involved with every decade of the past century? The American people do not even think about them and guilt. In fact, they are our protectors."

"Is this really so different??????"

"Most scientists are ethically very sound. But, I have to assume that there are some who would cross-over, perhaps for some large monetary number, and CHEAT."

Ex-Mr. President, grinning said "Are you saying that capitalists have no ethics? Be careful. I am now just a business man."

And they all exchanged a round of smiles. Most people have a price, or do they?

Mr. Murphy spoke up, "I know you all have other duties today but I want to leave you with one last problem to think about. There are rumors that there is a nanotech corporation being organized in London which will soon mass market all types of nanotechnology systems, for any purpose. No screening of clients. You only need money to obtain any standard or custom designed nanotech molecular system. We need to watch for such corporations and attempt to interrupt their 'business'.

3

IRISH MYTHOLOGY AND IRISH GODS

During the second week in June, Uncle Dagda Murphy and Jamie O'Reilly flew together to Ireland to visit their Irish family. Jamie had been there only twice, and not since his father was 'assassinated' when he was the American Czar of High Technology, six years ago. Uncle Dagda's sister, Katelyn Murphy, who married Grandpa Braden O'Reilly, was Jamie's grandmother. She had died before Jamie was born. But there were more than one hundred Murphys and O'Reillys; and all were somehow blood related in the Lough Ree area of Ireland. This was about one hundred kilometers directly west of Dublin on M4-M6. Jamie and Uncle Dagda were going to stay with Dagda's oldest son, Riley Murphy. Cousin Riley was semi-retired from the Oglaigh nah Eireann (Irish Defense Forces) and now was a first Lieutenant in the Cultaca an Airm (Reserve Defense Forces). He had won numerous military honors so had no difficulty being assigned in his home neighborhood. And Uncle Dagda thought it might be good for Jamie to spend some time with his son, as well as to have a military trained family member hanging around Jamie during his Irish sojourn.

As Uncle Dagda and Jamie walked through the Dublin International Airport, Uncle Dagda said. "Keep your eye open for Riley. He is a little bigger than me, looks like me, acts like me, has some hair, greying but still there. I tell him that he is trying to catch up with me as we are both developing that popular Irish monkish clear-top-of-the-head-look. We know the girls like that."

And he laughed as Jamie thought he was serious. So, Jamie started looking around very carefully. He knew Uncle Dagda had difficulty seeing distances. That he would not wear his glasses because every time he sat down to read, he took them off, lay them somewhere, and then would have difficulty finding them later. This would 'piss him off'. And he knew many good ol' Irish bad words. It was almost fun to listen to him rant and rave. Then if he happened to accidently bump into a pretty girl, he had an automatic excuse. A seventy-year old going on thirty—but no longer a serious stallion.

Suddenly Jamie spotted a guy waiting and looking at them. He seemed to be close to seven feet and must have been near 300 pounds, sort of looked like Uncle Dagda, and indeed had a one-half monkish hair style; bushy on the sides but bald on the peak. He did resemble a big branch on the Irish tree walking beside him. This guy would make a very big security component to watch over Jamie during the next few days while he was away from of his secure Boston home. Uncle Dagda would be leaving him there for a few days while he went to meet some contacts in Copenhagen.

Jamie's father was one of the first ones 'assassinated' with a nanotech killing system about six years ago. Soon afterward the older man/young boy had developed a father/son relationship, in addition to their partnership efforts in seeking the nanotech killers. Uncle Dagda was born and raised in central Ireland, but had spent the past thirty years with British M16, INTERPOL, and the American CIA. So, he knew both the North American and European security systems rather well.

Fifteen years ago, his brother in law, Jamie's grandfather, asked him to establish a private International Assistance and Anti-Terrorist Corporation (ISAAT), and gave him the first of several contracts to protect against and seek to eliminate certain international criminal organizations. The O'Reilly family owned a Fortune 500 international import-export company called CELT, Inc. And these days international shipping required more than a simple New York City security company. Therefore, this experience, plus the fact that his nephew was the US President, Jonathan O'Reilly, put him in a position to lead a worldwide effort to seek and eliminate perpetrators of the more than five hundred nanotech homicides during the past six years. Although they were not having much success.

So, Dagda had not resided in Ireland for many years. He only visited during select holidays. His oldest son, Riley, had never left Ireland. However, family and Irish solidarity remained snuggly intact. During Riley's military and police career he had been assigned to several of the dozen military bases in Ireland. So, he understood Irish security problems very well. Dagda told Riley about the not very successful worldwide nanotech homicide investigative efforts. Then he explained that Jamie now wanted to consider Irish witchcraft as a means of including it into these research efforts. It was determined to be a good idea. Riley agreed to take time off from work and would help in any way possible.

The two Irish giants, father and son, met in the airport corridor, shouted Dia is Muire duit/Hello, and laughed, hugged, slapped each other on the back, then turned to looked back at Jamie. Jamie was seventeen, well under six foot, dark brown/black hair and turquois-blue eyes inherited directly from his father. His 175 pounds weight did make him feel small next to these two genetic *brothers*. Maybe he would catch up with them, but he remembered that the Murphys were all big outdoor types. So!? He knew that it would be good to have some physical size around him; he and his three buddies might just be on the Conservatives 'hit list'. He did have one less finger on his left hand from his previous experience with these 'people'. And it would be a fascinating adventure. He was still a little afraid of the unknown. But he accepted the Irish greeting of Dia is Mire duit, laughing, hugging, slapping on the back, and became a true Irish brother.

And they headed outside to the parking lot toward the car. Cousin Riley and Uncle Dagda lead the way and began chatting in Gaelic and Jamie felt very lost. But once they were in the car and driving down M4 his curiosity began to take over.

"Uncle Riley," Jamie asked. "Where are your daughters and how are they doing? My mother told me to ask you."

"Aoife and Cliona are both married and have children, replied Uncle Riley. "And tell your mother that I now have three grandsons and one granddaughter. And your Uncle Dagda has three great grandsons and one great granddaughter."

All Jamie could say was, "WOW!" He was not exactly sure what the difference was between a grand-this and a great grand-that, but he would try to remember to tell his mom.

Riley's wife had died several years ago from kidney cancer and he never remarried. He lived alone in a small house near the military base at Longford.

And big son gave big dad a big smile. Dad returned the smile with a solid punch to the left shoulder which made the son almost drive off the road. The two of them just broke down laughing. Jamie only grimaced.

Once Jamie was sure the car was back on the road and under control he again spoke up. "Are you really going to take off from work and help me while I learn about Irish mythology and witchcraft? From my readings I understand that it will take me ten to fifteen years of hard studying to become a real witch." And he chuckled.

Riley smiled and responded, "I sort have a general plan. During these past few years, I have been the Commander of the Reserve Defense Forces camp near Langford. While there I have been involved with several legal problems involving witches in the area. There is a large and quite powerful coven nearby. A coven is a school which trains and teaches how to become a witch. In Ireland, witchcraft is a profession. There are many schools with highly trained witches teaching in the old languages and the old knowledge about the rites and rituals of Irish witchcraft. They then become a professional witch, provide appropriate services, charge fees, and pay taxes. They are something like the American personal primary doctors. Witch and 'patient' frequently become friends for life. You will learn all about this soon. I have picked a witch for you." And he laughed.

After a few minutes of driving Riley continued. "During my work with the witches and students at this coven, I helped them with their security and legal problems. I developed a close relationship with the High Priestess of the Coven of Morrigan. Her name is Banthnaid O'Keefe. Her coven is in the County of Roscommon. This region is where the legendary homes of Queen Madbh (Macbeth) and the Goddess Morrigan are mythologically found. The Priestess is a lovely lady. I have already briefed her about your problem and your ideas about using witchcraft as one possible solution. She found your ideas very interesting and is willing to spend a couple of days with you, teaching Irish mythology and witchcraft. What you do with this new knowledge you can decide for yourself later.

All Jamie could say was, "Super. That really is super! I want to learn all of that and more. I will be a good student and not disappoint you. She is your friend. Maybe she can become my friend. When can we see her?"

"She will see us tomorrow morning at 10:00 at her house in the glade. Uncle Dagda and I will join you so we can learn also. I am looking forward to seeing her again. She has a very different way of viewing and talking about life processes. You will learn this also, I think."

Uncle Dagda spoke up, "So now relax, lay back, enjoy the emerald green of Ireland, and I will briefly remind you of the history of Ireland such that you will better understand the Irish mythology lesson tomorrow."

"The first human settlements began on the island, now called Ireland, over 10,000 years ago. And it has been inhabited ever since. Near the fifth century BCE, Christianity arrived via the Christian monk, St. Patrick. For the next five hundred years the Pagan Irish and the Christian Irish were in constant friction. At the same time the immigration of one of the many pagan Celtic tribes from the mainland to the British Isles began. During those times, often the way of life of a feudal society depended upon the religious state of the current king of that particular region. As with Rome, when the emperor or King accepted Jesus, so did the people. This process is called 'Cuius regio, eius religio' in Ecclesiastical Latin. In the early ninth century the Viking raids began which led to external trade and foreign contacts, but also a decline in Christianity, replaced by Paganism."

"However, in the twelfth century the Catholic Norman/French invaded, which caused the Angles to begin to pay more attention to the neighboring island. Numerous mini-treaties between Normans, English, and the many little Irish Kings resulted in several years of killings and turmoil. Eventually, in 1261, Fineen MacCarthy defeated a strong Norman army at the Battle of Callan. This was the beginning of the attempts of the Irish to win back their occupied land. By the end of the fifteenth century, the central authority of the Normans and the English was all but gone."

"Unfortunately, just as the more modern era of Ireland began in the late sixteenth century, the current rulers of Ireland, the Fitzgeralds of Kildare, became unfriendly toward the English Tudor monarchs. Henry VIII, upgraded Ireland to a kingship, appointed himself King of England and Ireland, invaded Ireland, and by the mid sixteenth century England controlled most of the Irish land mass. Both Irish and French Catholics lost lands and titles; Irish and English Protestants gained lands and titles. After a failed Irish rebellion in 1789, the United Kingdom of Britain and Ireland was formed and the two parliaments were joined."

"So much for the long and bloody history of the Irish people. Now let Riley tell you about the Celtic people," Uncle Dagda finished up. He then looked over his shoulder at Jamie, who just nodded and smiled. He was eagerly swallowing everything.

Riley began, "The Celts were a group of people who occupied much of western Europe for more than a thousand years. They occupied the land from Italy to England. There were numerous tribes. In the early years of the Roman Empire, they defeated the Roman armies several times, and even captured Rome itself. They were basically called barbarians by the Romans, Greeks, and English. Scattered over several thousand miles, their major unification was in speaking one of six Celtic languages. The Celts, who migrated to the British Isles, spoke q-Celts or Giodelic and p-Celts or Brythronic. Giodelic developed into three forms of Gaelic languages spoken in Ireland-Gaeilge, Isle of Man-Gailck, and Scotland-Gaidhlig; Brythronic developed into two forms, Welsh and Cornish. It is my understanding today Irish Witches use Gaeilge and other old Celtic phrases for their incantations, divining, and enhancements. We can ask Banthnaid."

"So, the Irish, Welsh, and Scottish people all have a significant amount of Celtic blood and cultural extensions within their societies today. This may be why they are not routinely included in the historical lists of Angles and Saxons" Riley finished up.

Uncle Dagda again looked back at Jamie who was still fully awake and still drinking every word. They exchanged the father-son look. "I think we have filled your mind with enough information for now. Why don't you take a nap so the jet lag will not interfere with your learning of tomorrow."

Jamie closed his eyes, and before he knew it, he was unconscious and would not regain full consciousness for at least a month. He frequently remembered lying in a bedroom in Riley's house, but his eyes were always open onto a new strange outdoor world. His mind dreamed that all was good but not under his control. And his body was continuously sweating. It seemed that he was learning a new life system.

By the time the sun was half awake, Jamie was 'fully' awake. He had already spent two hours with his I-pad on-line reading more about Ireland and its witches. He was more than ready to go when the two jolly green giants, as he now thought of them, called him down to breakfast. For the next few days, he only had partial memories; he blamed this on jet lag, not on mind overload.

He remembered riding in the back seat of a red Fiat through a rather wild natural environment composed of much green/brown vegetations and many small hills and valleys and streams and big rocks. He did see a sign that said Roscommon. They pulled into a single lane rock road which led into a large dense forest. About ten minutes later they parked the car, got out, and walked for another ten minutes, arrived at a small well-kept village-like house with thatched roof. The cottage was white with green shutters; all shutters and windows were open and a middle-aged lady was standing at the front door waiting for them. She said nothing and handed a large thermos jug containing hot water to Dagda, a basket of food to Riley, and two blankets to Jamie. She picked up a jug of fresh spring water, then turned and entered the forest. They followed her.

They walked for more than fifteen minutes through thick green foliage composed of green shrubs and trees on an unmarked trail. Without her they certainly would have become lost. Suddenly they reached a small circular clearing surrounded by a perfect circle of twelve giant hawthorn trees, plus ancient boxwood and pyracantha bushes. It was as if they suddenly had a 100-foot high wall around them which was composed of trees and impenetrable thorns. She motioned for them to 'enter', and for Jamie to spread the blankets. She then sat upright and cross-legged on one blanket, motioned for Jamie to sit beside her, and then implied that the two men sit the same way on the other blanket. They all faced each other.

The weather was autumn mild even though it was mid-July. Continuous breezes made the semi-enclosure sleepy comfortable.

Finally, the High Priestess of Irish Witchcraft spoke, "We are here to attempt to become one with the universal giver of all life, Mother

Earth. All life comes from her. All life returns to her. We will first drink a cup of tea. Riley would you please serve us?"

Riley opened the food basket and took out four large coffee sized cups. Dagda poured hot water into each cup. The Priestess then added three different intact leaves to each cup and stirred. Riley gave a cup of tea to each of them. For the next fifteen minutes they slowly drank their fresh tea, looked around at the pristine nature created by several thousand years of life untouched by humankind, and said nothing.

The Priestess spoke again, "I welcome you to my home. I understand that you want to learn about our way of life, and maybe use our knowledge to do some good in the world. I totally agree with this. Let us begin."

"The tea will help you open your mind to your natural ancestors and the Otherworld. Please close your eyes and listen, feel, hear, reach to your surroundings, open your mouth and with your tongue taste the air. Hear these one-thousand-year old Hawthorn trees speak. They have seen much and have much to say. Listen to the birds and insects, they have a history millions of years older than ours—learn from them. Smell the numerous odors from the natural flowers that many people call weeds, from the nearby planted domestic harvest fields, and from the surrounding natural flowering trees and shrubs. If you concentrate you can feel Mother Nature giving up her summer harvest and preparing for another night as we are half-way between the Summer Solstice and the Autumn Equinox. It is time of plenty, feasting, of largesse. It is the time of the abundance of critical life needs—food."

She continued to talk in a quiet monotone voice, switching from English to old Irish to Gaeilge for the next hour. None of the males opened their eyes—Sleep—Trance—Semi-consciousness??? And not one of them would remember his thoughts during the most tranquil hour that they would ever have in their lives.

As noon time approached, the entire forest had become silent, no breezes, no noises, no smells, no movement. The Priestess seemed to have enchanted all forest life. Then she gently brought each human to a state of aware consciousness using a few select words of old Gaeilge. She rinsed out the cups, filled them with the cold spring water, gave one to each of the gentlemen, and watched as they each greedily drank it down. Somehow, they were very thirsty. She next opened the food basket and started serving lunch. She placed on three plates only uncooked foods—carrots, broccoli, cauliflower, small tomatoes, cucumbers, cheeses, and fresh bread. She also served to her new pupils a large glass of her home-made blueberry wine. There seemed to be nothing to say. Each male took the offered plate and slowly ate his lunch. Though not hungry, they somehow knew they were expected to eat. Then, one by one, they stood up, stretched, walked around for a few minutes, slowly entered the woods, found a tree, and did one of their natural things. Each actually felt very refreshed and really in super control of his life. Upon some unknown signal they returned to their seating positions such that the lessons could continue. They each wanted more.

The Priestess did not eat lunch; but she intently watched the males. "I will briefly review the Irish mythology and Irish gods. Tomorrow, Jamie and I, alone, will discuss Irish witchcraft."

So, the rules were laid down—today would be a review or lecture for all—tomorrow would be a special learning experience for Jamie only. And she began lesson number two.

"There are several Irish gods. I will only talk about a few of them. If you have any questions, please ask. The obvious first god is Dagda."

And she looked Dagda Murphy in the eyes and smiled. He just smiled back.

"Dagda is the High God or Great Father of the Irish. He is the god of abundance, male fertility, and the great provider. This is his time of the year. He is the god of sun, agriculture, and merriment. He has tremendous sexual and culinary appetites. And he is a giant of a man known for his physical strength and power, and family-children orientation. Father Dagda has one wife, Danu, and several mistresses including Morrigan and Boann."

Dagda has a gigantic magic club that he always carries with him. One end is very rough; he uses it in battle and to kill. The other end is smaller and very smooth; he uses it to bring the dead back to life. So, it is a magic club with the power of life and death."

Jamie couldn't resist looking at his Uncle and smiling. Uncle tried to ignore him.

"He also possesses several other magic objects. He has a mystical 'cauldron of plenty' which provides its own recipes and can cook unlimited quantities. Its motto is 'if you eat from me you will never go away hungry or unsatisfied'."

"Dagda possesses a magic female harp. With this harp he is the supreme maestro in playing the three noble strains: The Strain of Lament, the Strain of Laughter, and the Strain of Sleep. He keeps her on a hidden shelf, and it flies to him when he calls.

"He built and lives at Brugh na Boinne (Newgrange) which has a window that faces east over the sea and allows the sun into this stone/earth palace only on the day of the winter solstice each year. Thus, Dagda controls the shortest day in the year, or both the start and finish of every year. He has unlimited power and super strength from the sun. Today this location is a famous prehistoric megalithic passage tomb mound of which mythology predicts that one can travel to the Other-land."

"One Dagda story goes that one of his many children, a son named Oenghus Og, verbally tricked him and took over his home and lived there for many years. This son was born from Boann, Goddess of sexuality, fertility, voluptuousness, and abundant promiscuousness. Of course, she was the Cow Goddess. Within the society, Boann had but one such responsibility. The conception of Oenghus Og occurred at a special time when Dagda went to Boann's house to service her. In order not to get caught, when Elemhaire, her husband, came home from work at sunset, Dagda caused the sun to stand high in the sky for nine months and then fall to allow both the night and the new son to arrive. In this way Oenghus Og was conceived, carried, born and placed with foster parents while the husband was continuously at work. It is no wonder that many years later Dagda could not kick him out of the 'occupation' of his "house'."

Jamie gave Uncle Dagda a puzzled look, which went again unacknowledged.

"This most powerful of Irish Gods was involved in many battles and wars. For example, in the battle of Magh Tuierdh he moved several mountains and rivers to tilt the battle ground in his favor. Immediately before the battle he made love with Goddess Morrigan—more about her later—after which she promised to use her destructive powers to assist Dagda's people, the Tuath De Danaan, against their people. Soil, and Irrigation, as well as the Goddess of Fertility and Bounty.

She is the perennial Mother and the favorite mate of Dagda. Tuath De Danaan in Gaelic literature refers to the People of the Goddess Dana or Danu. So, Danu represents productivity in all of its forms. Large fertile garden areas are called Gort na Mor-Rioghna (field of the Great Queen). Large stone lined cooking pits are known as Fulacht na Mor-Rioghna (hearth of the Great Queen)."

"Lugh is the God of Light, Keeper of Agreements, God of Martial Arts, and God of Creative Arts and Crafts. Obviously, Lugh can and does participate in many forms of life circumstances. At the festival just before the Battle of Magh 'Tuiredh, he tried to enter the grand hall to join in the pre-battle feast. But the gatekeeper said that one must have a skill to enter and asked him to name his skill. He quickly said a harpist. No, one is already present. A painter, no one is already present. A warrior, no one is already present. So, he started listing his many skills, one by one. Each time the doorkeeper said that such a skill was already present as the Tuath De Danaan people had many very talented people in their tribe. So finally, Lugh became disgusted and declared that he was certain there was no one at the feast that had all one hundred of these skills that he had. He was admitted."

"Lugh functions as a King and Judge in his role as Keeper of Agreements. And he is a warrior with super martial arts training, and much physical talent and military skills. He was a senior leader in the Battle of Magh Tuiredh. He also fathered the legendary human hero, Cuchulainn, by a Milesian maiden named Dectera. And he used his magic and military skills to frequently help his warrior son during his son's many exploits and battles."

Jamie quickly spoke up, "Is that the Cuchulainn who stopped the entire Connaught army of Maedbh's on Magh Muceda (Pig-Keepers's Plain) by chopping down a monstrous oak tree and blocking the enemy army's path. And he declared that his army would surrender if any of the enemy could jump over the tree in a horse pulled chariot. Several days later, half of the Connaught army had tried, none had succeeded, and all were killed trying. Half of the enemy were eliminated before the battle had even begun. Finally, Maedbh arrived and ordered the rest of his army to go around the tree. So Cuchulainn tied himself to a large boulder in the middle of the path beyond the tree, killed the advancing army as they tried, one by one, to pass. And he killed most of the advancing army, fought to the death by being tied to the rock, and died standing on his feet. I think that today Cuchulainn is the most famous of the Irish heroes. Am I right?"

The High Priestess nodded positively. And Jamie grinned from ear to ear.

"Brighid is the Goddess of Poetry and Healing. Her major role is to protect the weak or needy such as children, mothers, and women during childbirth. She is thought to be a noble muse regularly using her magic in her work. She is a healer and known as the goddess at the bedside, hearth, and home. She performs many miracles such as healing the very sick, relieving the dying of their pain, assisting a problem pregnancy to positive completion, removing a problem fetus during pregnancy, helping to solve marital problems, helping to solve psychological, hormonal, and physical problems of men and women, and on and on. Today, she is almost as popular as St. Patrick, among the Irish people."

"Manannan Mac Lir is the Keeper of the Otherworld. He is guide and protector of the realms in the earth and sea. He is an illusionist, trickster, shape-shifter, and a mischievous god. He uses much magic and uses many different physical forms when moving into and out of the Otherworld or when traveling on the seas. Manannan has many magical objects: an instrument that controls the weather over the sea; a sword named Answerer which can cut through any armor; a ship named Ocean Sweeper which can travel at high speeds to anywhere he directs and does not require oars nor sails; a horse named Aonbarr who can travel as fast on water as on land. He always wears a great cloak of many colors so he can become invisible any time he chooses as he can always blend into background areas land or sea. His throne is on the Isle of Mann; this island is named after him."

"Goibhniu is the God of Protection and Charm. He uses many forms of magic to make swords and metal crafts. He has protective and therapeutic powers plus his magic which is called upon to heal everything from a major chest wound to removing a thorn from a finger. Goibhniu has one very special talent. He annually rules over the Feast of the Otherworld, known as Fledh Ghoibhnenn. All of those who attend this feast and drink a certain very strong beverage, 'a drink of the gods', stop aging and remain, physically, just as they are that night forever after."

"Ogma is a Warrior and Champion of the Gods. He has super strength and is the Patron of Languages. He is a weaver of words, phrases, and commands many languages. He is most outstanding in poetry and speech. With several written languages, he created the Ogham system of writing. When the Druids needed a coded language to avoid Catholic scrutiny, they used his system. It involves magical, spiritual, and special mind deciphering thinking to correctly employ the Ogham system of written symbols. This ancient script is still used today by poets, scholars, and seers. Ogma also was a hero in the Battle of Tuath De Danaan. Dagna had the greatest fighting skills, but Ogma had the greatest physical strength."

"The last of the Irish Gods that I want to tell you about is my soul-sister, Morrigan.

"Mor-Rioghain (Phantom Queen or Great Queen—Morrigan) is the Goddess of Strength and War, Inciter of Battles, Weaver of Magic designed to help or harm whomever she chooses, and Keeper of All Lands. She regularly initiates and is involved in battles and wars. One of her magical techniques is to shape shift to a crow or raven and fly over the battle-field to follow the flow of fighting. Morrigan enjoys the killing and slaughtering. She simply feels that this is necessary to keep the sacred land. In wartime, observing from above, she studies the two armies, decides which one she wants to win, and uses all types of magic to help or hurt either side."

"In daily 'normal' situations she uses magic to get her own way. Once, in disguise, she approached Cuchulainn and asked him to make love to her. He refused, but won the battle anyway. Overall, one could say that Morrigan was very feminine and beautiful but could readily display a selfish and ugly disposition. She was a lovely monster, cuddly but very dangerous. It is best that you are her friend, or at least that she likes you."

"All of the Irish Gods and Goddesses, as they are set down in Irish Mythology, are steeped in magic. Therefore, it is to be expected that the Irish people should be in tune with the ideas and concepts in witchcraft. Witchcraft is the magic created by witches. This is probably why witchcraft is an above table profession in Ireland. While in many countries, witchcraft is still a dangerous, fearful, and a forbidden form of existence. Witches are still hung or burned in many countries. So, we educate and train our own Irish witches; and we make extensive efforts to police their actions, At the extreme—suicide is acceptable—homicide is not acceptable."

Dagda asked, "I have a feeling that other systems of magic users, such as Gypsy magic or Voodoo, also do not agree with using magic for homicide. Would that be correct?"

Banthnaid answered, "In general I think you are correct. But problems occur because there is little or minimum control of magic makers in most countries. Most magic makers and magic users learn their magic, one on one, from a practicing magic maker. And many countries do not have special laws regulating the work/activities of such people. They simply fall under the laws for all citizens or immigrants in those countries. In Ireland, we are organized to investigate, judge, and ban Irish witches who abuse our magic practicing extremes."

Jamie asked, "I have heard that there is a World Witches Conclave that meets regularly. Is this true? What does this Conclave do?"

"I see that you have been doing some on-line research—very good. Yes, several professions that use magic in their working environment have organized and selected representatives to attend a certain meeting at certain times. Currently there are six senior witches, and each may bring two associates. Therefore, there will be eighteen of us from various parts of the world. We meet at various places, at random intervals, and discuss the problems of trying to maintain a viable profession which requires 'many secrets', and has been historically considered to be associated with the dead, demons, and even the devil himself. I am currently the President of the World Witches Conclave. We will be meeting here in Roscommon later this year. Because witches will never be universally accepted, and there will always be people who fear us and want to kill us, our small group and our meetings are kept secret."

The group of four continued discussing Irish mythology and comparing world mythologies, gods, and witchcraft for another two hours. Then they picked up their baggage, left the uneaten food for the forest animals, and returned to the little thatched cottage. Dagda, Riley, and Jamie all gave their sincere thanks, climbed into the car and headed back toward Longford. Tomorrow, Jamie would drive back, alone, and have his special lesson number three, specifically on Irish Witchcraft.

4

THE GOOD HONG KONG LIFE

Hong Kong is an island off the coast of China and has been inhabited for several thousand years. China ceded it to the United Kingdom in 1841. After the Opium Wars with China, in 1898, the British signed a ninety-nine-year lease to take political and military control of Hong Kong. This land lease also involved several miles of land to the north and two hundred and fifty islands in the Shenzen River. The deep-water harbor area made for a large natural ocean/river/land trading port. Before the British arrived, the area consisted simply of a small group of fishing villages. Now it is the military and international financial door for China. It is a very wealthy community, ranked with the world's sixth highest GDP income, supporting almost one half of the foreign capital that flows into China. Hong Kong is now a magnificent western style city and was officially returned to the People's Republic of China in 1999. The twelve million people still retain a limited degree of internal political independence. It is a perfect place for venture capitalism in the Orient. Three young business men will soon find this to not be so easy. In fact, there is much difficulty in the integration of the capitalistic and communist economic and social systems.

Quaid Gang Hu was his legal private name; he had changed his public name to just Gang Hu (Unyielding Tiger) to his Chinese friends and Tiger to his foreign friends during his schooling in

England. So today Mr. Hu (Mr. Tiger) was sitting in his tenth level Happy Valley private viewing box with two of his long-time school friends, Charles and Ameer, and watching the feature race of the afternoon series, the Victoria Racing Club Trophy. He came to the Hong Kong Racing Club a couple times every week.

Today had not been a good day. He had already lost more than a million Hong Kong Dollars. This next race was a handicap race in class 3, division 1, with ratings ranging from 080 to 060 on B Course at 1200 meters. He now felt lucky so he bet one hundred thousand HKD on Panther Run at 39 to win and 19 to place, and thirty thousand on Life of Beauty at 29 to win or 14 to place. Aggressiveness and confidence were in his blood.

His chauffer had brought Tiger and his old English and Arab school mates from his offices in Kowloon Down to Happy Valley via Hong Kong South (route 1) and Wong Nai Chung Road; he dropped them off at Son Dong Gate; they had lunch at the Moon Koon Restaurant; Tiger had his usual Cantonese seafood special of shark fin soup, and mantis shrimp with a few sweet vegetables; they were all on their second scotch and soda so the heads were yet clear. Last night Tiger had received a spiritual blessing, the promise of a nice victory from one of his favorite Chinese Gods, Sun Wukong, the tricky Monkey God. Impeccable's trainer, Y.S.Tsui, had told him that Impeccable was feeling really great today as he would be studding tonight and he knew it. So, his adrenalin was really high and he was on the big GO. Mr. Hu would soon find out if his go was high enough.

The three men, each in his mid-twenties, unmarried, Chinese, English, and Arab, were quiet, serious, and each had placed a bet in this last race of the day, albeit not a regular and serious business, but for fun. They had met as roommates at Trinity College in Cambridge University and later at the Cambridge Judge Business School. These are located in the heart of the city on Trinity Street as Trinity College is the largest and most cosmopolitan of the thirty-five Colleges in the city of Cambridge just north of London, England. During the last four years of education they shared a common personal and educational life style.

Each was from a wealthy family, each was an only child, each was above average in physical size but not in mental abundance, each was very common in looks but had unlimited pocket change for clothing, each was ambitious, and each developed his own mechanisms for getting minimal grades without the trouble of studying. Money can buy everything, at least in some places.

They each had the same continuing problem. They were under father's monetary control. But fortunately, they had loving mothers who wanted to see their sons successful, married, producing grandchildren. So often clandestine negotiations, in the presence of mother only, solved most major problems.

Their fathers had sent them to the best schools in England London and Cambridge. Upon graduation they were each given several million pounds for seed money to start up a business. Each chose to establish an international import/export company in their homeland. But after a couple of years, without regular monthly allowances, instead with monthly paychecks needed for several employees, they found out that establishing a business and competing in the international capitalist world, one needed to 'grow-up' OR get lucky.

Gang Hu is near average height for a Chinese, rather square, with very oriental facial features, and a flat face due to his Mongolian great grandmother. He is not handsome, but his quick mind, financial status, and aggressive personality usually allowed a dominating advantage with most people, and of course his English was British perfect. He was a typical hyperactive only boy child and much preferred the action in the streets as opposed to the lack of action inside classrooms. He was born in Shanghai and grew up in London and Shanghai. So, the Shanghai Horse Club's Race Track provided Tiger with his summer entertainment when a boy with daddy's (and mommy's) money.

Shanghai is the largest populated city in China and ranked number one in commerce and finance. It is situated at the mouth of the largest river in eastern China, the Yangtze. In most developing countries, including China, the rivers have been the central transportation for hundreds of years before roads become available. The location of this river provided the Quaid Family with ample business opportunities. For more than six generations they have used the river and were the river's major smuggling importers-exporters. The Family 'businesses' had established connections with several British shipping firms which purchased contraband, such as opium and heroin from India, and brought it to Shanghai. The Family then smuggled it down the

Yangtze River and sold it to the several million people living along the river and its many tributaries. The Quaid Family businesses are still very active to this day. Gang Hu is simply not directly active yet. He wants a business of his own, not under family influence. It should be related to his different view of the modern western world. He wants something more. He just doesn't know exactly what that is.

Charles Somersham was born on the 600-acre family estate, Somersham Golden Meadows, just north of Colchester in southeastern England. His father, Baron George Somersham had inherited the title through the British peerage system given to an ancestor in 1833 by King William IV from the House of Hanover. Charles only hoped he would live long enough to assume that title; his father was a big strong robust outdoor type. Charles took after his mother and is well over six foot, slim, not athletic except for horseback riding; he has light red hair and green eyes from his Irish Marquesse Grandmother, a narrow face with light freckles and a beaked nose. He has a shy and gentle disposition which is one reason he and his father do not talk to each other except when required. With a dominating father and his willow tree personality, he is protected by mother. Barroness Somersham takes care of her son's needs and wants before he even asks.

When the three fellows met at Trinity College, about ten years ago, Charles easily fell into step behind the aggressive Chinese Tiger and the sophisticated playboy Arab, Ali. Both Tiger and Ali were horse lovers. And since the Baron bred Irish racing horses at Somersham Meadows, which is less than an hour drive from Cambridge, it was only natural that many weekends involved horseback riding over the open hills and vales of southern England. The Boars Head Inn, located half way between the estate and Cambridge, routinely provided an evening with a roaring fireplace, mead, meat, and bed partners when so desired. Charles just sat back and enjoyed his foreign buddies.

Ali Abdel Aal is the youngest and only male child with three older sisters, finally making his father a "real" man. His father, through an arranged marriage, had established the family as a major shareholder of the large Alexandria Petroleum Company. The family already owned another oil producing company, the Desert Black Gold Corporation, just south of Cairo. And because he was the only son, someday Ali's inheritance would be substantial. He was waiting not-so patiently.

Ali was a little over six foot 2 inches tall with a professional swimmers' bronze body, dark eyes, hair, and mustache-chin beard, womanizer and a lover of small pleasures. His mother was a beautiful 'Cleopatra' Egyptian lady from a wealthy Cairo family, hence the second oil connections. A typical wealthy Arab boy, he grew up with horses. As a teenager he went to schools in England, mastered his British English, and spent childhood weekends at the English Riding Academy in Hyde Park. And his grades reflected his priorities. He was more successful at studying the warm opposite teenage sex than cold paper books. And his school grades reflected these priorities. But he was an expert at cheating, had plenty of money to pay someone to his do his home-work, and he eventually graduated from high school and went on to Trinity College.

At the end of the Victoria Racing Club Trophy race, the winner was Grand Mary by a nose. It had not been a good day for Tiger, but Ali had called it correctly for his third win of the day. Ali now had more than a million HKD in his suit pocket, so he would decide which night club to go to for a small celebration, how to celebrate, and pay for the entire evening. He chose one of Tiger's private clubs. This club had no street address so only Tiger's chauffeur knew where to go and how to get there, and later how to leave. The chauffeur picked them up in Tiger's Crystal Import-Export Company's limousine and they started up Route 1 through the Cross-Arbor Tunnel toward Kowloon, turned left onto Gascoigne Road and immediately exited near the Kowloon Cricket Club. Nearby the driver identified a side street entry for an establishment called the Red Dragon. It was a member's only private club which proudly fulfilled their motto 'Whatever You Want We Have It'. Tiger had a lifetime business membership so all possible accommodations were available to him and his guests. But sometimes you had to reserve for special attractions in advance; tonight, they had called ahead.

At the door of the club the three ex-roommates punched in Tiger's entry code, passed through the electronic security, and entered the main level with ornate Red Dragons on every wall. They were escorted to their private room on the fifth floor, sat down in comfortable arm chairs surrounding a small round table, ordered whiskeys around, and Ali asked the critical question, "So, Tiger, are you comfortable here in Hong Kong and away from your family in Shanghai? Don't you think it would be easier to get your business really in motion if you worked with your father and uncles?"

In three years of effort Tiger's Crystal Import-Export Company was only grossing a few million American dollars annually. Tiger angrily responded; with his heavy losses at the race track he was not in a good mood.

"Do you want me to become a crook? Most of my family's businesses involve illegal smuggling. You and I became citizens of the British Commonwealth after we finished school in Cambridge. I could be extradited to England if 1 am caught playing the games my family plays. You are probably in the same situation. Dual citizenship must play out in international trading and commerce treaties. This socialist society here in China doesn't function like a capitalist society. Laws are not rigidly enforced. And palmed cash will buy what bank checks cannot. But in the UK, one must watch for the security cameras on every street corner." And he laughed at his own joke.

"Yes, of course you are right," responded. Ali. "I do have similar problems. In my little Sandstorm Import-Export Company, I maintain books for clients who wish to pay in cash or gold, and keep certain transactions off the books. Many of my clients, especially those involved in drilling activities and pipeline repairs, prefer to avoid the tax system in Egypt, even though it is not nearly as rigid as in the UK. Most of my business friends think Cairo is on the other side of the moon." And he laughed at his joke.

Charles asked, "Do you guys also have to annually file personal income and business tax reports to your second 'homeland', the UK?

"Yes and no," said Tiger. "My company is not registered in the UK. I have no UK source income. My residence and domicile are here in the Peoples Republic of China. Plus, UK and PRC have a double taxation treaty which should protect me from the UK tax man. But I am very careful with my company's imports and exports in all of Europe. The European Union and the UK are not eye to eye on all business and commercial taxes. I do not yet understand. If I should have a problem with a Hungarian company and Hungary tries to extradite me, will the UK reject or support such extraditions?"

Ali added, "My response is similar to Tigers. I have avoided the UK in my business efforts because I am not sure where I, and my

Saudi registered company, stand on certain potential legal situations. This is especially true with the level of corruption and the quantity of palm money floating to government officials, UK and Saudi."

"What if I could answer some of your questions and provide a few turtle shell business transactions?" Charles inquired.

Both friends looked at him with smiles on their lips. Charles was always the pure one and balked when illegal or near legal or clandestine events happened during their previous multi-year relationships. It was Charles who chided the Chinese and the Arabs for their less than honest business practices. Was Charles now alluding to something less than English pure?

Hearing no response from his buddies he continued, "My Green Meadows Import-Export Firm is registered in England, UK and EU. And we are doing all right. We are sending electronic components to South Africa, importing fresh food such as fruits and vegetables from the Caribbean area, shipping toys and Christmas gifts from Sweden to the USA, and others."

"We are all in established and continuous trade areas. The competition is terrible. We are the last ones at the table and the food is almost gone. What we need is a new product that is not yet in the marketplace let alone on the table. We need to find this product, get involved with it, and establish a first order monopoly before word gets around. And I have such a product!"

And again, the air was quiet. Charles had a new idea. Impossible. But miracles do happen.

So, Tiger spoke up, "Are you going to tell us or is it an English secret?"

Charles smiled, looked at his buddies, soon to be business partners, and dropped his voice to a whisper, and motioned that they should come closer to the small round table.

He spoke quietly, "From an English medical/science friend of mine I have learned about a different type of product that must be shipped under maximum secrecy and security. But it could lead to a very lucrative trading arrangement in a short time. Everything about such a deal would have to be clandestine, and if we are intercepted there could be severe punishment. If we successfully accomplish this 'new business' with great care, the arrangement could expand and continue for many years. Later, in a more secure setting, I will explain in greater detail. For now, I am talking about billions of English Pound Sterling. And the key word is nanotechnology."

Two big grins filled the faces of Charles ex-roommates. It would appear that ethics was not a current problem to worry about. Just wait.

And another nano-tech weapons systems for international distribution begins.

In three days, Charles and Ali would be returning to London and Cairo, respectively. So, they asked the waiter to refill the drinks, bring the food and the girls, in that order. They also told him to turn down the covers on all three beds as they were planning to celebrate all night.

5

JAMIE AND IRISH WITCHCRAFT

THE NEXT MORNING JAMIE was up and driving down the road toward Roscommon by 7:00. He arrived in the woods two hours early; so, he just moved back his car seat, opened his latest book on Irish Witchcraft, lay back, and read until class time, 10:00. Then he got out, locked the car (big city habit), walked toward the little thatched cottage, psychologically prepared himself for the next lesson from the High Priestess of Irish Witchcraft, Banthnaid O'Keeffe.

As he arrived at the cottage, he was met by two crows and one raven. The crows flew and landed, one on each shoulder. The raven circled his head and encouraged him to follow. The four of them went to the back yard and into a small flower garden filled with beautiful native Irish flowers such as amaryllis, Easter lilies, bog rosemary, and clover shamrock. The Priestess was sitting on a garden chair, drinking tea, and waiting for him. Jamie went to her, realized she was rather pretty, though a middle-aged lady, kissed her hand and said.

"Good morning Mrs. O'Keeffe." It was what Riley told him to say.

"I am nervous, because I am afraid that I will not be good enough to learn from you. You know so much that I feel like a little boy with a new mother who I am meeting for the first time. I will try my best, but I may not learn fast."

All three birds flew into the air, circled the two of them three times, settled nearby, each facing away from Jamie. They seemed to be establishing a security barrier.

Mrs. O'Keeffe returned, "Jamie, please do not lie to me nor try to win my favors with compliments. I am a witch. I read minds. You do learn fast, in fact quite fast. And apples do not make me happy. If you want to understand witchcraft, begin to find a soul-brother among the Irish Gods. Simply be my friend. And this will make me happy."

Jamie turned very red in the face, dropped his eyes, and said, "Yes, my Lady."

She smiled and poured two fresh cups of tea, one for each of them, motioned for Jamie to sit in the adjacent garden chair. She sat back down, laid back, listened to the forest sounds, smelled the forest trees and flowers, and sipped tea. Jamie mimicked her. After a few minutes, the Priestess said:

> "I am happy that you want to learn about Irish witchcraft. Wealthy people usually come to me, explain their problem, pay me a fee, and I correct or solve their problem. They have no interest in witchcraft, or how I solve their problem. They only want a quick and easy way to a solution. Now I know your background. The American O'Reilly family is politically and financially rich. So, with the help of your three uncles, you could do the same thing—purchase a solution from me. But you have chosen to learn. For this I will give to you my full attention. And believe me, you will be a better man for doing so."
>
> "Yesterday you began to trust me. You must continue to do so, or you will not be able to correctly use what you learn. Let me begin with Folklore or Mother Nature's little friends, who can be good friends of witches if they are properly understood."
>
> "I have a tribe of fairies living here in my flower garden. They prefer to live among the foxglove, so I grow those flowers for them. But they can go back and forth between here and the Otherworld. There are so many fairies here in Ireland that a literary genre referred to as Fairy Folklore

generates numerous children's books, films and movie cartoons, CDCs, and a variety of childhood entertainments."

"I have many fairy friends, so I see them and talk to them often. I do not just live here alone. And when I have no specific students to teach or magic to work, they come and keep me company. They are usually only a few inches tall, have wings, fly like butterflies not dragonflies, have two arms and two legs but never walk, can be very lovely to look at, but they have difficult and selfish dispositions. Only after you get to know them can you really enjoy their dis-continuous childlike activities."

"You will find most of them living in Raths or Ringforts. These are raised mounds which contain the remains of ancient settlements. They are clustered in many places in Ireland. Smaller Raths or Ringforts were once villages. Large ones were once ancient royal castles. Dagda's home, Brugh na Boinne, is a large Ringfort. You may not have noticed any fairies in Boston. But I assure you that they are there as they immigrated along with their 'offspring'."

Jamie spoke up, "When I go back, I will try to find them. I would like to have them as my friends, I think."

"Now let me describe the education and training of an Irish witch. Most witches are educated in a Coven. I teach witchcraft from my Raven Coven located here in this forest. You were in one my 'classrooms' yesterday. There are three different levels or degrees of learning, each requires several years of study. I give all of my lectures and 'field experiences/rituals' to a maximum of two or three students at one time. These formal lessons usually last one complete day, perhaps twice a week. Otherwise it is the responsibility of the student to learn—books and on-line. And yes, there are regular tests which one must pass to advance within the learning levels. There are first, second, and third level Priesthoods or Priestess-hoods. After many years of study and practice one can become a High Priest or High Priestess of Irish Witchcraft."

"Not everyone reaches the higher levels. Those who do not simply are limited to less difficult or less critical levels of craftwork and must so market themselves at that level after they graduate and begin seeking clients. Only a High Priest or High Priestess may establish a

Coven and become a teacher of his profession. So, we are an organized educational system that is teaching and graduating people who have a viable place in our society; they use witchcraft for problem solving."

During the learning process there are two critical areas. We use ancient Irish and Gaelic languages for all craftwork. So, you must learn these languages very well. And you need a soul brother or soul sister. He/she must be one of the ancient Irish Gods as I described yesterday. Morrigan is my soul sister. Only they have the power to help you in your work."

"What is our work—to solve problems of our own, of family, of friends, of our living community—such as plants, animals, and humans. And of course, to solve the problems of clients who pay for a 'correct' solution. We are human and we do have minimum financial needs for basic living."

She smiled. Jamie smiled also. He was beginning to really like this unusual lady.

"How do we solve these problems? During the evening/night, when alone and with an open mind, take the problem into the forest, sit on the earth, become one with Mother Nature, contact your soul brother or soul sister, discuss the problem with him/her. Once you have determined a 'good' solution, you must select a 'good' magic ritual/method of accomplishing this solution. This is where one's limitations begin. At each level of education, you master several rituals and magic methods. So, a first level Priest would have mastered only one or two rituals/methods which he can use to solve the problem. A higher Priest has many rituals/magic methods available which he uses. And he is continuously learning more. It is his profession."

Jamie asked, "What do you mean by rituals/magic methods?"

"Magic includes a variety of rituals, chants, spells, and magic circles which allow for control of physical appearance and disappearance, invisibility, partial and full hypnosis, positive or negative incantations, future prediction by palm reading or tarot card reading, divination of past-present-future, past and present family spirit connections, natural cures for both physical and mind diseases, shape changing (to animal or human), contagion, mind control, spell casting, and more."

Jamie's mouth had dropped open, his eyes glazed over, expression frozen. Finally, he said, "That is unbelievable. Is this true? Can a witch really do all of that?"

"No, a witch cannot do all of that. Usually a mid-level educated—trained witch can do only a few of these. One or more rituals/chants are necessary for a single magic method requires many hours of practice; if the ritual is not performed perfectly, there can be negative feedback of the person trying to perform it. The spirits can help, or they can punish. Punishment can lead to a person's death. We are human. Our minds can only contain a limited number of languages, rituals, and chants. Even the very highest level of High Priestess is limited to several rituals/magic methods. During your education and training you select which rituals and chants you wish to master, approach a witch who has mastered them, learn everything from him/her, and continuously practice to guarantee that everything is always perfect."

"I apologize if this is too personal, but why did you decide to become a witch?"

"It is all right. I am not from several generations of witches. I have no genetic connections to any past witches. And there will be no kin following me."

"Many years ago, my husband and three children were all suddenly killed in a bus accident. I wanted to die, but a close female friend of mine told me how a witch had helped her when she lost a twin sister in a car accident. So, I spent many hours talking with this witch lady and decided that I could yet make a positive contribution to my life by helping others. I started studying and learning Irish witchcraft. I found Morrigan as a soul mate and re-directed my life. I never forget my loved ones, and I have found peace in helping people through witchcraft."

"I do not think that I want to become a witch, but I do want to get closer to Irish witchcraft. How do I do this?"

"All right. You have a difficult task. I do want to help you. So, let us consider a special arrangement. If you will spend the next few weeks learning and accepting Mother Nature, learning about and trying to find a soul brother among the ancient gods, I will help you in your efforts to identify and eliminate these nanotech killers. How about that? Later if you want to continue to learn more about Irish witchcraft, I will help you find someone near your home in Boston to teach you."

And Jamie thought for a few moments. He was not sure if he was capable of mastering this. But he could try, so he responded, "Yes, I want to try to do this. And I want to meet Dagda, as he has already become my friend."

"I am not surprised that you chose Dagda, since you have such a deep love for your special Uncle. OK. Here is what you need to do. I have several ancient books on ancient Irish languages, and on Dagda and his exploits. I will loan them to you, and I want them returned when you leave Ireland. For the next five days you come to me and we will learn to feel Mother Earth and how to communicate with her. Then for the next two weeks, you will go and live in Dagda's ancient home, Brugh na Boinne, Newgrange. It is about an hour drive north of Dublin. As I mentioned, it is a large Ringfort, famous and open to tourists during daytime. But that is fine, as you will need to 'live' there during the night when everyone is gone, all will be quiet, and the spirits will appear."

"You can go there, find a hotel or take a tent and camp out, whatever. You will remain there for fifteen days. Read and study these books and eat and sleep during the daytime. At night, go to the Ringfort, and learn to feel the home of Dagda. Walk, explore, and seek out the many spirits who lived there over numerous years. Send to him messages that you want and need his help to battle world killers. Sit and listen to all of the talk among all of the spirits."

"I will give you three sticks. After five days, I will send to you one of my crows. If you are making progress and want to continue, give him one stick. Continue feeling the home of Dagda at night for five more nights. This time I will send one crow and one raven. If you are making progress and want to continue, give one of the sticks to the crow and the raven will give to you a small bottle containing five leaves. You are to use these leaves as follows."

"Each of the next five nights, at midnight, prepare one cup of tea using only one leaf. Drink this tea. It will make you invisible but capable of seeing in the darkest dark. Go to the Ringfort. There will be a guard at the door, but he will not see you and the door will unlock for you. Directly enter the multi-roomed ancient dwelling, go down six levels. There will be a lock on each level, but they will all unlock for you. This can take you on a path to the Otherland. At level six, follow the corridor straight ahead. Take the fourth passage on the right. This passage will not be locked as you enter but will lock behind you after you enter. Continue for about one hundred meters and you will enter a large domed chamber. Sit here and feel for Dagda. This is his war room where he planned all his major battles with Morrigan and his generals. Communicate with all the spirits who come to you and wish to know you. Be honest with them and they will be honest with you. You may make many friends. But be non-aggressive, courteous, patient, and remember what you hear. Dagda may just watch you and not say anything. But he will be there, listening. He may just study you for the first night or two. After four hours, leave by the reverse route that you entered."

"Continue this each night for five nights. If Dagda decides to become your friend, and it is too early to talk soul-brother, he will communicate with you in his way. Or he may think you are not worth knowing and that your quest/problem is not one he wants to share. If he wants to help, he will communicate directly with you, tell you how, when, and where he will help you. And you will then always have an ancient Irish God as a true friend. At the end of five days, I will send a crow to you. If things are positive, break the last stick into two pieces, give them to him, and he will return them to me. I will then know that we will indeed be together in the future. I will communicate with Morrigan and inform her of the situation. It is very possible that these two gods might want to work together to help you/us solve this problem. If you remember, the two of them often worked together during battles."

"Now follow my instructions very carefully. Dagda's house is a large circular mound, two hundred meters in diameter and surrounded by a five-meter high stone wall. There are no windows, one major entrance and two secret entrances. It is a labyrinth of underground rooms, many zig-zag corridors, closet sized rooms and auditorium sized rooms, several levels, some corridors go up, or down, or dead-end. Some of these corridors go into the Otherworld. Do not get lost, or we may not see you again, ever. Is this totally understood?"

Jamie swallowed, looked the priestess in the eye and reluctantly said, "Yes my Lady."

"Later, you can leave my books with Riley and he will return them to me."

Mrs. O'Keeffe stood up and said, "It is a pleasure getting to know such a fine gentleman. I feel positive about our future efforts. I will see you tomorrow morning, same time, same place, same garden. After tomorrow's learning session I will give to you the books to study."

Jamie stood and she walked him toward the front of the house. Suddenly she disappeared. Jamie turned only to find himself alone. Yet he was not surprised. And he knew he would see her tomorrow, so he was not worried. Maybe over the next few days he could get to know and understand her better. He remembered that Riley said she had a different way of thinking. He was certainly right.

Over the next few days Jamie followed the High Priestess Banthnaid O'Keee's 'orders.' He found out that Irish mythology was not just fantasy but could be a functional means of civil weaponry. So, he remained in Ireland all summer, and learned. What did he learn?

He learned that the Great Father-Chieftain-Druid-King-God Dagda has total control over nature and weather. He has super physical strength. And using Druid magic has control over men's emotions as well as life and death with his double ended staff. In summary, Dagda is believed to be the Irish God of Life and Death.

Jamie visited Brugh na Foinne many times, spent several additional nights there, and left with the feeling that he had communicated with the ancient Celtic Gods. He was not certain if he had 'talked' directly with Dagda, but knew he had 'talked' with Dagda's war buddies. And he felt that when he needed help in his battle against Korrectorizer and his Committee of World Conservatives, Dagda and his men would be there. He perceived the battle would be in Ireland, and it would be very lethal. {He was very right.}

He was also certain Morrigan would fight. She specialized in shape-shift from human to animal to non-human forms. And with Dagda's super strength, any attack would certainly be too powerful for a 'human' enemy. And Jamie thought that if the battle were too difficult the gods of Celtic mythology, Tuath De Danuann, would jump in and help his children.

When Jamie finally returned to Boston and school, he decided to not tell everything to his Uncle Dagda. He assumed his uncle already knew, somehow. What he now needed was a 'proven' suspect/candidate enemy. He knew that was now happening.

6

COMMITTEE OF NANOTECHNOLOGY CONTROL I

At 9:00 o'clock on the last Friday of February 2035, the second Committee of Nanotechnology Control in the Division of High Technology met on the second-floor conference room in the Federal Trade Center Building on Constitution Avenue in Washington, DC. The second committee was composed of:

- Mr. Gerald McGriff, the US Attorney General as Chairman
- Mr. Dagda Murphy, President of ISAAT as Co-Chairman
- Mr. Thomas Bradmier, Director of the Office of Science and Technology
- Mr. Harold Thomson, Director of British MI6
- Dr. Ulda von Eulenberg, Deputy Chief of INTERPOL
- Dr. Lawrence Batly, Director of Chief Medical Examiners' Office, NYC
- Mr. Leopold Mueller, Director of European Central Bank
- Ms. Dorthy Lawess, private lawyer in international trade
- Dr. William Stronger, Chairman of Nanotechnology at the MIT in Boston

- Dr. Joseph Barkley, Chairman of High Technology at the Univ. Chicago
- Mr. Boursher Femer, Director of ISAAT in Europe

Chairman Mr. Gerald McGriff opened the meeting. "I thank you for joining us in our attempts to identify and incarcerate the people who have killed, in a gross macabre fashion, more than five hundred people in eleven different countries during the past six years, by using nanotechnical weapon systems. This is our second committee. The first one was not quite successful. The focus of that committee was on science and technology. It was not enough. We now will focus on science, business, banking, communications, business, and family. This committee is larger, more diversified, and will cover the entire world. However, it will still concentrate on nanotechnology, both for curing and killing."

"The other committee had identified seven people as prime candidates for direct involvement in these many nanotech-homicides. They were: Dr. Boris Kukrynisky-Moscow, Dr. Frans Gunter-Munich, Dr. Mario Kemps-Buenos Aires, Dr. James Walters-Ottawa, and the three Chiang brothers-Nanjing-Berlin-Los Angeles. A few months ago, the three Chiang brothers were found dead at their ancient castle in China; cause of death not determined. A few days ago, Dr. Boris Kukrynisky was found dead in his own bed; cause of death not determined. We did perform official on-site interviews with Drs. Gunter, Walters, and Chi Jiang. The others were protected by their foreign citizenships. So today, from the original seven, we have only three strong candidates. We currently closely monitor Dr. Gunter and Dr. Walters. And we monitor, as best we can, Dr. Kemps is South America. Within one year four of seven candidates are dead, also probably due to the nano-killer systems".

And the entire group was shocked. Did this mean that labeling a scientist as being possibly involved in nano-tech homicides puts him in the bull's eye? Or does it imply that those who are now dead were involved with the Committee of World Conservatives and there was a major disagreement. There was obviously a 'management' problem among the nano-tech assassins.

"Are there any questions, or should we come back to this latest information later in our meeting? If not, I will ask Mr. Murphy to brief you of new suspects that we want you to consider moving up to candidate a status."

Mr. Murphy began, "For the past few months we have been continuously monitoring for select words and phrases using the electronic spies that we have at the US National Security Agency and INTERPOL. We have a list of more than fifty suspects worldwide. When we add to this data, which was originally collected from human contacts, we have tried to narrow the field down to seven possible new candidates. Including the current three, we count ten individuals that we could investigate in ten different countries. The manpower necessary to do this will more than deplete our current funded budget, of which ninety percent comes from the USA. So, unless the European Union, ASEAN, or other funds become available, ten candidates will be our current limit."

Mr. Thompson asked, "Can you briefly explain what information or data that you will be seeking from each of the candidates? Maybe we can assist in some areas, at least in Europe."

"Thank you," responded Mr. Murphy. "We originally identified the suspects using science related data. So now, we will seek information concerning:

- Personal – family, close relatives, daily habits, non-business electronic communications, relaxation time activities, luxury vacations, excess personal income, investments on self and family, extra expenses such as schooling, maintaining elderly or handicapped, special nursing care, etc,
- Professional – business confidants, senior colleagues, select junior, colleagues, select booking personnel, personal secretary, daily work habits, degree of control in office, laboratory, or factory, international business travels, all electronic communications, annual reports such as IRS or government tax statements, quarterly tax records of any company with major controls, checking of all foreign affiliates or clients, special monitoring of suspicious transactions and international shipping, record of local and foreign bank accounts (where available)."

Ms. Lawess asked, "Do you think this will be enough information to identify and arrest, especially at the international level?"

"We hope so" answered Mr. Murphy. "But we are certainly open to new ideas, and assistance."

Mr. McGriff spoke up, "We think all of this can be also accomplished in the USA because any suspicion of or direct involvement in nanotech homicides is legally similar, but not yet equivalent, to terrorism. Many European countries have also recently passed, or at least introduced bills into their legislative system, to establish laws linking nanotech homicides with terrorism. However, most countries of the world have not made such a linkage. We will simply obtain as much info and data as we can on who we can and where we can. Does that help you understand the direction we are going and the quantity of the problem?"

Mr. Murphy said, "Many of you know my Director of the European Division of ISAAT, Mr. Boursher Femer, sitting here. I am sure that he would accept any assistance on investigations in Europe."

Mr. Femer quickly replied, "Yes, any assistance for our European efforts will be greatly appreciated and could allow more funds for other more difficult areas of the world. As you will soon see, we really do need more assistance in Europe."

Mr. Mueller asked, "Has the European Union or any of its members promised any money in the near future?"

"I am sorry to say, no," Mr. McGriff responded.

"Not to change the subject, but please allow me to turn to our new list of suspicious individuals, who we are proposing to you for investigation, concerning their possible role in international nanotech homicides," said Mr. McGriff. "We will continue to monitor Drs. Gunter, Walters. and Kemps. And we will initiate electronic and surface investigations, but not yet a person to person or on-site visits, of the following:"

- Dr. Anneka Andersson, Stockholm, Sweden
- Mr. Faustino Mariniti, Rome, Italy
- Mrs. Yaritzma Azevedo, Brasilia, Brazil
- Dr, Albert Langdon, London, England
- Mr. Haruki Takahashi, Tokyo, Japan
- Dr. Edward Kline, New York, New York
- Dr. Lin Liang, Hong Kong, China

"In general, the doctors are scientists in some field of chemical engineering or nanotechnology; while the Mr. or Mrs. are business or banking people involved in some areas of international finance or commerce. Each person has been identified from electronic surveillance technology, a soft follow up investigation of their place of business, and/or identifiable non-compatible relationships between their level of living and personal income. As we obtain more of a significant amount of data and information concerning each of these candidates, we will brief you at each of our regular meetings. And we request that no written materials leave the meeting room unless special permission from Mr. Murphy or me. Now are there any questions?"

Dr. von Eulenberg inquired about timeframes. "Do you plan to investigate all candidates at the same time? Or do you have a set of candidate priorities for your efforts? If priorities, how did you make your decisions concerning the sequence?"

Mr. Murphy responded. "Our budget and manpower are not sufficient to continue to monitor Drs. Walters, Dr Gunter, and Dr Kemps, plus investigate all seven new candidates simultaneously. So, yes, we established priorities. It seemed most logical to begin in-depth investigations in countries where we will receive assistance or at least no resistance to our efforts. So, we plan to begin in Sweden, Italy, England, Japan, and the USA. After we have a reasonable amount of info/data, and our eyes and ears are in position to continue monitoring, we will move on to China and Brazil."

"For a timeframe, I hope we can complete the easier ones this year and the more difficult ones, next year. Brazil, Argentina, and China will require some special efforts."

Mr. Mueller spoke up, "In your past investigations, did the personal information and electronic data reveal any critical information that was not observed by just looking closely at the working or business structures?"

Again Mr. Murphy responded, "Let me answer that by giving you a couple of examples:

- Dr. James Walters, Ottawa, is a nanotech scientist. He had a Columbian doctoral student whose father is the head of a major drug cartel. Currently Dr. Walters has sort of a partner-like relationship with this Dr. Wilbur Sanchez and has helped him set up new nanotech laboratories in Bogota. Supplies, chemicals, reagents, and biologicals have been sent from Canada to Columbia. No identifiable 'black' money has changed hands. Dr. Sanchez regularly visits his former mentor and vice versa. And Dr. Walters has three children studying in universities in Canada and the USA. Their tuition and expenses are paid from three separate bank accounts at the Central Bank of Columbia. Again, nothing obviously illegal. We are certainly monitoring all of Dr. Walters's professional and personal bank accounts, his general financial situation, and his Columbian friends—hard evidence—none.

- Dr. Franz Gunter, Munich, is a nanotech scientist. He has a company, Nanosolar LTD, which has several subcontractors and several banks that he and his company routinely use; so, determining who moved first, to where, for what, and how often in that financial forest is difficult. Less difficult is the fact that Dr. Gunter's mother and father are both in expensive nursing home centers in Munich. Their expenses are paid for by three different Chinese banks and two German banks. Dr. Gunter has clients in China, the mafia called Chinese Five Snakes, and in several European countries, all for curative therapies of course—hard evidence includes data that Dr. Gunter shipped a 'forty-pound package' to Turkey just before the Istanbul Ciraghan Palace massacre two years ago.
- Dr. Mario Kemps, Buenos Aires, is a nanotech scientist. He has been designing and producing nanotech systems for 'cures' and selling abroad for several years. Local information is difficult to obtain because Argentina is non-cooperative. The only hard evidence includes data that Dr. Kemps shipped a 'thirty-pound package' to South Africa at a time just before the Bloemfontein diamond mine massacre."

"So, monitoring personal lives, including financial status, is helpful, but these people are very bright and probably have excellent professional and financial advice. What we are seeking is not unusual.

The candidates whom we investigated closely have several suspicious financial relationships, business and personal, intermixed. All is not necessarily illegal, at least not yet. Again, this is why we must have continuous monitoring, ear and eye, on each of our candidates."

Mr. Sugimura asked. "How much help can we continue to expect from the American Central Intelligence Agency and National Security Agency?"

"That must be minimally expressed," replied Mr. McGriff. "Let me say that we are using CIA and NSA information and data daily. Most of our electronic searching and monitoring comes to us via the NSA. If there should be a hit' from a ship, truck, train, or even a car, such as it might be carrying a suspicious nanotech cargo, we can arrange satellite pursuit, inform local or international authorities, and have the vehicle stopped and searched. Remember, in the USA and EU laws which cover terrorism, there are some aspects of nanotechnology where we currently have the highest level of jurisprudence."

"Let me give you an example of my question," continued Mr. Sugimura. "If NSA identified a nanotechnical product problem concerning a Japanese citizen in China, could I find out about this problem before the news media? Of course, I would impose a committee need to know situation."

And he smiled—always a touch of the Eastern way.

That brought the first round of laughter. Every committee member could experience such a problem. Just how informal were committees such that committee members could try to rescue friends or countrymen? Worldwide such things were not uncommon. They were just simply more common in the Far East and South America. The question went unanswered.

Dr. von Eulenberg cleared the air. "When do you anticipate our next committee meeting?"

"I plan to meet twice a year," replied Mr. Murphy. "Perhaps early spring and early winter, assuming our investigations go without major problems."

"Earlier Mr. Femer suggested that he could use direct help from sources outside of the ISAAT in Europe. What type of help are you requesting?" asked Mr. Thomson.

"If the Europeans on the committee could possibly return for an hour or so after lunch, maybe we can determine what you can provide and match that with what we need. We have some investigative areas covered better than others. And maybe Mr. Sugimura could give us some additional assistances in Tokyo and Hong Kong," Mr. Femer replied.

Ms. Lawess asked, "How many nanotech homicides were there last year?"

Mr. Murphy answered. "Using the same Medically Unexplained Sudden Death criteria (MUSD), and counting only high-tech scientists, scientific entrepreneurs, or political supporters thereof who were killed, five deaths were reported in two countries. And yes, we do hold back from the reports on the nanotech pathology. Such decisions are made by authorities above my pay grade." And he had his chance at his 'committee' joke—he smiled.

After a few moments, Mr. Murphy continued. "Actually, the basic logic behind incomplete reporting any of these MUSDs is thought to help minimize any type of negative public response against high technology research."

The discussions of right-wrong, human ethics, self-preservation, or negative public backlash, would it or would it not be playing into the hands of the enemy—such ideas were batted around the table for several minutes. Each committee member needed to express his feeling about sudden nano-tech initiated homicides.

Not all committee members agreed with this idea, and they began to speak up. Mr. McGriff spoke up, "We are forgetting about our original and still major target, and that is Korrectorizer and his Committee of World Conservative Industrialists. They apparently have only struck three times since the Istanbul mass murders on October 29, 2032. We do not know when, where, or how they will strike next. There are many high-tech scientists who are unprotected all over the world. We hope that one of these candidates will help us find him, her, or them, before the world loses more high-level brainpower."

The Committee of Nanotechnology Control meeting continued with more questions and answers/educated guesses for the next two hours, adjourned and broke for lunch. Mr. Sugimura and the European members then met again with Mr. McGriff, Mr. Murphy, and Mr. Femer. They spent some time exchanging information and ideas of how and where in Europe to concentrate their efforts. It appeared that with this second major international effort, now having new restrictions and laws in the USA and Europe, using a larger modified committee with more international clout, would indeed be successfully established in another attempt to identify and incarcerate those involved in the worldwide nanotech homicides.

Later in the week Mr. Murphy and Dr. Stronger had both returned to work/offices in Boston. That Friday afternoon, Dagda joined the two O'Reilly brothers in Jonathan's law office on the top floor of the O'Reilly Building for late afternoon tea. Dr. Stronger would join them later. Dagda briefly reviewed the pertinent actions of the meeting of the Committee of Nanotechnology Control, provided names of the old and new 'candidates' who were now current investigation targets.

William Stronger arrived, poured his tea, joined in the conversation and asked, "Have you recently talked with your nephew, Jamie, and his Four Musketeers? Remember we would still be totally in the dark if they had not jumped in and found a major source of the production of nanotechnology homicide systems, plus a general explanation of a rationale for targeting high tech scientists and their funding entrepreneurs."

Jonathan agreed, "I feel that they should be kept in the circle. Each boy lost a father and family members. They deserve to continue in their own way. I know Jamie wants another chance, call it revenge if you want to do so. His father, our brother, was one of the first to go."

"Jamie and I are going to listen to the Boston Pops Concert next week," said Dagda. "I will update him concerning the three candidates remaining from our past investigation efforts and give him a list of the seven new candidates. You are right. They worked with us extremely well, and we would not know nearly as much today if they had not, shall we say, maneuvered outside the law and entered places where we could not go. And I agree, they do plan to continue their quest to find their fathers' killers. Do you know what they are going to do? They are going to learn about ancient witchcraft and try to use this as a new weapon."

The other three gentlemen all smiled, looked at each other and tried not to laugh. They knew these 'boys' were serious. And they had been successful last time.

Dagda said, "Don't laugh. I bet you a million dollars that they will have more success than we do using this rather unorthodox approach at fighting the bad guys."

Each just nodded in positive agreement!

7

KEF AND VOODOOISM

THE LEGOASE FAMILY HAD taken justice into their own hands when they 'imported' a Hungan/Priest from Haiti to perform a black voodoo spell on Kef's father's boss, Mr. Jonathan Saatfordam, who was the Co-Founder and Vice President of the Saatfordam Diamond Mines in Bloemfontain, South Africa. Mr. Legoase was the manager of a working crew at the mines. One night the entire crew of 212 workers suddenly and simultaneously died, apparently by breathing a contaminated air source. Kefentse Legoase's father was one of the victims. Each miner was found inside the cave, laying on the floor at his work station, with no lungs in his body. The lungs had digested/dissolved. These macabre deaths were not reported to the news media. And no specific causative agent was identified, but a toxic 'something' was reported to be in the air. The other miners working in the mine believed that this massacre was orchestrated by Mr. Saatfordam. This group of victim-miners had been demanding to unionize. Mr. Saatfordam said no, never, no. It was the way of this white man. So, one year after the mass death investigations, finding that no guilty party had been identified by local security officials, the case was closed, and Mrs. Legoase acted.

Kef and his buddies of the Four Musketeers understood the type of justice that had been meted out. And they learned and decided that maybe witchcraft might be an approach that could be used to fight the World Conservatives who were orchestrating these nanotech homicides. In the five to six years that they had been battling these people and their nanotech killer systems, they had won a few minor battles, but were losing the war, so far. Using ancient witchcraft might provide them with a possible new secret weapon. There were not many 'attacking' options out there for a bunch of teenagers.

After watching the Voodoo revenge in motion, Kef approached his mother and asked her opinion. "Mother, do you think that black voodoo could be used to fight these World Conservative Industrialists and their nano-weapons? My 4-Pack needs some help; we are too young to learn about and use nano-technical systems to fight back. Maybe we can learn and recruit some help from another direction. Maybe witchcraft will work as a weapon for us. What do you think?"

Mother thought for a moment and finally replied, "I cannot tell you to stay away from this powerful medicine because I have recently used it. It is very curative. All the families with loved ones who were killed in the mines told me so. Each family is pleased to see some real justice. I too feel justice was victorious. Revenge is not always a bad thing. If I help you, you must promise me that you will find and recruit an experienced and very skillful Voodoo Priest—hungan or mambo. These priests are everything to their people—healer, confessor, magician, doctor, confidential advisor, and prophet. Voodoo is a religion of Black People. And Haitians are the most advanced. Voodoo reflects the social structure of the believers. It provides a means to remove all types of illnesses and corrects misfortunes that always seem to fall on these people. Similar to Christianity, its leaders use spirits/souls, and it involves the supernatural world or natural world events which mankind does not understand. I will arrange a meeting for you with my hungan before he returns to Haiti."

Kef's older brother Baryti, a senior level technician in the CT Nano nano-company in Cape Town heard about this proposed session with their mother's hungan. Baryti and Kef had been traveling together when their father was killed in the Saatfordam Mines massacre. They went to the mines, found their father, prayed over him, brought his body back home, and buried him in the family cemetery. So, Baryti also had a very strong personal motive to want to be involved with efforts which might help to identify the people and laboratories that manufactured these nano-weapons. He was a lab specialist in nanodrugs. In addition, he wanted to protect baby brother.

So, one week later, on a dark cloudy day, Kef and Baryti went to the old rented house where the Haitian hungan temporarily resided. For the past several weeks the hungan had been teaching and holding sessions, three times a week, for 'interested people in need' in the Cape Town area. He had generated much interest, especially with rumors of his possible involvement in the suicide of the diamond mine owner.

As the brothers arrived at the old wooden house, they saw that the front door was open. They knocked and entered. There was only one large living room and a small bedroom-kitchen off to the back. Immediately to the right of the door was a small round table. The house was dark and empty. A strange music and strong smell permeated the air. Weird 'things' were hanging from the ceiling. Also, they saw flags which had numerous non-readable 'symbols' painted on them. Both fellows suddenly felt cold chills due partially to a cool down draft coming from somewhere above them. They looked around and only saw the table and three empty chairs; on the table was one large alligator tooth, two small mice teeth, and three lit candles. Hanging above and to the side of the table were the heads of two roosters, recently sacrificed, as they were still dripping blood.

Kef became very nervous, looked back at the entry, and judged the distance to the door just in case he needed a fast exit. He was a super athlete and knew he could be out the door in less than one second. But he knew overweight big brother was not fast at all. He glanced over at Baryti, who was also showing signs of nervousness. He started to say something about coming back later, when a sudden scream occurred in the back of the house.

A black cat suddenly flew past them and out the front door. They heard another quiet noise at the table. Turning around they saw the hungan sitting on one of the chairs. His eyes were shut, but he motioned for them to sit in the other two chairs. They did so.

On the table in front of them were two glasses of hot 'tea'. He motioned for them to close their eyes and slowly drink. As they did so the music, smells, and air drafts continued very strongly. Kef began to cautiously open one eye and study the little old man who was very dark but smooth skinned, had reddish freckles, frizzles of stringy gray hair at the temples and long gray eyebrows. One could guess his age to be 80+ years. The room was so dark Kef could not tell if the hungan's eyes were open or shut, but he was certain he also had very dark eyes. The obviously powerful old man wore a brilliant red and gold robe and began softly chanting. This only made the boys more nervous.

After a few minutes, without opening his eyes, the hungan spoke in their mother's voice. "I know why you are here and what you want. Because of the recent happening, our laws allow me to only teach to you, not do for you. After I have taught to you, the older will remain here, and the younger will go beyond. Please ask no questions. All will happen as needed."

"I will begin at the beginning. About three hundred years ago, West African Blacks were kidnapped and taken to the so-called New World, especially the colonies of Saint Domingue, then Haiti and Republica Dominica, and now Dominican Republic. They were 'employed' as slaves with no pay. By colonial law they were required to be baptized and become Catholic within one week after arrival. The owners were responsible for this. The slaves accepted baptism but were never given church instruction. Over several years many blacks formed their own small 'black' church. But white Catholic Priests were discouraged from going out to the plantations where they might observe the cruelty and harsh treatment of the slaves, but this did not occur. How could the slave and his owner share the same God who taught peace, equality, and brotherhood? So, the Voodoo social religion/structure was transplanted from Africa and blossomed in Caribbean America, but separate from white man's Christianity."

"As the black slaves began gathering under the Black African trained or self-trained priests, numerous gods, beliefs, rituals, practices, and charms/amulets of Voodooism were born and accepted as a major way of life. In the beginning the social infrastructure developed around secret night time Voodoo gatherings. A basic Voodoo oriented infrastructure developed and matured. After the French revolution, a slave revolt in Saint Domingue, led by Napoleon's former generals who were exiled along with Napoleon, was successful. Haiti became independent; slavery diminished; and for many years the entire island suffered through a series of power-hungry presidents and continuous wars. But Voodooism was the life source for the common mode of the black civilization. It was the linkage for the Black Peoples of Haiti, northern parts of South America, and many of the islands in the Caribbean Sea, most of whom were forcefully transplanted from Africa by the white Europeans."

"There is no hierarchy of leaders such as priest-bishop-cardinal-pope in the Voodoo Priesthood. The oum'phor/humfo/Voodoo temple is where Voodoo services/ceremonies are held. There may be one or several humfos. All is under control or guidance of a Voodoo Priest, houn'gan/hungan or mam'bo/mambo. All may have several rooms or chambers; each chamber and altar may be reserved for the worship of a single god. All power in Voodooism resides in the humfo. Therefore, the hungan or mambo, equivalent to the emperor or empress, are the supreme everything to his or her people. And each call upon one or more of the LOA or supernatural spirits/souls/gods for assistance. Younger son will soon see this when he goes beyond."

Kef and Baryti exchanged puzzled looks. Kef swallowed twice. He did not want to go abroad.

"The humfo usually contains one hungan or mambo and a few servants. Or it may contain more than one hungan or mambo and adepts which are surrounded by many houses and buildings which accommodate Voodoo adepts, trainees, acolytes, initiates, assistants, believers, visiting pilgrims, and the sick, destitute or needy. It may be a small village with a focus upon helping people with natural and supernatural illnesses. A humfo may have only a limited few. Or it may have many men, women, and children—a close knit community which provides its own sustenance."

"The major source of financial support is the reputation of the hungan or mambo for healing, mentally or physically. People come from great distances and will pay much money to be treated and healed by a famous Healer. We cure many types of physical and spiritual problems. OR they come to learn their future-fortunes from a famous Prophet known to have great insight or second site. It is common for such a hungan or mambo to regularly service wealthy businessman and government leaders, in addition to the poor. Most of the income for supporting the humfo comes from such services."

"Services vary depending upon the hungan, his chosen LOA or GOD, and the ability of the humfo to assist in carrying out these services. They will usually involve a ceremony, incense, music, dancing, chanting, incantations, and human trances, while using a variety sacred items such as gourds containing beads, snake bones, animal charms, and animal sacrifices. An intercourse between the known and the unknown worlds will be established. The LOA will communicate with the hunan who will serve as the god's mouthpiece. During the mystic trance the problem will be given and a solution will be received. This solution will be interpreted and/or implemented for the believer who gave the problem."

"I understand that you need the assistance of special Black Voodoo medicine, therefore a Voodoo Priest or Priestess. But before you can ask for this medicine you must find the source which requires this special therapy. In the meantime, Younger Son, you shall go beyond and learn about Voodooism. And when you identify the 'target mind' which needs curing, tell you mother, she will contact me, and I will support your appeal to the Humfo of the Voodoo of the Caribbean and South America, the Black Cleopatra. Her humfo is near Port au Prince in Haiti. She is a direct descendent of the Egyptian Queen Cleopatra, who was black inside and white outside. But you must be prepared to pay a high price for her services."

The hungan stopped talking and suddenly fell into a deep sleep. The two brothers looked at each other and shrugged their shoulders. Kef motioned that they should leave. Baryti agreed. After a few moments, the hungan had not moved, but started to sing in a strange language. They slowly, quietly, and carefully got up and quickly left the house.

As they walked home neither understood nor could explain what had happened. They would ask their mother for help.

One month later, on the third Sunday afternoon of June, Kefentse Legoase glanced out of the window of the South African Airlines 360Airbus as it dropped down over the island of the Dominican Republic and Haiti. It approached the Aeroport International de Port au Prince on the west side of Haiti. The view was the rugged mountains, areas of naked rocks and shrub, and some areas of heavily treed forests. This was the largest tropical island in the central Atlantic Ocean. He could see areas of cropland and pastures, especially in the large valley east of the Haitian capital, Port au Prince. The distant Gulf of Gonave was a beautiful dark blue with numerous boats and ships of all varieties. The shoreline west of the capital was one of the heavily populated areas and that was where he was going. Queen Cleopatra's Humfo was located high up in the mountains directly south and above the city of Carrefour. This would require some land travel time.

The trip was smooth, the landing gentle, but finding the transportation for the two-hour ride through the crowded city filled with many nice houses on the sea shore, and many not-so-nice houses elsewhere, was difficult. He spoke no Creole or French, but finally with help from some of the natives he purchased a ticket on a city bus at a bus terminal near the airport. An hour later, before he entered the bus, he telephoned his mother and told her all was going as planned—no problems. It was a hot day but his T-shirt and shorts were fine. He had heard that city buses and most houses did not have air conditioning, so he was very properly prepared for a hot summer.

The bus ride up to the humfo was long, hot, and tiresome. Kef thought back to the final decisions with his buddies. He had talked with Jamie who had met with his Uncles Dagda, Jonathan, and Jackson. They all agreed that there was adequate evidence to place at the top of the hit list a certain Dr. Mario Kemps and his laboratory in Buenos Aires as being directly involved in the South African diamond mine massacre. Jamie passed this information on to Kef; so now Kef would learn about Voodoo witchcraft in Haiti, and maybe later they would cite or declare this Dr. Kemps as a potential target. Kef's family and the families of the miners who were killed donated money such that he could go to and spend time with a Voodoo witch and his/her humfo. Kef's mother arranged with her hungan who obtained permission from the Black Cleopatra for Kef to spend a couple of summer months as a trainee in her humfo in Haiti. The request was accepted when based on the concept that Kef would train this summer and continue as a trainee this fall. If it was possible and he decided he could try Voodoo witchcraft as a career, he would have priority to join the witchcraft school.

It was late afternoon as the bus arrived in Carrefour. His timing was lucky because the last south mountain bus was leaving from the Carrefour terminal in fifteen minutes. So, he quickly purchased his ticket and climbed onto this bus going to Queen Cleopatra Humfo and nearby villages. Most villagers had come to the 'city' for shopping and were going home. The rock-asphalt road was one car narrow much of the time, required a climb to 12,000 feet, had numerous places requiring hairpin turns around mountain ridges. It was a most difficult forested mountain climb for an overused old bus that struggled all the way; but eventually it ended up on the high mountain plateau, three square miles of flatness that contained numerous associated buildings and provided spectacular views of the sea on both the north and south sides of Haiti.

Indeed, the ride was very bad, but the humfo location was very good. The bus stopped in a small park; he climbed down, looked around, and counted more than a dozen buildings surrounded by a lovely green forest. He had no idea where to go. Suddenly a young man tapped him on the shoulder and said in English, "You look lost. You must be Kefentse Legoase from South Africa."

"Welcome. My name is Asahel Leobia. I am a Haitian, and a third level adept here at the Queen Cleopatra Humfo. I will be your guide, translator, and partial teacher while you are studying here."

Asahel was twenty-five years old, clean shaven, with long curly black hair, and was a very handsome young man. He was born and raised in a middle-class neighborhood of Cape Haitien on the north coastline of Haiti. And Kef would soon learn that Asahel always knew where he was going in life, and would help him in his further decisions.

"Bring your suitcase and I will take you to your dormitory room so you can get settled. Then we can go register your arrival and entry into the Voodoo training program. You will soon see that Queen Cleopatra runs her program very much like a professional school or college. As you know, if you successfully complete the three-year program here, plus a one-two year traineeship at a location away from Haiti, pass an exam given by the Queen, you will be a Voodoo Priest. I know that you will like it, as I do, and perform very well."

Kef swallowed. He wasn't planning all of that. He responded, "Thank you. Yes, I am happy to be here in such a beautiful location. I am anxious to learn everything. When do I start classes?"

And they continued talking as they walked toward the administration building. Asahel said, "You will start immediately. The registration office will give you several pamphlets and books in English which you can look over tonight. Tomorrow, I will take you on a short tour of the humfo and introduce you to other trainees and some of your teachers. You will probably not meet Queen Cleopatra or any of her three daughters until sometime in year two or three; They teach the final courses of White and Black Voodoo magic. And of course, they give the final ritual examinations—pass or fail."

So, Kef and Asahel visited the registration offices, picked up study materials, checked in the dormitory for men, dropped off his suitcase in his new bedroom, and went into the dining room to join in the evening meal which was winding down. There were only eight people at the tables. Asahel introduced Kef to all of them. They welcomed him and told him they looked forward to helping learn the Voodoo way. It was getting late and Kef had been up for the past twenty plus hours. So, he ate quickly and went to his room—everyone had a single bed room with one bed, one chair, and one study desk. There were multiple bath-toilet-shower rooms on each floor. Asahel told him he would meet him downstairs for breakfast in the morning; Kef was asleep before his body hit the bed.

At 9 AM Asahel was waiting for Kef in the dining room; they would eat and then begin a short tour of the humfo. With nearly five hundred people living, working, and schooling in more than eleven buildings, it was much larger than Kef anticipated. But the dormitory for men and the eating facility were in the same building, so he was not yet lost. The nearby village had a population of less than a thousand men, women, and children, who were 'peasant' farmers who provided food and maintenance services within the humfo. It was a very positive symbiotic relationship.

"I know you went directly to sleep last night," Asahel began. "So, I brought a summary of the educational program. Go, select your breakfast, let us sit down and eat, and then we can go over it."

Kef, now finally wide awake as his biological clock was at mid-afternoon, chose his breakfast from a limited selection of foods, mostly fruits, returned to the long table and sat with Asahel and four other fellows. He quickly downed his meal. He was still hungry but was afraid it would be bad manners to eat two breakfasts on his first morning. He looked around, and picked up a copy of the Voodoo Educational Program. They started going over it.

Asahel began, "The program is very different from any high school or university education with which you might be familiar." And he pointed to page two and began going over the voodoo training ideas as established by the Queen Cleopatra's Humfo.

TRAINING FOR THE VOODOO PRIESTHOOD

List of courses: A-courses year one; B-courses year two; C-courses year three.

A1 – Voodoo History

A2 – Organization of the Humfo—religious and lay leaders of the Voodoo Society

A3 – Religious Symbols and Artifacts

A4 – Gods and Goddesses—the Pantheon

A5 – What Gods Can and Cannot do

B1 – Ceremonies and Rituals

B2 – Chants – Rhythms—Prayers

B3 – Physical Health Care and Problems

B4 – Mental Health Care and Problems

B5 – Plant and Animal Active Extracts

B6 – White Magic and Black Magic

C1 – Participation in Minor Ceremonies and Rituals

C2 – Participation in Major Ceremonies and Rituals

Asahel explained, "All courses are tutorial and continuous. Each course is taught by an adept/teacher. You will meet for one 2-hour period twice a week, either in the morning or afternoon. Exams are given only when your teacher determines that you have successfully completed the course. This educational format is similar to the educational programs at Cambridge and Oxford Universities in England. A trainee may enter the program anytime, discontinue for short periods, and re-enter. He simply is required to satisfy his teacher that he has learned and knows the subject matter of the course. The trainee has four years to complete and pass the three-year program. During this week you will meet personally with each of your adepts/teachers for each of the five courses in the first year of the program. I will be your teacher for course A4—The Gods and Goddesses of the Pantheon."

"And how do I go to a class?"

"You do not. Teaching/learning is not always accomplished in a classroom. Your teacher and you will decide where and when to meet. You have already been scheduled to meet with your other four teachers later today, between 4 and 6 o'clock, one by one in the library. They each speak English so you will not have language problems. When you talk with each one, you will be given a synopsis of the course and the key overall objectives. The two of you will establish certain hours on certain days of the week to meet in your teacher's office, a small library room, or other convenient locations. He/she will be your only teacher for that course, just as you will be his only student for that course. Any questions?"

Kef was a little puzzled and asked, "So the teaching and final grade for the course comes directly from the teacher, just like high school; but the scheduling of course is what—random?"

"In general, classes are not lectured; and they will always be arranged jointly by student and teacher. You will see that some teachers prefer lecture type covering of the subject matter, while other teachers will want much discussion of what you learned from your pre-reading/pre-study assignments. There are many ways to learn, in addition to a single teacher standing in from of a classroom of thirty sitting students and talking in a one-way direction about the subject. This does not allow for maximum learning and also good understanding. It simply makes teaching easier for the teacher. Your learning here will be a 100% tête-à-tête communication with each of your teachers. You may even get to know and like some of them. Now, you and I will meet every Monday and Wednesday mornings at 8:00 to 10:00, in my office. OK?"

Kef could only reply, "That seems like a good way to learn. Yes, I like it. Let's get going." And laughed at himself.

The two of them stood, went outside, and began a walking tour of the center of the large/village of Queen Cleopatra Humfo. They began near the north parking lot and main entry into the complex of buildings.

"This is the major road associated with the entry, but there are several small roads through the forest which sort of surround and provide car and truck service access to the back of some of the buildings. Toward the north and west is the Humfo Village, about one mile. The villagers provide much necessary service to the humfo such as fresh fruits and vegetables, breads, prepared foods, building maintenance, janitorial, and housekeeping services. Located there is small state school which is available for all the children of the area."

"As we enter this gate, straight ahead you can see in the center of the complex of buildings is the temple. You can see it is built on eight large tree trunks as support columns. They support a pyramid shaped thatched roof with a smoke hole in the center. All sides are open. It will seat six hundred people on the surrounding benches. The earth floor drops down to a large stage-area which has the poteau-mitan center post in the middle. The poteau-mitan contains several spirits and forms the pivot point for many dances. All feasts, ceremonies, dances, and rituals are performed here. It is the center of our lives. You can enter and look around whenever you want. No doors—no keys—no do not enter signs." And he laughed out loud.

They began walking through the complex of buildings. "The major buildings form a large rectangle around the temple. As you can see, all of this area around the temple is one continuous walking plaza. That first building to the left of the temple contains the health clinics, the adjacent building is a small hospital/hospice. Both physical and spiritual diseases are treated here. As you can see, both of these buildings, as well as most buildings, are three to four floors. And only the hospital/hospice have elevators. All buildings are built with hand cut trees from the local forest. The building beyond the hospital is the women's dormitory. And beyond that is a four-floor library with over one thousand books."

"On the right side of the temple complex is the dormitory for men. Be sure to recognize that if you want to sleep indoors every night, However, there are several nearby camp sites where we sleep outdoors, for comradery of course!" And he winked at Kef.

"Both dormitories have food services for all members of the humfo. The next building on the right contains most of the administrative units.

That is where you registered and picked up your books and pamphlets yesterday. Continuing on the right is a large more modern styled two floor building for visitors and guests. Beyond that is a large house where Queen Cleopatra and her daughters live. Immediately to the left of this area is a dormitory for adepts. I live there where we have our own food service and small conference rooms. There are currently 21 adepts. And then around to the library again. The first floor of the library also contains classrooms and conference rooms."

"Outside of this large rectangle of buildings and houses there are several support buildings and houses under control of the mambo. In fact, the mambo makes all decisions; so be aware and do not create problems for her. She is known to have recently placed a curse on the Haitian Foreign Minister, who subsequently died in a tragic airplane crash."

The two of them were rapidly becoming friends as they slowly walked around. Kef asked many questions. Asahel gave many answers. Asahel introduced Kef to various people. Kef felt that things were sort of divided into male and female areas, but working was totally integrated. Kef would soon learn that most ceremonies required both sexes participating. He met several members of the humfo from Africa. And he easily used his Swahili to talk with them. They agreed to join him for lunch at a café 'out' near the village café, on the south side of the complex which overlooked the Caribbean Sea—spectacular views.

Kef liked the overall set-up, no fancy buildings or landscaping, just lots of natural shrubs and trees. A tropical island like Haiti has rains and hot weather year-round, so plants grow whether you want them to do so or not. It was a very natural setting with pastel and faded colors on the wall of buildings surrounded by forest, sea, clouds, and sun. The numerous flowering plants were all local and transplanted into locations around the buildings in the plaza area. The atmosphere was very quiet, no vehicle noises, only birds and forest animals, very relaxing. He began to understand how with a little concentration one might be able to reach up to God or god or Gods or gods or they might reach down to you. And then new things might just start to happen.

Near noon Asahel showed Kef his room in the dormitory for the adepts. They then separated and would meet back there at 3 PM to discuss their course. Kef went to the little South Café to meet the humfo Africans. He was pleased to learn that the five of them were from five different countries. And thus, Kef spent the next three hours learning about these neat guys, and listening to their understanding of Queen Cleopatra, the functioning of the humfo, and their understanding of Queen Cleopatra Voodooism.

At 3:00 he joined Asahel in his second-floor dormitory room. The adept's rooms were rather large as they accommodated one single bed, a study area with book shelves, three chairs with a large round table, and a small couch. They also had their own small kitchenette and nearby a shower/toilet. They lived here and taught up to three students at one time from these rooms.

Asahel welcomed him and asked, "So what do you think of our forest mountain top home and school?"

Kef gave him a thumbs-up-gesture.

Asahel just grinned. He then sat on one of the chairs around the table, motioned for Kef to sit on one of the other chairs. He took out his course synopsis of Gods and Goddesses of the Pantheon, opened it and said, "I will briefly review the major concepts that will be covered in this course."

"LOA—Gods and goddesses originate from male and female spirits. That is why there are many. Most live in the Pantheon. They are supernatural, mysterious, and natural in a way most mankind does not understand—and most arise from the dead. Their presence and strengths depend upon the specific tribal rituals and death rites of the tribe or of the Voodoo priest performing the death ceremony. And there are many variations in the music, rhythms, chants, language, prayers, ceremonial symbols, sacrifices, and the specific spoken phrases, as well as even how the death occurred. We are talking about the spirits from our ancestors, the humans that came before us."

"There are many classifications of gods such as Rada Mysteres, Congo Mysteres, Ibo Mysteres, and Pethro Mysteres. We will discuss these groups. And there are certain 'senior' Gods and Goddesses who are accessible to all Voodoo priests. These include: Legba who opens the doors/gates to the mysteres, Dahomy acts as an interpreter of the many gods, Agwe who is the god of the seas, Siren who is female songstress, Damballah-wedo is the serpent god, Simbi is the guardian of water, Sogobo is the god of lighting, Bade is the god of winds, Agau is the god of the earth, Ogu-badagri is a war god, Loco is god of vegetation, but Zaka is the peasant god of food crops, and on and on. We will look at many of these gods and compare their roles in the lives of Voodoo believers."

Kef quickly asked, "If you want to reach a certain spirit from a local family, how do you do this.?"

"That is a very intuitive question. Yes, you would need new information concerning specifically that spirit. This information would come from the family. Personal items from that spirit when he was a warm being is very helpful. Perhaps a tuft of hair, a tooth or a body bone; something that has 'genetic units such as DNA'. Then you can work out a new specific set of ceremonial symbols, chants, and prayers, and a specially designed ritual to try to reach that specific spirit. You will learn about this during your third year when you take the C-courses with the Queen and her daughters."

And he gave Kef a big smile.

For the next hour the two of them continued discussing the Gods of the Pantheon and Voodoo life. And then near 4:00 Kef went next door to the library to meet with his other four adepts/teachers. He was directed to a small study room and was introduced to a very pretty middle-aged lady wearing a bright multicolored dress and large black rimmed glasses. They shook hands, sat down and began a conversation.

"My name is Mahalia. I was born in Haiti. I am a second-year adept. And I know that you are Kefentse from South Africa. How did you decide to come here to Haiti and become a Voodoo Priest?"

Kef was shocked. He was not ready for such a straight question. He swallowed and quickly thought. Fortunately his mouth was as fast as his championship feet, so he came up with story about that he had not completely committed himself to the priesthood, that he needed to learn more about voodooism, that he always wanted to learn about witchcraft, he had one more year in high school, his mother was pushing him in this direction, for the present he was in an open learning mode.

Mahalia smiled and did not really believe any of it, but opened the synopsis for her course anyway—course A3—Religious Symbols. She gave Kef a copy. He opened it and they began a review of the course material.

"I wish for us to meet here in this library study room on Monday and Tuesday afternoon at 2:00. Is that all right with you?"

Kef nodded affirmatively. What else could he say?

"During the year we will learn about the many symbols used in voodoo and how we use them. If you look on the first page of your synopsis you will see a list of the major ones which include: veves, asson, assein/asin, assoto, bakas/talismans, ouangas/amulets, ritual flags, ritual signs, joukoujou, ku-bha-sah/LaPlace's sword or cutting blade, and many perfumes or aromas."

"To give you an idea just how important these are let me briefly talk about a couple of them."

"First and of high importance is the veves. These are special designs traced on the ground with maize flour, wood ashes, or coffee grounds. They can also be placed on ceremonial objects, even food. The veves are astral forces which are personified star-ancestors. The ancestors, in turn, are personified by the LOAS, the spirits and the mysteres. During a certain ceremonial rite, reproduction of specific astral forces represented by the veves obliges the LOAS, who are represented by the heavenly bodies stars, moon, planets—to descend on earth. Different rites require different veves—Rada rites require white or yellow flour, Pethro rites require certain leaf powders, etc."

"Most veves include the serpent as a transmigration of spirits/souls. All voodoo veves have three astral planes which are arranged in a diagram according to the magical attributes of the LOAS. This becomes complicated as it also requires the Omnipotent or father and the Omniscent or the mother. These three planes correspond to a serpent-synthesis which is ophi- (serpent), os- (mystere), or ophitomorphic. In other words, the planes unite to form a macrocosm, which include the elements of the microcosm or 'human being'. The serpent has five heads—pentamorphic—which correspond to the five degrees of the LOA."

Mahalia suddenly stopped, saw Kef's eyes had glassed over, and asked, "Are you following this?"

"Not really," he replied.

"Good, that means that you are honest and simply have a lot to learn. This is just one Voodoo symbol that I have begun to describe. In any given ceremonial rite several symbols will be used. In this course we will learn about all of them, and how and when to use each one. I will give you one more example."

"The assein/assen is an iron object, usually a rod with a round plate like area fastened horizontally onto the top. The rod may be a simple rod or cross, or a complex design such as climbing-intertwining snakes or branches. Hermetically this represents LOAS of fire and the forge. Candles or fire are placed on top of the assen. Sacrificial offerings are also placed on the plate area. Every Voodoo Priest has his own personal assen."

The two of them talked for a few more minutes. Kef thanked his new teacher, told her he would see her next Monday, and quickly left, and went down the hallway to his next new teacher for his 4:30 appointment.

Kef knocked on the door, was motioned inside to meet a tall slim blue-eyed black man. "My name is Nwadinkpa. I am a second-year adept from Nigeria. I know you are Kefentse from South Africa. I asked to be one of your teachers because I thought that when you finish your training you might return to Africa and practice Voodooism using Swahili, not English. So, if you want, we can speak in an African language."

Kef's eyes lit up and he replied, "I am pleased to meet you. And yes, I would be happy to so study in your course—A1—Voodoo History—Right?"

"That is right. We will analyze the history of the movement of voodooism away from Africa, and the role white people versus black people played in this immigration. I would like for us to meet on Wednesday and Thursday afternoons at 2:00 in my room in the adepts' dormitory room 305."

Kef could not have been happier. In fact, things were going almost too well. He had sort of planned to stay only a couple of months, return home, finish high school, and then go to college and study nanotechnology, following in his older brother's footsteps. He just wanted to learn 'some' voodoo magic. He promised himself he would not change his mind.

And the two African brothers spent the next fifteen-twenty minutes glancing over the course content. Some Kef already knew; but the way Nwadinkpa would present it would be fascinating. It was as if he believed that a great loss had occurred from Africa when the center of Voodooism moved west. There was great interest in moving it back to Africa where there were 1000 times more black people. Because of the African comradery, they planned to sometimes get together for evening meals where they could discuss potential involvement of voodooism in the future life of Africa. If he decided to go back home, this might be a good present to bring back to his African people.

Kef hurried to Room 211 in the adepts' dormitory for his 5:00 appointment. He knocked on the door. No one answered. He waited for a few minutes and started to leave. Suddenly the door jerked open, and there stood a bald headed, middle aged, overweight, a very light brown man, with amber eyes. This was a Haitian, Toussant De Beau, born to a black father and a white French mother. He was rather world famous in his specialization area of Voodoo Gods. He invited Kef inside the room. They introduced themselves, but Dr. De Beau explained that he had just been called to meet with a 'believer', so would have to leave quickly. They sat at the round table, and opened the synopsis for Course A5—What Voodoo Gods Can and Cannot Do.

Dr De Beau explained, "This course explores the advantages and limitations of gods in life, death, and post-death situations. They can protect, confer certain powers or facilities, cure various mental or physical illnesses, assist in the use of the supernatural powers, create or solve problems, help identify future events, see into the mind, and many more things which we will talk about during the duration of the course. We will not only talk about what a god can do, but how we can use such strength to solve problems."

After a fast fifteen minutes of reviewing the course, they agreed to meet in this room Tuesday and Friday mornings at 9:00. Each left in a hurry as they were both running late for their next connections. Kef did not like this Haitian.

Kef returned to the library and found his next adept/teacher, Nadege, a pleasant looking young Haitian lady with a large afro hair style and who was wearing a Celtics T-shirt, shorts, and tennis shoes. She had a lovely smile, immediately shook hands, and hugged Kef. She was a very warm person and of course he had to compare her with his last teacher contact. This course had to be more fun. Her course was A3—Organizations of the Humfo. Nadege had a university degree from Tufts University in Boston, USA; and she loved American sports, especially football/soccer. When she learned that Kef played middle fielder for the South African National Soccer Team last year, she hugged him again. She played middle fielder for the women's soccer team at Tufts while in school there. After this unusual introduction, they both sort of forgot the Organizations course and talked international football/soccer for the next fifteen minutes. Kef promised to join the Humfo's soccer team, which played on Saturday morning. They agreed that Nadege would teach Kef on Thursday morning at 9:00 and Friday afternoon at 1:00. And Kef would teach Nadege on Saturday morning at 9:00—different sports of course.

After they completed their new and unique humfo organization, knowledge for skills, they said a warm goodbye, shook hands and hugged again. Kef took his copy of the course synopsis and returned to his own dormitory room. Things were very good here. He was sure that he would learn a lot and develop some ideas about how to fight against the nanotech killers.

That evening he called his mother and told her about the humfo 'campus', teaching program, explained each of the five courses for the first year, and his current feelings about voodooism. He had already decided to stay the entire two months, but asked his mother if they could pay for any time longer. It was one thousand dollars per month which included all expenses. He told her he still planned to come home to finish high school. Next year was next year.

8

THE GOOD LIFE IN LONDON

Charles Somersham loved England and London, especially. He was born and grew up in Colcheser, a city so small everyone knew your business before you knew your business too—small. And college in Cambridge was very good with the mass of continuous youth, energy, action, and noise; it was fantastic, when he was of the age to enjoy it. But now that he was in his late twenties, the age for controlled energy, to try to really make something out of your life, London had it all. There were distinct areas of intense energy, areas of focused productive activity, and places of quietude in the numerous heavily treed parks. Charles preferred anonymity, or at least the opportunity to disappear from the world in the middle of the ten million people around him. Gentle people must be able to select periods of action and not have them thrust upon them.

His mother was the daughter of Irish nobility. And due to his ancestry from the House of Hanover, he could take what he wanted when he wanted. As long as his family was successful in breeding his maternal family's Irish racing horses, and as long as he was close enough to the Somersham Golden Meadows estate so he could ride his favorite horse, Gentle Black, every week, he was almost happy. To complete his life, he needed a 'more' successful business.

London is not only the capital of England and the United Kingdom, but also the world as far as Charles was concerned. It was settled more than two thousand years ago, conquered by the Romans, and a walled city named Londinium was built. In the fifth century, Rome collapsed, and Londinium was deserted. Nearby Angle-Saxons built a new settlement and named it Ludenwic. In the ninth century, attacks by the Vikings drove the people back into the old fortified area now called London. It became the largest city in the region, a major trading center, and the politically dominant power in the southern part of the British Isle. During the nineteenth century, London was the most populated city in the world, and the royalty adopted it as their city. Samuel Johnson, poet, writer, and author of the first English Dictionary was quoted as saying:

'You will find no man, with any degree of intellect, who is willing to move from London. NO SIR! When a man is tired of London, he is tired of life. For London has all one needs for the complete life.'

Today London houses both city and national governments. London proper has a two-tier government—city wide containing thirty-three small locales. The city is administrated by the Greater London Authority with a Mayor of London (executive) and a London Assembly (legislative); all are located in the City Hall in Southwark. Each has its own mayor.

London is also the seat of the Government of the United Kingdom located in the Palace of Westminster while the home of the British Royal Family is in Buckingham Palace. Many government departments are located nearby including the Parliament and the Prime Minister's Residence, 10 Downing Street.

London generates about one quarter of the UK's GDP. The economy of the London metropolitan area is the largest of any city of Europe. In fact, London is one of the top five financial centers in the world. Of Europe's five hundred largest companies, more than two hundred are headquartered in London. And seventy five percent of the worlds Fortune 500 companies have offices in London.

It was for all of these reasons that Charles Somersham chose to establish his Green Meadows Import-Export Firm in London, and why he was having lunch with Gregory McCorland at the City of London Club, patronized by the Duke of Edinburgh. Mr. McCorland was a descendant of Mary, Queen of Scotland, whose son became James VI, King of Scotland and Ireland. His wife was the daughter of an Irish baroness. So, similar to Charles, Gregory's father was a Lord, and through the royal peerage system the McCorland family inherited several hundred acres, complete with castle, in the highlands on the east coast of Scotland. He was an only boy, but had three younger sisters, was in his late twenties, and was using the family money to establish businesses in London. So, the two of them had much in common—birds of a feather—.

As Charles was escorted to Gregory's table, he again looked at his new friend, they had only met a few weeks ago at a cocktail party. Indeed, Gregory was very Scottish—tall, lanky, reddish rough skin, long blonde hair in a ponytail, almond eyes, obviously a strong and decisive personality, a person who tells you what he thinks, a no-nonsense person. You would always know where you stood with him. He thought to himself, 'I do believe things could work out with a proper business partnership'.

Arriving at the table Gregory immediately popped up, bear hugged Charles and said rather loudly, "welcome to the only German club in England." And he burst out laughing.

Charles grinned and responded, "Then how do you explain being a member?"

"Why? Would you like to be a member?" returned Gregory. All we have to do is to talk to the clubs' senior patron. The problem here is that this specific 'German' patron has been living with that English Queen Elizabeth II for so long I hear he no longer speaks to foreigners. Therefore, you will have to ask him yourself." And he burst out laughing again.

Charles thought to himself again, 'this guy really has a sense of humor. And he is not wrong. But an Englishman cannot say such things.'

Gregory continued. "And how is the importation of bananas from the Caribbean and pineapples from Mexico?"

"Probably as rewarding as the importation of copper and potash from Brazil?" replied Charles.

He knew that Gregory also had an import-export company, CMcMetals, Inc. And that neither of their companies could be called successful.

"If I did not have to pound the bushes in the Amazon looking for something warmer than cold metals." And he glanced at the blond waitress in a short skirt who was going by and smiled at her.

"That is one thing about London," declared Charles. "There is much good money to be had, but the competition is ferocious. Among my business friends they seem to go in and out of a business venture every three or four years. Sometimes they profit from a tax loss they can take when they go out, but it always takes a while to find some new venture capital to start up and to go again. And then you need to find a product that is not already in the 'educated' market place. Or one can go abroad to some country that cannot spell the word business profit. But they know the word money. And ethnics of any type has not arrived."

Gregory said, "Do you mean Africa, or South America like I am doing?"

"What about that new drug stuff that you were telling me about recently? You gave me to understand that it was just entering the international market place. And if we moved now, we could beat the rush."

"Do you see that middle-aged gentleman sitting there in the atrium near that small lemon tree? He is wearing a gray-blue jacket, black slacks, with a grayish receding hair line, and smoking a Turkish meerschaum pipe."

Charles answered, 'I see him. So?"

"Four things come to mind. His name is Dr. Albert Langdon.

- First, he has lineage from the House of Windsor. This makes him our royal kin.
- Second, he is a Professor at the Hammersmith Hospital and Research Center and is currently creating and producing nanotechnical drugs. These are new types of chemical substances which can cure very sick people or kill/assassinate, in macabre-secret ways, non-sick people.
- Third, he is past President of the City of London Club, so he is the correct person to talk about membership.
- Fourth, Dr Langdon is a horse lover. If you mention to him that your father breeds racing horses, he will probably beg you to join the club."

And he again laughed at his own joke.

Gregory called the waitress over, ordered wine, soup, and salads for two, and said. "After lunch, he will smoke his pipe. We are already sitting in the smoking area of the dining room. And I know you will want to smoke your briar pipe, so I will then invite him to join us and introduce him to you. I will start the conversation with horses, especially Irish vs English racing horses. Then we can slowly switch the conversation into business. The last time I talked with him he was seeking a couple of businessmen who would join him in a venture that would export and sell his nanotechnical drugs. He has a couple of his well-trained doctors dealing with drug 'sales' within Europe. He really needs to introduce these 'drugs' into the other international marketplaces. And I know that you have close colleagues/business friends in China and the Middle East. Is this all right?"

Charles could only respond, "Super!"

Albert Langdon, also of royal ancestry grew up in the elite children's school called the Royal School of Science. He entered at the age of three, graduated at the age of fourteen, and finished his PhD and MD from Oxford University at the age of twenty-three. He had a brilliant science mind and saw biological cells as little people and played with them as such. He developed tremendous insight into human life and death, via controlling tissues, cells, and their molecules.

Dr. Langdon taught and studied at Hammersmith Hospital and Research Center for twenty years. He performed the chemical-drug related research and gave his findings to fellow scientists to test in 'intact' human beings. Working with real people was boring. So, he routinely used cell-tissue cultures and small animals as first tests, humans became second tests by his medical students and colleagues. Using these methodologies, he discovered the entire concept of nanotech molecular systems. He learned how to target and control the functioning of almost any cell in the body. If he wanted, he could have fought to be rewarded with the Noble Prize in Biochemistry, but he preferred to remain less well known, as he had other ideas.

Born into royalty does not mean born into money and wealth. The Langdon family was born into the House of Windsor, but on the lesser side of the tracks. Grandpa Langdon lost everything in gambling. So, Albert grew up outside the royal circle, and regretted it very much. Because of this trick of fate, his life-long goals involved wealth and controls of human life. He was rapidly accomplishing both.

An hour after the nanotech doctor joined the two businessmen, each gentleman had drunk an extra cup of tea, and they had much discussion about horses and 'new born' drugs, Charles, Gregory, and Albert seemed to be developing a warm, possibly even a profitable, relationship.

The three of them would go together to the Epsom Derby next month. Charles and Gregory went to the horse races about every month. Charles's father would be racing one of Charles's favorite horses from Golden Meadows flat racers, a three-year old filly, named Lovely Dancer, in the Epsom Derby. No filly had won this race in more than twenty years. So, the odds would be very good.

Charles was bragging about his father's Irish race horses, "In England the fastest horse wins the Gineas. The luckiest horse wins the Epsom Derby. And the best wins the St. Legar. My father said he was feeling lucky, and I hope he is right. We have won one race out of nine races this year, a couple of show and place, not good. Winners sell their offspring. Losers or non-winners eat oats."

"I have a feeling that this race will be good for the Irish. I found a four leafed shamrock today," replied Dr. Langdon.

And horses continued to dominate the conversation for the next hour.

9

AYKUT AND THE GYPSIES

Aykut Turan had heard many rumors and even strange things about the colony of Roma or Romanian Gypsies living in the Belgrade Forest, up near the Black Sea, just north and west of Istanbul. He was curious about them and of course about Gypsy Witchcraft. Through a contact in his father's bank, Isbank, he was able to identify a Roma-Turkish family near where he lived. He went to their house, explained who he was and that he was doing a research paper for his college history course on Romanian Gypsies. The father of the family spoke Turkish and Romani, was a gentle middle aged man and worked only part time; the family had five children and was always in need of money; so Aykut agreed to pay him a fee and the two of them would drive one hour, one way, to and from each day, and visit the gypsy colony and learn about 'authentic' gypsies. Aykut was now nineteen and had a small car. They would make this trip several times during a week-long visit.

Two weeks later, early on a bright sunshiny day, Aykut picked up Mr. Mirceau Iancu from his house and drove in his Fiat convertible west from Istanbul on the E-5 or London-Delphi autobahn. Mr. Iancu was average size, with dark brown skin, black curly hair, and large black mustache. He was a laborer at various construction projects in the Istanbul area, and had no high school degree, so he was rather shy in riding in a 'topless' car with the son of wealthy banker. Also, this son was near six-foot tall, more than two hundred pounds, and working on a college project. The two were of different ages, social backgrounds, education, and 'plans' for life. So, they had little in common and the drive was a long-quiet hour.

As Aykut left the autobahn and drove north through the beautiful emerald green forested mountainside toward the small Turkish-Roma town of Sulukale, he reviewed the brief history of the 'Roma' or 'Gypsies' that he learned from his on-line research.

"The gypsy people originated in northern India, but in the ninth and tenth centuries many gypsy tribes moved west into the lands around the Persian Gulf and Caspian Sea. They then eventually split into three groups: going south into Turkey, into Egypt, and on into Europe. By the fourteenth century they had settled in Bulgaria, Romania, Moldavia, Hungary, Bosnia, and the Balkans, eventually eastern and central Europe. But with their mobile lifestyle, settled is not a proper word. They continuously moved within these areas of Europe. Today, most European countries have developed laws that restrict migratory movement of all nomads, especially gypsies, within their boundaries. Currently there are large groups of gypsies in Bulgaria, Romania, and Turkey.

'After the western migration and because of their swarthy skin, colorful clothing, and nomadic and mysterious lifestyles, the Europeans decided they resembled ancient Egyptians. Hence, they went through a series of names such as Egyptians, Egypcions, Gyptians, Gyptenians, and finally Gypsies. This large migration of Eastern nomads created many problems for the already numerous land-established groups and regions of Europe. So, these immigrants/nomads created stories supporting their patronage by the Mughal (Muslim) and Indian (Hindu) emperors, Ottoman and other Islamic sultans, various European princes, kings, emperors, and even the Pope. They proclaimed that they had permission to wander and beg for alms.'

'These unusual people became specialists in entertainment and special skills such as such as palm reading, fortune telling, tarot cards, animal care especially horse care, curative arts, metal crafts, and the occult arts which today we call gypsy witchcraft.'

'Apparently the English were one of the first to use the word Rom or Roma for male gypsies. This was associated with the invasion of the British Isles by the Romans. Also, as Eastern Europe began to settle into national states and countries, the new country of Romania had a large population of gypsies. Today these people are also referred to as Rom or Roma and speak Romani. Few still live in 'wheeled' houses, and most are Christian or Muslim depending upon the specific country where they live. Their life-styles have changed only according to their monetary needs and social requirements.'

Aykut slowly drove down a long heavily forested mountainside into a lovely valley and entered a small Turkish looking city, with numerous 1-2-3 floors of drab gray-yellow stucco and stone buildings most with red tile roofs, both rock and asphalt streets, and a central area with numerous shops and stores surrounding a large water fountain; all parking was on the side of the street. People were dressed in and out of modern fashion. Children wore blue school uniforms as it was early morning and they were on the way to a large central school building which contained all grades. Most men had facial hair, wore dull colored slacks, and colorful long-sleeved shirts; the older men frequently had on wool vests or jackets and flat caps or hats. A few business types wore jackets and ties.

The women's clothing was of two types. Some wore more modern style dresses or skirts, blouses, and sweaters; but many women wore bulky pantaloons, bright colored thick overshirts or blouses, and covered their hair with scarves. Most people wore open sandals or shoes and were obviously on their way to various kinds of work. Only the young ladies dressed in French or Italian style blouses and short skirts, plus wore an abundance of cosmetic and had long hair. One could easily tell the single from the married ladies. But it was difficult to tell the Gypsy-Turks from the non-Gypsy-Turks.

Mr. Iancu directed Aykut to turn down a side street and soon they stopped in front of Ayfer's Supermarket. Ayfer Kurana was Mr. Iancu's aunt, or his mother's sister. She was expecting them, so she was waiting at the front door. Her three daughters were also present for the introductory merhaba (hello). They then returned inside back to work.

Mrs. Kurana was a short stout middle aged mother and businesswoman. She dressed appropriately in a nice light green dress, blue sweater, and red scarf. She had a smooth natural skin color which glowed, and graying hair. She was obviously a competent and successful member of the business community. Mrs. Kurana immediately came forward and began, "Welcome to Little Roma."

She kissed Aykut on both cheeks and carefully eyed him as she knew that this rich boy Turk needed her help. So, up front she wanted to let him know he would learn an authentic gypsy's feelings of gypsy history, and then they could start bargaining. After all, she needed a small fee too.

Aykut replied, "You are close to the Black Sea. You must have a lot of good fish for sale."

"Yes," she quickly responded. "Today we have more than ten different types. However, it is hamsi (sardine) season, so they are the best buy. I can offer you one kilo for two (Turkish) lira."

"I will give you one lira for one kilo or two liras for three kilos," he countered. "And I will pick them up later today when we return to Istanbul."

They looked each other in the eyes, and the market owner laughed and said, "You are my kind of child, but you are too big to be a gypsy. A deal!" They shook hands.

Her brother had been standing there waiting for some attention from his aunt; finally, she welcomed him with the standard cheek to cheek kiss and a hug. They then walked to a neighboring tea garden; sat down at a plastic table on hard plastic chairs and were immediately served Turkish rabbit blood tea (as the saying goes due to the color) in small glasses.

Aykut began to explain his reason for visiting them. "Thank you for seeing me. I am in college and want to write a research paper for my history class on Romanian Gypsies. I want to talk with gypsy families who have been living in this region for several generations. I cannot speak Romani, but Mr. Iancu will help translate where needed. And I do want to talk with someone who practices the occult. I have a special interest in Gypsy Magic."

Mr. Inancu butted in, "My mother's family are of multi-generation gypsy life. Ayfer Hanim can tell you everything and direct you to many other multi-generation families in the area."

Mrs. Kurana ignored her nephew, obviously not needing his help. "My great grandmother is over one hundred years old. No one really knows her age and she will not tell anyone, or really does not know. She has her own little house up there on that hill." And she pointed somewhere upward east into the rising sun.

"She is Princess Luminitsa. She thinks queens are old women, so she is still a princess. But she is certainly the most famous old witch in the entire region. She has trained many young witches. And she still practices her magic for anyone with money." She looked at Aykut and chuckled.

"After you and I have talked, I will send you to a couple of multi-generation gypsy families living near here and you can talk to them. Later I will arrange for an appointment with Princess Luminitsa, which means Little Light. But you must go to see her with me, not by yourself. I do not want the Istanbul police coming to me later and asking me to where you disappeared."

This time when she met Aykut's eye she did not chuckle. Aykut understood. The old princess was a powerful old lady and could be dangerous.

For the next couple of hours Mrs. Kurana answered some of Aykut's questions; and where she was not knowledgeable, she proposed to identify someone in the area who could try to answer his questions.

She explained: "In general, gypsies prefer the outside world, nature. They believe that trees and flowers, birds and bees are pleasures to be shared by everyone. All Gypsy Magic is accomplished under the open skies with the assistance of the sun, moon, and the earth's children two and four legged. The Romani word for God is Duvvel or Del; the word for Devil is Ben or Bengh. God is believed to be a positive force; the Devil is thought to be a negative force. The earth was not created; it has always been there. The Earth is called the De Develeski; the Devine Mother. All life comes from Her and returns to Her."

"The Gypsy saint is St. Sara or Sara la Kali. She is also known as the Black Sara. It is said that St. Sara assisted the land and water travels of all three wise men in their journey east to Bethlehem for the birth of Jesus Christ. Today there is a statue of St. Sara at the Church at Saints Maries de la Mer on the Ile de la Clamargue at the mouth of the Rhone River in France. Every year, on May 25, thousands of gypsies make their pilgrimage to the church."

"Our original beliefs were pagan. But over the years of wandering through numerous lands with different ethnic and religious peoples we have blended a mixture of pagan and non-pagan, mostly Christian and Jewish teachings and beliefs, although most gypsies in our village are nominally Muslim. Assimilation for protection has always been a way of live for nomads."

And again, she looked Aykut in the eyes and grinned. Aykut was young and a Muslim, but she knew already his life's experiences had forced him to mature early. She had checked him out before he came to the village. He just returned the grin.

"Gypsy births and deaths take place in bender. Outdoors, a small tent-like structure is created by bending and attaching several tree branches to the ground and hanging several blankets over them. Birth takes place here. Later the newborn is baptized here to aid the child against the many negative mental and physical forces he will be confronted with during his life. Death also takes place in the bender or out in open nature. When near death the person is dressed in his best clothing and laid on blankets. Family and friends gather and quietly eat and converse until death occurs. The deceased is then placed in a wooden coffin and buried somewhere in the forest. The grave in not marked."

"The Romani word for ghost or spirit is mullo. This word is also used for the living dead such as vampires. There are many gypsy stories about the mullo. Some are true; some are not true. Even though you are young, I am sure you will understand this next explanation."

"The mullo has an insatiable need to have sexual intercourse. If he was married before he died, he will regularly return to have sex with his widow. If he was denied marriage to a young lady before he died, he will regularly return from death to have sex with her. If a mullo re-establishes a regular sexual arrangement with a previous lover, he may ask, and if yes, then assist that lover in joining him in his vampire life. It is common for a married woman to have a long-time lover, only to later discover that he was a vampire. Some gypsies claim that vampires, as lovers, may or may not be visible to his lover during the sexual act. So, lovers and sex are to be carefully used in our lives."

Aykut turned very red in the face during the telling of the gypsy beliefs of the vampire. But he just smiled and nodded for Mrs. Kurana to continue. He was aware that the Dracula Castle is in north-central Romania. It had been a major stronghold of the gypsies for several hundred years.

"One other set of beliefs you should know about is that of the sabbats. Related to the mysterious life of the gypsies living in their wheeled houses in the dark forest, their strange singing and dancing, which were considered to be the that of witches, sorcerers, and evil doers, normal people were afraid to go near or through the forest at night. This was well known and used to strike fear into 'normal' peoples' children. It was these sabbats or nightly gypsy parties that diffused into the entire forest and brought night dangers of many kinds. Or so believed non-gypsies living near gypsy colonies."

As lunch time approached, Mrs. Kurana signaled to a boy waiting nearby. The boy immediately ran across the street to a restaurant. In five minutes, he returned carrying three plates of takeout meals. Each plate contained tavuk doner kabap/grilled chicken, baked potatoes, steamed rice, green peppers, and a mixed green salad with cucumber and carrot slices—olive oil and lemon juice dressing. A second quick trip across the street and the boy returned with hot fresh village bread cut into large pieces, and ayran/dilute plain yogurt with salt. They then slowly ate their meals and continued discussing gypsy life.

After lunch Mrs. Kurana said. "It has been good to meet you and know that some city Turks are good people who still recognize that there are gypsy groups hereabout. I do have other work to do, but I will immediately arrange for you, beginning with tomorrow, visits with local multi-ethnic gypsy families who can describe to you various ways of gypsy life such as: certain magic spells, sickness and healing, divination, methods of warding off all types of evil, and ways to predict future happenings. If you have other areas that you want to learn about just let me know and I will try to find someone to explain those areas. Oh! Your three kilos of hamsi will be ready by 3:00, in ice, which will keep it good for several hours."

And again, she smiled. He returned the smile. They might even become friends before the week was over.

She went back to the store. The fellows returned to Aykut's car. They would drive around the village for a short time to become familiar enough such that they could find the locations of his 'new' gypsy families tomorrow.

As they arrived at the car a potential problem occurred. There were two large puppies asleep in the front seats. They had no collars so they must be village strays. Mr. Iancu was embarrassed, so he waved his hands and shouted for them to get out, down, and away. The puppy near him in his seat panicked and jumped out and ran away. However, the puppy in Aykut's seat stood up and barked at Mr. Iancu. When Mr. Iancu tried to grab him and throw him out, the puppy scratched and almost bit him on the arm.

Aykut quietly told the dog to settle down, held out his hand, and gently called the animal to him. The 20 kilos/45-pound fellow looked Aykut in the face, then jumped directly into Aykut's arms, and started licking his face. Aykut immediately saw his Amber. Two years ago, his six-year old buddy, Amber, saved his life by eating a piece of chocolate cake that had a nanotech poison in the white frosting. Both his father and dog died a similar macabre death at the same time by consuming this nanotech molecular system. This puppy was obviously a 'hybrid', probably part Turkish Kangal and something else. He was light golden brown with sparkling amber eyes that could stare you down. He was a carbon copy of his previous Amber. Memories came to Aykut's mind. Tears came to his eyes. He felt that this was a gypsy gift. The puppy had declared him as friend and master. He had no choice but to take him home, at least for now. And he was certain his little sister would also fall in love with Amber II.

Aykut had Mr. Iancu 'fetch' a bottle of water and some cookies from the store, while he and his new buddy settled into a get-to-know-you-mode, even to the level of belly rubbing. With the treats, the dog quickly learned to love everyone, even Mr. Iancu. So, for a couple hours they petted the dog and drove around and learned about the village. Near 4:00 they picked up their cold hamsi and started back toward Istanbul. As they entered onto the London to Delphi autobahn, Aykut looked in the rear-view mirror. What did he see but a light golden brown dog with head sticking up into the wind, watching Aykut. It was a reincarnation of his first four-legged love.

The next day, with the convertible top down, the threesome, and with a dog's head up in the wind, they drove back to Sulukale. They arrived near mid-morning and went directly to Ayfer's Supermarket where they obtained names and addresses of the gypsy individuals or families that they would talk with over the next several days. It was well organized as they would meet for a certain period with each one. Today they would meet with a family in the afternoon, Wednesday morning and afternoon with two other families, and Thursday morning a single individual. Punctuality was not important for any of these meetings as each would take place in their homes. But on Friday at 10:00 in the morning the last learning session would be with Princess Luminitsa; this meeting should be punctual!

So, after lunch Aykut drove to their first interview. The Sarikaya family lived on the right side and maintained a health clinic on the left side of the same building. The clinic was composed of four rooms. Up front was an office, for tea serving and waiting and talking with patients. Beyond this room were two rooms, one for growing selected plants and preparing plant extracts from the growing tables and from outdoors. The other room was a cold room for storage of fresh and prepared 'drug' extracts.

Mr. Sarikaya was a sixty-six-year old widower who practiced Gypsy Medicine. This medicine involved both preventive and curative treatments using various herbs, certain plants, selected nutrition, and secret magic involving the physical and spiritual. He lived in the neighboring apartment with his son, daughter-in-law, and three grandchildren. They each worked with him in the clinic. Most of the beneficial medicines were prepared by family members using ancient gypsy recipes and formulas. He is officially licensed as a Turkish pharmacy, not as a physician's clinic. He is not a medical doctor. But he has a large clientele with a broad variety of health needs.

As Aykut, Mr. Iancu, and Amber II drove up to the clinic, Mr. Sarikaya was informed by one of his grandchildren that his special guest had arrived. The entire family met them at the door, welcomed them inside, and of course served tea, Amber waited in and protected the car. There were several children playing nearby and Amber had his eye on these possible temporary playmates.

Mr. Sarikaya soon asked, "I was informed that you want to learn about gypsy medicine. We do not use factory made medicines in our clinic. We prepare our own medicine which we call medical extracts. Having said this, I can explain how our preventive and therapeutic systems work, if you want to so learn."

Aykut immediately complied, "Yes, thank you, I want to learn how you care for the health of your people."

Mr. Sarikaya began. "The Romani word for which is shuv'ani/shuvani, female, and shuv'ano/shuvano, male; chuvuhani is the word for the wise and most knowledgeable one. A shuvano, such as myself, must have the knowledge and wisdom to be able to bless and to curse, heal and make sick, make good or make bad, perform social taboos and rites and rituals such as baptism and marriages. We are never considered evil or repugnant or disgusting by any gypsy anywhere anytime. And we do provide a necessary correction or adjustment for most medical, personal or social problems.

I specialize in healing or sickness situations. I know every single plant for one thousand miles in every direction and how to extract the medicinal components. Many of my extracts, plus my gypsy magic, will prevent and cure problems that many 'modern' medical doctors still do not understand, and pharmacologist ignore. I give you several examples: baldness or hair thinning, immediate cure for pains such as headaches, eye inflammations, toothaches, nosebleeds, ear problems, stomach aches, asthma, heartburn, warts, liver-kidney-urinary bladder problems, diarrhea, constipation, arthritis, female menstrual irregularity, fungus-bacteria-virus infections, obesity, stress, and on and on. Today, neither modern pharmacists nor modern physicians know how to prepare drugs. They only know how to sell them or proscribe the selling of them."

"Do either of you or a family member have a specific health problem? If so, just name it and I will show you from which plant we will make the cure, and even how we prepare the curing extracts. With this knowledge, in the future, you can treat the problem for free."

Aykut answered first, "Yes my mother has arthritis and frequently has a bad case of constipation."

"Very good. First for constipation. Remove the inner bark of the white walnut or the butternut, boil it in water until you have a thick syrupy solution, add white flour, let partially dry, roll it into large pills, dip the pills in sugar, and take two a day, morning and night. Also, dandelions, both stem and leaves, contain a mild laxative; so, these can be eaten as a component of green leaf salads."

"For arthritis there are several remedies. One of the simplest is to stew a few celery sticks with leaves in milk; eat the celery and drink the liquid. Do this every day for as long as in needed. Another easy one is to soak lentils in water overnight. Drink the lentil extract the next day. The same is true for soaking walnuts in water and drinking the walnut extract the next day. You can also boil dandelion root in water for one half an hour, cool, and drink a full glass every day. Similar extracts of juniper berries and rubbing the extract on affected areas every day is a good preventive. Any or all of these remedies can and should work, and they are not expensive."

And Mr. Sarikaya smiled for the first time. He had been serious in defending his life's work in front of this rich young Turkish boy. He did not know the boy's parents, and not all his remedies were 'approved' by the Turkish Department of Health Services. He did not want any government officials snooping around. So, he wanted to be forthright in convincing these people that Gypsy Medicine was a good approach to prevent and possibly cure many health-related problems. They were not competing with government certified surgeons, orthopedics, ophthalmology, gynecology doctors and so on. Thus, he was trying to be honestly careful, or carefully honest, or both.

"Mr. Ianchu, are there any health problems in any members of your family with which I might be able to help you?"

The response was yes. "I frequently have heartburn. Do you know any way to prevent this?"

"Good. There is one excellent recipe. We use as a special tea prepared as follows. Place in to a pint-sized jar a large handful of crushed fresh blackberry leaves, pansy roots, white oak bark, fresh rose leaves, and fresh or dried sage leaves. Store these in an airtight jar for several days. Invert and mix every day for several days. When you want to make some tea, place a large tablespoon full of the now dry mixture in a cup. Pour boiling water over the mixture, cover, and let it seep for fifteen minutes. Strain and let cool. Sip one such cup of cold tea three times a day, morning, noon, and night as needed."

Aykut spoke up, "This is another one of your non-expensive extracts?"

Mr. Sarikaya and Aykut simply smiled at each other. They both apparently liked open-straight talking people.

Suddenly they heard some loud barking at the front of the clinic. The three of them ran out the front door and found Amber standing on the hood of Aykut's car, barking, and looking toward the side of the building. They went around the building and saw two teenage boys hassling a little girl. One boy was holding the girl and the other was trying to take her backpack. She screamed that her money was in her back-pack. The two of them finally managed to get the pack and, with it, took off down the road, They were fast and Aykut could not catch them. So, he pointed at the running boys and told Amber to get them. In a flash Amber caught up with them. He grabbed the pants leg of the boy that had the pack and brought him to the ground. When the boys saw what had brought them down, they gave out screams, dropped the pack, scrambled up and took off running down the road without looking back. Aykut told Amber to stop. He did. He then pointed at the girl. Aykut went and picked up the pack while Amber went over to the girl and started kissing her face. It was if he was trying to console her. Aykut gave the pack to her. As it turns out she was Mr. Serikaya's youngest granddaughter. And they all petted and thanked the new four-legged hero who pranced around in circles like all heroes do.

After a few minutes of quiet and looking around to see if there were any more problems, Aykut rewarded Amber with a handful of protein treats and put him in the back seat of the car. The three gentlemen spent the rest of the afternoon looking at pictures of native plants that contained extractable medical components, watching how various extracts were made from some of these plants, and becoming convinced that Gypsy Medicine was good. It was custom designed, certainly a lot cheaper than conventional medicine, and probably better, less side effects, most of the time. It was indeed a good learning day for Aykut's research paper on the lives of gypsies.

The threesome returned on Wednesday and Thursday and spent time learning about gypsy social life with the several families of gypsies. But it was Friday that provided the more exciting interactions.

On the last day of their venture they visited the **Parlor of Syeira—Learn Your Fortune and Future.** Princess Luminitsa had taken sick a couple of days ago, so they would spend some time with a key student of the Princess, Ms. Syeira, who had already begun to see many of the

Princess's clients. She was a long-time student and almost a daughter of Princess Luminitsa. She would probably soon inherit the Princess title if she so desired.

The three of them drove up to the small two-level house and parked in front. Amber waited in the car. Aykut and Mr. Iancu walked up to and entered through the open door on the first floor. Inside was a one room parlor which was decorated in bold red and gold motifs on the floor, walls, and on every curtain. In the center of the room was a small round table with a green tablecloth filled with red and gold designs. In the center of the table was a large glass ball which had a cloudy interior. There were three armed chairs, cushioned in red and gold, surrounding the table. As soon as they entered the empty room a green parrot in a corner hanging cage suddenly sang out, "Your guests have arrived. Come and help them as I can see that they need your help. Aaaak. Welcome."

From a doorway in the back of the room a fiftyish lady with shoulder length bright red long hair, bold red lipstick, and thick facial make-up entered. She wore a gold-green-blue shawl over a blue-turquoise long dress. Her hair was partially covered with a bright red and gold scarf. She smiled and said, "Welcome to the World of the All Knowing, Mr. Aykut Turan and Mr. Mirceau Iancu. I am Lady Syeira. Princess Luminitsa, my magic mother, sent you to me and told me to teach Gypsy Magic without a fee. She is becoming crazier every day to ask such of me. Only for her will I do this, and one time only. And I know we shall become friends and then you can pay double. Or the next time you win the Turkish lottery, promise me you will share half of it with me." And she cackled loudly. Aykut grimaced, smiled, shook her hand and said, "Thank you very much for seeing us and helping me with my school research paper on gypsy life. Mrs. Kurana told me that you were taught by Princess Liminitsa and were as good as her in your future predictions. Is this true?"

"I am the best shuvani of dukkering in the world." [Duk is the Romani word for hand. She was referring to palm reading.]

"I am also very good with charms and spells, tarot cards, and reading tea leaves."

Aykut responded, "I wish to learn about gypsy divination. Could we please start with the tarot cards, then tea leaves, and last, read my palm? If you do all of this, I will pay your fee for just one, teaching me about my hand."

Lady Syeira looked Ayku in the eyes and said, "Mrs. Kurana told me that you would try to bargain with me. So, I am ready. For teaching you all three gypsy tricks I will charge you for one and one half. Is that a deal?"

Aykut noded in the affirmative.

She began, "Today there are hundreds of decks of tarot cards in existence. Each reader simply selects a group of decks that he likes and uses only these most of the time. A tarot deck is made up of seventy-eight cards composed of two parts—Major and Minor. The twenty-two cards of the Major Arcana show various figures such as Death, Hierophant, High Princess, Clown, and Hermit. The fifty-six cards of the Minor Arcana are divided into four suits: cups or goblets, pentacles or wheels, wands or staves, and swords or knives. Each suit runs from Ace through Ten, plus the Court Cards of Page, Knight, Queen, and King. Each of these is differently represented on the cards of different tarot decks, from simple numbers to elaborate scenes."

And she opened a deck and laid the cards on the table, face up, and pointed out examples of the Major and Minor, and the various types of the suit cards.

"In general, the reader must keep in mind that the cups are associated with love and close relationships, pentacles indicate money, wands represent sexual feelings, and swords imply troubles or misfortunes."

"The person for whom the reading is being made is called the Querent. This person may choose nine to twenty-four cards from a freshly shuffled deck. These are then laid out, face down, on the table in the shape of a five-pointed star, or a variety of other shapes can be used. The reader will choose the final shape. Certain rules are used in laying down the cards and in the sequence of turning them over, one by one or in groups, and in the reading of them by the Shuvani."

"One card is selected and placed in the center of the table. This card is used in subsequent reading, and the Querent is now asked to concentrate on a particular problem or question that is critical to him. A proper reading of the spread deck should provide an excellent answer for him, which may be apparent to him, or he may need assistance in finding the answer."

"As the cards are turned face up, usually one or two at a time, the Shuvani must create a story or sequence of events which have meaning or significance in the Querent's life. Most of this interpretation is a result of the Shuvani's own feelings, sensations, intuitions, and perceived insights of the Querent, and the Querent's response to the cards as they are turned face up during the time of the reading. The Shuvani will study the face, especially the eyes, and the body reactions of the Querent. The concept is to provide an answer to the Querent's problem or question, or to predict something important in the Querent's near future. Certainly, if you can help him, he and his friends will come to you often. So, an excellent Shuvani, like me, is never broke."

And Lady Syeira smiled ear to ear.

Aykut quickly caught on and the two of them laughed together. Mr. Iancu just sat there wondering what was so funny. Again, Aykut appreciated the openness and honesty of these gypsies, even though they had a historical reputation as liars and thieves.

"Now the reading of the tea leaves has only a few rules and most people can learn to do this if they know the rules. The rules are as follows:

Serve your client a cup of loose-leaf tea in a round white porcelain cup. The client should drink most of the tea, then take the cup into his hands. For a female, the cup should be rotated counterclockwise three times using the left hand; for a male, the cup should be rotated clockwise three times using the right hand. Have the client turn the cup over and place upside down on the saucer. As they do this the cup should be swirled to spread the leaves around the bottom and sides of the cup. Let the cup drain for a couple of minutes and engage the client in conservation to learn more about him. Pick up the cup, turn it upright, and carefully and slowly begin to 'read' the interior distribution of the leaves."

"You are looking for all types of shapes, symbols, numbers, faces, letters, straight or curved continuous lines, geometric figures, animals, plants, physical objects, and on and on physical things. Lines are roadways or future life movements. Broken lines are broken promises. Bells, triangles, and evil eyes mean good luck. Shapes near the handle refer directly to the client. Shapes on the far side of the cup away from the handle refer to family or friends. Shapes on the left side are usually negative; shapes of the right side are usually positive. Shapes at the top of the cup refer to immediate times; shapes at the bottom of the cup refer to future times. There are many natural interpretations from easily recognized shapes such as an airplane would mean a distance journey; a boot would be protection from dangers; a rainbow is hope and good luck; a steeple or minaret is self-ambition; a hammer is hard work ahead; a wheel is progress; a question mark is for an unknown; a monkey symbol is wealth; a flower is for festivity or celebrations; and you can make a list of numerous shapes to look for and help the client find the answer to his problem or his future life."

"OK, let us turn to dukkering. This is a special area for the client because the palm of his hand will not change. What I find there is there for life. Are you ready? Are you certain you want to do this?"

Aykut swallowed and thought for a few seconds and then said, "Of course." He moved his hand forward, but he really was not sure.

He thought to himself, "What secrets do I have to lose? The macabre death of my Father and my best four-legged brother was something I do not want to share.'

He started to withdraw his hand. Lady Syeira looked Aykut in the eyes and realized there was reluctance here. She asked Mr. Iancu to leave the room until she had finished. This seemed to satisfy Aykut, and he again moved his hand toward the center of the table as Mr. Iancu left the room.

Lady Syeira took Aykut's right hand, studied it for a minute, and began. "The hands reveal much about a person. They tell if he is a laborer or a desk worker, confident or uneasy about himself, meticulous or careless precise or nonchalant, indication of potential diseases such as rheumatism, and on and on. For example, you have hard and pointed hands. This tells me that you are very energetic and have much perseverance. The length of your fingers and palm are the same, so you have good balance in making life judgements, and you have excellent instincts. Your hands are somewhat soft, and the skin is heavily lined, so you are rather impressionable. Your hands are long, so you have much capacity for detail. Your fingernails are curved at the bottom which means you have a good head for business. And the nails are thin which tells me you may have delicate health."

"Obviously. you are right-handed because you gave to me your right hand to read. So, on the palm of your right hand there are several dominant lines. The top horizontal line just under the base of the fingers is the heart line. Your heart line is long, narrow, deep, and has good color. This indicates that you have a good heart, a strong and happy affection. These branches near the first finger side of the heart line imply that you are heavily affected by several people. Each branch is different therefore gives a different meaning. For example, this long branch that extends up toward the first finger says that you will be successful in life. Absence of branches means a loveless life with the opposite sex. While a short heart line indicates unhappiness and jealousy."

"This next major horizontal line across the palm directly below the heart line is the headline. Your headline is even, long, and narrow. This tells me that you show strong judgements, have much determination, and usually a clear mind with much energy. This small fork near the end of the headline implies that you have both imagination and much common sense. The headline and just below, the lifeline, join near the thumb. This tells me you have need for self-confidence. This, along with the unbroken heartline also tells me you have much common sense. If this line were short, it would imply that you lack spirit and balance and need help with ideas and creativity."

"The lifeline starts near the headline and curls around the thumb to end near the wrist. You have a long, deep, and unbroken lifeline which implies you will have a long life with little illness, and that you have good character. Pale, shallow, or a broken lifeline indicates a short lifetime with poor health. You have many branches on both sides of the lifeline which says you will have a rich and dignified life. These do not turn downward which would indicate poor character and poverty. You do not have any stars or crosses near your lifeline which would indicate chronic health problems."

"Let us look at your thumb and fingers. The overall character depends on the thumb. If the thumb is pointed-apprehensive, square-love of truth, spatula-prone to exaggerations; for the first phalange if long-need for protection, if short-excessive changeableness. Your thumb is square, and the first phalange is long."

"Look at your fingers: in your first finger the third phalange is the longest-pride and love of rule, your second finger the first phalange is the longest-melancholy, your third finger the second phalange is longest-love of work, and in your fourth finger the second phalange is the longest-industry and common sense plus love of argument."

"Now let us look at your finger mounts. This is the area at the base of each finger where it connects to the palm. If the mount is full and fleshy, we consider it as excess; while if the mount is flat and sort of fleshless, we consider it absent. Now, in your first finger, Jupiter, the mount is excessive, so it implies you have honor, love of humanity, and a good mind. In the second finger, Saturn, the mount is rather flat which implies sadness and misfortune. The third finger, Apollo, is rather flat, this says that you are not an exciting person. And I see in the fourth finger, Mercury, neither fleshy nor flatness. Excess would imply treachery while flatness indicates negativity."

"Look at your Mount of Venus, this is the fleshy area in the hand which attaches to the thumb. Yours is in excess which tells me you have some inconstancy, coquetry, vanity, and sensuality in your personality."

"And these three short lines which parallel the lifeline and the fingers as they cross the headline. Starting on the thumb side of the palm and reading left to right we find the lines of fate, fortune, and health. These lines are difficult to read as they may begin and end at different places. The fate line tells about a lifetime of success or failure. The fortune line shows fame and riches, prosperity, or poverty. And the health line implies a strong or weak constitution."

"So, I do not just casually read these three lines. If a client is serious about having these lines analyzed, I make ink copies of both hands, study them for several days, then meet with him and discuss my interpretation including how and why of my predictions. This is expensive, but important. So usually only certain people, businessmen, politicians, and lawyers can afford this personal information. And I make it a special charge to guarantee that is tax deductible."

And again, she smiled at Aykut and gave a low chuckle. All he could do was return the smile. But he thought that this was enough.

Aykut only had a few questions to ask, then he thanked the Lady Syeira, told her he would call her in a few days, make an appointment with Princess Luminitsa, and return as he would have more questions by then, and pay her fee. He was thinking of the nanotech killers and asking for any possible assistance. And he had enough. Much of what was told to him about his hand was true, and that was kind of scary. That someone could tell very personal things about him just by looking at his hand. Enough for now.

The three of them hopped into the car. Amber could tell something was wrong with his new master, so he went, head down, and laid on the back seat. They drove straight back to Istanbul. The conversation was minimal.

10

COMMITTEE OF NANOTECHNOLOGY CONTROL II

At 9:00 AM on the first Monday of November 2035, the new group of international experts, who were responsible for trying to identify and stop the world-wide nanotech homicides, met for the second time. Mr. Gerald McGriff and Mr. Dagda Murphy had called the meeting. Mr. Murphy and his ISAAT had produced a complete update on the three 'old' candidates from Buenos Aires, Munich, and Ottawa, whom they had investigated during the past few months. And they also had much information on some of the 'new' candidates from Stockholm, Rome, London, and New York City. Hence, the Committee of Nanotechnology Control, was again held in the second-floor conference room in the Federal Trade Center Building on Constitution Avenue in Washington, DC. Chairman Mr. McGriff, looked around the room, and seeing all seats occupied, called the meeting to order.

"Welcome to Washington. Weather wise, today is beautiful. But I promise, stay a few days and we will have ice, snow, cold, closed highways and airports. The only continuous hot places in this city are geometric oval and pentagon." And he waited to see how many committee-mates were politically alert. And he saw smiles everywhere.

We have a lot to cover today, so if there are no critical questions, let us begin. He hesitated, and looked around the room to confirm that all committee members were in attendance and ready to work. Hearing no questions, he called upon Mr. Dagda Murphy, Vice-Chairman and President of ISAAT, the company leading the investigation.

Mr. Murphy opened his presentation. "We have made remarkable progress during the past several months. Let us begin with the three remaining candidates who we believe are directly involved in the world wide nanotech homicides, Drs. Kemps, Gunter, and Walters. As you will remember the other four of the initial candidates, Dr. Kukryknisky and the three Drs. Chang brothers, were all killed probably by nanotechnology systems."

"First, let me describe our new information and data concerning Dr. Kemps from Buenos Aires. Dr. Mario Kemps is a brilliant man, but a loose cannon. Not only has he had four wives, seven children, and currently has a harem of several teenage black girls, but he has a large research team of nine academic trainees. He produces several types of nanotechnical systems or nanotech molecular systems, 'sells' his systems to anyone, has monetary accounts in several foreign banks, and a bunch of unsavory business friends. We have data which shows that the nanotech killer, which was used in the Bloemfontein Diamond Mine massacre, which killed 212 miners when their lungs were dissolved/digested, came from Dr. Kemps' laboratories."

"We have information that a bio-toxic labeled package left the Kemp Laboratory, on May 29, 2032, and traveled on the ship, Cooked Goose, to the mid-Atlantic. There it met another ship, Black Sage. Satellite pictures show that on June 12, 2032, there was an exchange of packages between the two ships. Cooked Goose went on to Gabon, while the Black Sage traveled on to Madagascar, and docked at Mahajanga next to another freighter ship, Lost Voyage. The two ships sat side by side for three days. We have no hard proof that any packages were exchanged, but we do have witnesses who say the captains and senior crew members had a 'super marlin dinner' and a 'rum' night for all. We were told that this was normal for two captains who have known each for a long time. The Lost Voyage left Madagascar and landed in Cape Town, South Africa on June 30, 2032. It immediately loaded and unloaded much cargo, and left for Montevideo, Uruguay, on July 1, 2032. The same day a local delivery truck picked up three 'newly arrived' large packages from the Cape

Town docks, and took them 'north', then disappeared. There was no Kemps' laboratory labeling, but there was Argentina labeling on one of the packages. The diamond mine massacre occurred on July 4, 2032."

"Overall, our data followed the smoke from South America to South Africa, but found no smoking gun. Knowing the background of Dr. Kemp, and now we have a probable *modus operandi*, we will monitor his shipping of bio-toxic labeled packages from his laboratory very, very carefully from now on."

Mr. Murphy looked around the room to see if there were any questions, but no one spoke up, so he continued.

"The type of information and data that we uncovered for Dr. Franz Gunter is similar, but different, in character. We believe that the nanotechnical system that was used to massacre most of the attendees at the World Congress of High Technology and Entrepreneurs at the Ciragan Palace in Istanbul on October 29, 2032, originated in Dr. Gunter's laboratory in Munich, Germany. Dr. Gunter performs university and private research involving the production of a variety of nanotechnical systems. He has an excellent program with a large salary. But because he has very sick parents, he has special needs for additional income, hence we believe he produces and sells specially designed nanotech products (custom specials). The Istanbul nanotech killer system, embedded in the frosting of a cake, when eaten, a few hours later caused the bones of the targets to dissolve/digest which morbidly killed 325 people."

"A package, probably containing a nanotechnical system was sent from Munich on October 3, 2032. It left Germany by NZQ express truck and traveled to Bucharest, Romania. From there it went by train to Chisinau, Moldova, and then by automobile, with an unidentified driver, to Odessa, Ukraine. We next traced it onto a ship, Ice Flower, Greek registered, and on to Istanbul, October 28, 2032. It docked and loaded and unloaded cargo over the next three days, and left the day before the massacre."

"We have eyewitnesses that a European stamped package containing laboratory supplies came from Ukraine, was off loaded, and that a Dr. Semra Akman picked it up and signed for it. We were not able to identify any such person in Turkey."

"Most of the information that we have involves customs and duty stamps at entry and exit point in several countries. If we could have found this Akman, we might have been able to pursue legal charges against Dr. Gunter. Turkey would have probably cooperated and we could have had our first arrest in four years of efforts. At least we did manage to obtain our first nanotech killer system from the Istanbul massacre. So, a first smoking gun, but no human 'accomplice.' And we have a second *modus operandi* to closely monitor."

Ms. Lawess asked, "Were you able to obtain any related boxes or packages from Istanbul? If so, were there return addresses or stamps that one could possibly use to identify Dr. Gunter as the original sender?"

"That is an interesting question. We do have a package from Istanbul, and we have copies of permits that were filled out and stamped in most offices between Munich and Istanbul, including Istanbul. Some of the stamps are incorrect or missing. It is probable that the 'lab-tech supplies' that were sent was switched to another box on route, or even possibly to a third box. Such shuffling would create problems if we had intercepted the shipment on route, or even now with the custom permit copies—a clever maneuver."

"Just how large is this box or package that can carry enough nano-weapons to kill a couple hundred people?" asked Mr. Mueller.

Mr. Murphy answered, "Dr. Stronger, can you please reply to this question?"

Dr. Stronger responded, "How many people can you kill with a single drop of black mamba snake venom? Many! One could kill several hundred people with a few milliliters of a powerful nanotech system if you can properly place it into the body to destruct a single cell life requiring system heart, lungs, certain areas of brain, red blood cells, etc."

"A box to ship milliliter or gram quantities is very common. Practicing physicians routinely use such to ship biopsy samples to special analytical or diagnostic labs. The key is the ultra-frozen state that the sample must be kept in. The nanotech system must be maintained at ultra-cold temperatures, on dry-ice or in liquid nitrogen. If unfrozen for a few hours it will self-destruct."

Mr. Murphy turned to Dr. Stronger and nodded. Dr. Stronger again took up the explanation.

"A large cardboard box, as an example, could be six to eight cubic feet outside, 2×2×2feet. It would have 4-6 inches of Styrofoam lining on all sides, and an 8-12 cubic inch chamber inside which would be filled with dry ice. Several vials of your nanotechnical system, first frozen in liquid nitrogen and then placed, frozen, within the dry ice chamber. Everything tightly sealed. Ninety percent of the weight is dry ice which will slowly evaporate through the walls of the box during a few days. So, if you know the weight of the box with and without the dry ice, decreased weight on route, via measurement, this will let you know when it is necessary to open and add new dry ice to prevent any loss of nano-system potency. Therefore, this ultra-frozen state will only last a few days. The critical part in the shipping is to have enough dry-ice to be able to refill if the shipping distance exceeds a few days."

"Most companies ship bio-toxic, chemo-toxic, radioactive, and heat sensitive raw materials using this system. Many doctors do not have proper analytical tools in their facilities, so they use this mode of shipment to send bio-samples to a neighboring laboratory for analysis. However, the package must, by law, be carefully identified and labeled with information describing the hazardous nature of the contents and the name, address, and telephone number of the original sender. There must be sticker labels on the outside of the package stating exactly what is inside that is toxic, explosive, radioactive, room temperature destructible, etc."

"Shipping any dangerous or sensitive biologicals or chemicals with this carton-package system is not the problem here. All nanotech systems will self-destruct within a few hours at room temperature. So, the problem is to maintain an ultra-frozen state during travel especially if the travel is more than 3-4 days."

"What I have described is a large package system similar to one needed to ship 50-60 small plastic centrifuge vials, each at 2.25 ml in volume. With high potency this could supply enough of a nanotechnical system to kill 400-500 people. But for a shipment time of three weeks, it would require several re-loads of dry ice on route."

Mr. Murphy continued, "The cleverness of the organizer of this Istanbul massacre is that he laid two distractions for us, and we fell for them,

1) "The 'smaller' Haydarpasha (Istanbul) family massacre used a simple nanotech system placed in the drinking water. It came from Syria. And we had word that it was probable that this same system had been delivered to Istanbul for the science congress. Authorities thus carefully watched the water supply for the participants."
2) "On the last evening of the congress two hired musicians were caught entering one of the dinner ships; they had bombs in their instrument cases. After this, there was a general relaxation because it was thought that the mass assassination attempt was probably interrupted and all would be well. Wrong."

"These two distractions cleverly changed the thinking away from a month-long shipment from Munich to Istanbul, a very long time for maintaining a heat sensitive nanotech system, or the simple approach of a drinking water containing 'killer'."

"But now we know something about the person who organized this massacre of several hundred of our best scientists. Korrectorizer is an American male, probably working somewhere in Washington, DC. But this is all we know at this time. We do have several leads that we are following."

Mr. Murphy suggested they take a short break, stretch their legs, have a cup of coffee or tea and some sweets, and discuss this Istanbul massacre report. Thirty minutes later they again sat down to begin to hear more not good news.

"We will return to the Dr. Gunter investigation later, if you wish," Mr. Murphy began. "Let us look first take a quick look at Dr. James Walters, Ottawa, Canada. We do not have much pertinent new data or information concerning him at this time. We are monitoring him closely as there is much possibility that he is 'selling' his nanotech systems to the highest bidders. He needs money for his three children in three universities."

"I want to now give the floor to Mr. Femer as he has primary responsibility for the investigation of the European candidates.

Mr.Femer has been very busy and has data and information to present for Dr. Anderson, Dr. Langdon, and Mr. Mariniti."

Mr. Femer began his presentation. "We want to brief you about the three European candidates. I will begin with Dr. Anneka Andersson, Stockholm, Sweden. Dr. Andersson is an outstanding medical research scientist in the Division of High Technology at Sweden's largest medical research center, the famous Karlinska Institute."

"She is tall, blond, blue eyed, divorced, thirty-nine years old, but regularly exercises so she looks close to twenty-nine. She has a large group of young researchers in training. Most of her students/trainees are male black Africans from northern and central-west African countries. It is claimed that they take turns in her bed, but that is not our problem. We think, but do not have conclusive data, that several of her African researchers are stealing or taking some of the experimental nanotechnical substances with them when they return to visit their parents, using them, testing them I suppose. During the past couple of years several villagers, from villages which are near some of the student's home villages, have been found dead. Each was found in a different morbid state. Local health care services found nothing which might have caused such deaths. And of course, there was neither modern medical nor pathology diagnostic systems available to even guess what might have been the causes of death. So, all such deaths were disregarded."

Dr. Barkley quickly spoke up, "Are you telling us that this professor is letting her students, young men who are in their upper twenties, take home dangerous nano-substances? Playing with them in the laboratory under her supervision is one thing. But taking them home and testing them on their neighbors is something else."

"No, I did not mean that Dr. Andersson is giving her students permission to do this. We have not had an interview or on-site-visit with her. So, I do not know if she is even aware of this, and/or if they are doing it behind her back. I think that we do need to speed up our investigation of this laboratory and schedule a téte-4-téte with the professor, without and with her African male students."

Ms. Lawess commented, "If those African students are not Swedish citizens, and the deaths they are causing are occurring in the countries where they are citizens, but the weapons are coming from abroad and entering their countries illegally, do you realize what kind of legal mess this would cause? Oh Boy!"

And there was several minutes of light discussion. When it quieted down, Mr. Femer began again.

"Let me give to you what we have concerning Mr. Faustino Mariniti, Italian extraordinaire."

"Mr. Faustino Mariniti is 59 years old, a wealthy business-playboy. As a child he inherited a fortune from an old maid aunt and established an import-export company, apparently such that he could 'travel and test the world's flowers' as he is known to say. He claims to have sampled the ladies from all countries in the world. He is founder and President of World Global. His company owns five small container ships and six cargo ships that carry legitimate and contraband packaged products around the world. He recently purchased Health Care Products, JH. This is an Italian company that specializes in manufacturing and distributing over-the-counter drugs and cosmetics. Of course, he controls the world-wide distribution of many of these products also."

"His World Global has been caught at least a dozen times in the past few years transporting illegitimate merchandise. Each time he has managed to buy his way out of trouble. Most recently he was found with high technology supplies that he was delivering to Libya, Liberia, Somalia, Algeria, and Cameron. If a ship is caught, he flies to that location, and simply 'bargains' with the police and judges, his ships and employees are always allowed to go their own way. A major portion of his shipping involves Italy and Africa.

Mr. Mariniti has a long history of business corruption, most recently in the field of drugs and cosmetics. He has no concept of right or wrong, good or bad. He also has a couple of less than honest company directors, and several unsavory business contacts in several developing countries. These are countries not capable of high-tech manufacturing; but World Health Organization reports show that there have been several macabre deaths in the 'back regions' of several of these African countries."

"There is a club entitled Support Italian High-Tech Science (SIHTC) in Milan, Italy. It supports the research of several high-tech research professors in Italian universities. Mr. Mariniti is chairman of the board of directors and throws elaborate parties for the recipients and their associates of this support money once a year. Our observations show that he is very popular with many of these professors."

"We think this is a bomb ready to explode." Mr. Sugimura asked, "Did I notice that most of the African country destinations where he was caught had ocean access? Does his import-export business include Pacific Ocean access to nations such as India, Japan, or China?"

"That is a good question. We have not looked at this. But certainly, most of his ships do seem to remain in the Mediterranean and Atlantic Ocean."

Ms. Lawess commented, "You are considering Mr. Mariniti as a suspect in the nanotech homicide problem, not because of production of nanotechnology systems, but the possibility that he could be a distributer from 'friendly' Italian manufacturing locations to his routine African ports. Is this correct?"

"That is the heart of our thinking in the monitoring of this businessman."

Dr. Barkley, "Due the extensive international interactions of nanotech design, manufacture, distribution, sales, and consumption, are the legal systems in place to service this group of spider webs, each possibility in a different country?"

All faces turned to Mr. Gerald McGriff, recent past Attorney General for the United States of America, but not the world. He replied, "Not yet. To my knowledge, worldwide, there are not yet adequate comprehensive mechanisms in place for apprehension, incarceration, nanodrug testing, detention, extradition, judicial assemblies, trials, and imprisonment for suspects caught with involvement in nanotech homicide systems."

"When arrests are made, usually the first legal proceedings take place in the country where the homicides occurred. An official 'legal' individual responsible and a designated test laboratory must be available in several places in the world to evaluate the status of the nanotech system to cure or to kill. And international laws must be put into place specifically for high tech killings and/or massacres. Such laws are not yet in place. And we have not yet trained enough forensic teams with nano molecule system analysis capacity."

"My understanding is that most of this is being put into place in Europe, Japan, Canada, and the USA. Perhaps that is why we are more concerned about the lack of cooperation with African and South American areas."

He looked around. All was quiet. The problem seemed bigger than life. He nodded to Mr. Femer.

Mr. Femer began again. "I would like to now report to you about Dr Albert Langdon."

"Dr. Langdon is a sixty-nine-year old high technology scientist who is currently bitter with the world. He teaches and performs his research at the Hammersmith Research Hospital in London, England with a team of more than a dozen student assistants and post-doctoral students. He has won several international prizes for his leading research on the specific homing MoABs currently being used in his nanotechnical molecular systems. He has stated that he can target any cell, tissue or organ in the body. Dr. Langdon has been nominated for the Nobel Prize in Chemistry and Biochemistry several times during the past twenty years, but never won. He always claims that he doesn't have any friends in the Swedish Parliament, on the Nobel Prize Committee, or even in Sweden, from where the awards are chosen."

"During the past few years, he has regressed away from the international science community, and now makes/synthesizes only nanotechnical systems for the many types of lung cancer, but resists sharing and publishing all of this data. He has decided to go into manufacturing these systems and to lease them to the highest bidder. Dr. Langdon declares that he does not need the million dollars from the Nobel Prize. He will get rich in his own way and to hell with what people say."

"So why are we concerned? After all lung cancer is the number one cancer killer in the world. Now I ask

Dr. Barkley to help me explain this cancer problem." Dr. Barkley responded, "There are two major types of cancer, small and non-small cell, and with a total of eleven subtypes. This is one of the problems with this cancer which is treatable but rarely curable. Each subtype is treated with surgery, radiation therapy, and low-tech drugs. Dr. Langdon has developed a homing MoAB system for each subtype of lung cancer. He then attaches to each a specific nanotech-carrier five arsenic atoms complex. When the specific MoAB-nanotech-arsenic carrier binds to its specific cancer subtype, the cancer cell will be killed. The arsenic atoms enter the mitochondria of the cell and short circuit the 'electrical' energy production mechanisms. Because the MoAB is designed to only recognize this one specific cell, and not normal lung cells, the side effects for this type of drug therapy is minimal."

"However, I have learned from my graduate students, who learned from Dr. Langdon's graduate students, when they get together and chat at international cancer conferences, that they are preparing MoABs for normal lung cells, of which there are three subtypes. Dr. Langdon has been developing a nanotech carrier-arsenic attached system for each normal type of human lung cell. He successfully tested them on normal lung cells in vitro tissue culture (and killed the cells). They claim soon the laboratory will need to test them in vivo, in live humans. This would be cancer drugs for human normal lung cells. Why? Do you think he really plans to do this? His students do not know nor say!"

He turned and nodded to Mr. Femer.

"We have recently learned of more than one hundred cases of 'unusual' deaths of villagers near Manaus, Brazil. Three villages were involved; every member of eighteen separately located families died with an unusual-not known lung disease. Autopsies showed that the villagers may have died of a gonococcus bacterial infection of the lungs. Usually this bacterium does not kill. However, the lung pathology also showed numerous malformed lung tissue areas which had to be caused by 'something else'. We are suspicious that Dr Langdon is already testing his latest nanotech molecular systems for lung tissues. Biopsy samples were taken and tested from several villages with both normal and abnormal lung tissues."

An additional thought to dwell on. Many cancers are now treated using a nanotech molecule attached to a drug or a heavy metal plus the appropriate MoAB to successfully treat cancer patients. So, this type of cancer treatment is in use, often.

"I will add one interesting possible circumstantial component. There is a Mr. Gregory McCorland, who is President of McCMetals. His import-export company deals mainly with Brazil. In fact, his ships routinely go up and down the Amazon River to Manaus every month. This Mr. McCorland and Dr. Langdon both belong to the

City of London Club, have lunch there, together, often. Is there a possible collaboration here? Both Dr. Langdon and Mr. McCorland have been moved to the top of our hit list."

"Let us stand and take another short tea/coffee break, bat around this new information, and then we will cover one more candidate," added Mr. Murphy.

So, they did. Twenty minutes later they reformed and started again.

Mr. McGriff asked, "Does anyone have any questions? We will later have time to open up the floor to all current candidates. Mr. Murphy, will you please detail the American candidate?"

Mr. Murphy began. "Thank you. Our last presentation, whom, we consider to be a candidate of major indirect involvement in the world-wide nanotech homicide war. He certainly is a 'leader' in the nanotech field in the USA."

"Dr. Edward Kline retired at the age of fifty-six from New York City University. Dr. Kline is a good, but not great scientist. He just did not have the brain power, the sixty hours per week endurance, or necessary work energy to climb up the academic ladder of success. And he was spending more of his time in university teaching and less in the research laboratory. He was twice voted as the most outstanding teacher by his students. This usually implies that he has not been in the research laboratory all day every day."

"Several years ago, he left the university, leased some space on the tenth floor of the Kanjera Building on East 14° Street, in Manhattan, and established his own company, Kline Nano-Systems College. He set up his own classrooms, a couple of simple laboratories, and taught nanotechnology to private sector business-science oriented companies one-year courses. American businessmen did not need him as they had their own American university resources. So, he designed his teaching program for foreign advanced/experienced laboratory technicians working for drug, cosmetics, or medical diagnostic companies. Usually, major monetary support came from these companies' governments. Within five years he was teaching nanotechnology to more than fifty such laboratory technicians from 'companies' in less developed countries such as 15 from China, 9 from Nigeria, 6 from Brazil, 5 from Venezuela, 4 from Libya, etc."

"During the past couple of years, he has been traveling to several of these countries to assist them in designing and initiating nano-tech research programs. And of course, he receives special (non-taxable) fees for this special teaching. He has effectively quadrupled his salary and provided several less developed countries with the capacity to manufacture their own nano-tech systems. And he does have several foreign bank accounts."

"Three interesting examples of companies whose technicians were educated in Dr Langdon's classes, and who plan to design, manufacture, test, and sell nanotechnical systems include: an unregistered company owned by the Barinas brothers drug cartel and located outside of Caracas, Venezuela; an unregistered company owned by the Bush Oil Foundation and located somewhere in Libya; and a multifunctional laboratory established and controlled by the Chinese Triads (mafia) in Hong Kong."

"We see these potential 'uncontrolled nanotech factories' as a major problem for the world. The solution will require both local and international legal coordination. I can only hope that will be possible someday."

Dr. Batley spoke up, "I guess this is one of the disadvantages of democracy plus capitalism. Today you can walk down the street and carry a legally permitted gun. It can be loaded and ready to shoot. And you cannot be arrested until after you shoot (at) someone. The police must wait for someone to be shot (at) before the potential killer can be accosted. But if there is a shot, the 'potential' killer can be arrested on the spot. Smoke-gun-possible death."

"Not so with a nanotech weapon system. Today, you can carry a tiny needle with a half drop of a nano(weapon)system in the tip of the needle. You can bump into someone and 'accidently' stab them. The prick will be felt but will hurt for only a few seconds. The pain will immediately go away. Nothing will happen. So, you go on, and he goes on. Only during the night will that someone die. He did not die on the spot when you were with him. So, you must not have killed him.—No smoke-no gun-no death."

And the committee members looked at each other. The answerless questions flew. If this is a high technology way of street killing today, how can it be prevented, and what is in store for tomorrow? Is one half gram of lead equal to one half drop of any nanotechnical system? Is it always so easy to deliver? Is it so fast and soundless that it would probably prevent any potential witnesses? And dying several hours later, by yourself, in your own bed, certainly causes maximum problems in the subsequent homicide investigation.

Mr. McGriff looked around the room and said, "Before we begin a general discussion let me inform you of the positive side on nanotechnology in medicine. I assigned one of my senior staffers, Dr. Marion Joseph, to identify and list terminally ill patients who were suffering with non-curable states of various diseases, and who subsequently were cured with a nanotechnical system. The search was limited to the past three years. Using several international health care data bases, she was able to identify more than two hundred-sixty patients in eleven countries. These included several diseases such as primary cancers and cancer metastases, plus diseases of the kidney, liver, lung, and brain. Again, this illustrates that this nanotechnology can be used for good and bad. The molecular target in human cells is in the hands of the designer of the drug or of the user/controller."

Now there were several moments of complete silence by these international intellectual administrators. Finally, Mr. McGriff opened the floor to a general and specific discussion on any and all aspects of the many reports. The discussion lasted well past noon. After lunch the committee reconvened for more analysis of the international nanotech problem and the search for control possibilities.

11

AVATAR PLANNING CONFERENCE

Each of the Four Musketeers studied to learn something about witchcraft. Jamie (Ey'tuka) went to Ireland and learned about Irish mythology and the World Witches Conclave; Li (Tsu'tye) had difficulty as there were many forms of witchcraft and mafia relationships in China but finally focused on Shamanism; Kef (Na'via) spent several weeks learning about voodoo in Africa and Haiti; and Aykut (Mo'ata) went to a small village in Turkey to study Romanian gypsy witchcraft. So, they each had varying degrees of success in learning ancient witchcraft and how it is used for both white and black endeavors. It was time to share their learning and new experiences, identify possible targets, and determine how best to use their new knowledge and friendships to 'eliminate' or 'neutralize' these targets. Jamie's Uncle Dagda had helped them with target identification. But they would have to decide which witchcraft methodology to be utilized—when—where—how.

Ey'tuka initiated the conference with a privately, newly encrypted telecommunication satellite call from Boston to Los Angeles, Cape Town, and Istanbul. "Ey'tuka is here."

In response he heard:

"Tsu'teye is here."

"Na'via is here."

"Mo'ata is here."

Ey'tuka continued. "Thank you for responding so quickly. I have learned that twice in the past, when we were slow in connecting via the old encryption system, that was when we were intercepted. It is possible that this is how we were identified. And that is why Mo'ata now changes our encryption system every few months. The new voice recognition return system works very well from all locations. Our next probable means of identifying and fighting these nanotech killers, with witchcraft, must be kept top secret."

"But first let us update each other on this new possible form of warfare. I want to ask each of you if you are certain that you want to do this. My father was nanotech killed seven years ago. I will never completely recover. I am placing all those negative memories deep in my memory bank, and they only surface when I am depressed. Basically, I remember him as a beautiful, loving father. And I try to keep those positive memories near the surface where I can refer to them quickly and easily. But I am slowly becoming more focused, more mature and, at least on the surface, a 'normal' person. I do want to try to eliminate some of those killers and achieve some personal revenge. If we can do this, I think my periods of depression will be shorter and further in between. So, I want to try to use witchcraft in this war."

Na'via spoke up, "If you will remember my father and his entire 200-man mining crew, his many work buddies and friends for more than thirty years, were all killed. The owner of the diamond mines arranged this massacre and was justly punished. Now remember, Mr. Saatfordam was not killed. He committed suicide by jumping from the roof of his mansion and broke his neck. Yes. I would like revenge on the manufacturers and collaborators of this un-forgettable mass murder, in my opinion; I want revenge for my father and his friends and the many wives, sons, and daughters."

"My soul would never rest if I did not try to find my father's and my most beautiful four-legged brother's killers," said Mo'ata. "It all happened only four years ago, but it seems like yesterday. And there are the more than three hundred high tech scientists and their entrepreneur partners who were all killed at the Ciragan Palace in Istanbul with a bone digesting nanotechnology system. My father was one of the sponsors and responsible for this World High Technology and Entrepreneurs Annual Conference; therefore, was he partially responsible for the associated massacre? I do not think so, but some people partially blame him. If I can contribute in any way to finding those killers, my mother, my little sister, and I, and of course all the Turkish people, will begin to have some peace of mind. But they must be identified, located, eliminated, and these nanotech killing weapons must stop. I have already made this my life's goal."

All was quiet for several moments. Everyone was waiting for Tsu'tey to respond. Only two years ago did his father, an outstanding Professor of Nanotechnology, during a family conference at his grandfather's castle in Shijiazhuang, China, execute his two fraternal twin brothers. He had learned that the two of them were involved in manufacturing and illegally selling nanotechnological substances. Via Tsu'tey's clandestine investigations of the families' nanotech companies, his father became convinced that some of these substances were nanotech killer substances. So, he used his own designed nano-killer substance to execute both brothers, to cut off their heads, to bury the heads in their childhood play areas high up in the mountains near the castle, and then he committed suicide.

Tsu'tey finally, very quietly, said, "My mother died when I was a child. My father became my mother. Now, for me, all my genetic family are dead. You guys are the only remaining 'genetic' family that I have. I will, I must, spend the rest of my life trying to eliminate this international disease involving nanotechnology warfare. My uncles might be dead, but I am now senior family male; therefore, I now own and control my father's USA factory, and my uncle's factories and distributors in China and Syria. I plan to learn Asian witchcraft, go to China and work with you to help destroy those people. Nothing shall stop us!"

And with that comment there appeared to be a general agreement to get on with it, go forward and no looking back. Each boy, becoming man, had reason to be highly motivated. They had youth, energy, and 'identified' targets, thanks to Uncle Dagda.

So, Ey'tuka offered to go first and briefly explain what he had learned about Irish witchcraft. "I spent several weeks in Ireland learning about witchcraft with Ms. Banthnaid O'Keef, who is the High Priestess of Irish Witchcraft and current President of the World Witches Conclave. The Conclave is an international group of different types of senior level witches from all over the world. I learned a lot from her. There are many forms of Irish witchcraft, all are linked to Irish mythology."

"In Ireland, all of the new young witches are trained in schools taught by a priest or priestess of Irish Witchcraft. Witchcraft is a profession which provides a service for fees and is controlled and taxed just like any other profession such as a doctor or lawyer. Each priest/priestess has an Irish god as a soul brother/sister. When there is a problem to be solved, the priest/priestess calls upon the soul bother/sister and the two of them work out a solution. The solution usually involves one of magic methods such as hypnosis, mind control, and spell casting, A variety of rituals, chants, and magic shapes/signs using ancient Irish or Gaelic languages are used. The witches can solve most physical and mental/spiritual problems, and personal and family problems."

"I spent several days at a large Ringfort, underground stone home of the King of the Irish Gods, Dagda. At night I entered his underground war room and spoke to the many warrior spirits that lived there. God Dagda did not speak to me, but I talked with his colleague, Goddess Morrigan, who gave to me a gift from him. It was a saber tooth tiger's large canine tooth hung on a silver chain. It is magnificent. But it is very heavy. I do not wear it all the time, yet. All in all, it was a fascinating experience. I am convinced that we will receive assistance from the Irish Gods in our war efforts against the nanotech killers."

"Oh, and yes I am continuing to study and learn more now that I have returned here to Boston. The High Princess of Irish Witchcraft has assigned one of her graduates to teach me."

The emotional one in the group Na'via, spoke first. "Did you really talk to spirits and a spirit god?"

"Yes," Ey'tuka answered. "I sincerely think that I did. And that is what is important about magic. Not that it really happened, but that you think and believe it happened."

"I agree with Ey'tuka," added Mo'ata. "Let me tell you about Gypsy Witchcraft and you will also agree."

"I spent a week interviewing several families of Romanian Gypsy Witches in a small village in Turkey just north-west of Istanbul. Each of them lived within the local community of Romanian immigrants and migrants and local Turks. I too had a fascinating experience."

"The Gypsy witches rely upon Mother Nature as well as the ancient spirits for their witchcraft. They do have several gods, especially the

Mother Earth God—all life comes from her and returns to her. This is their major belief. The Romanian Del/God is simply all positive forces in life; the Romanian Bengh/Devil is all negative forces in life. As perpetual landless immigrants living in wheeled houses, these people had their unique 'secret' lifestyles for hundreds of years. But as governments required them to settle into landed houses, most did so and adopted the local religions and somewhat of an imitation of local lifestyles of their neighbors. But they still rely upon their witches to solve most of the physical and spiritual problems of the individual and family."

"How do they do this? Gypsy Witches are the world's experts in plants and curative extracts from plants. I spent most of one day in the laboratory of one such gypsy who was an expert on selected plant extracts; they can successfully treat heartburn, migraine headaches, digestive system problems, arthritis, stress, skin abnormalities, and many others. They have also the means to cure or cause certain debilitating diseases such as 'difficult' knees, hips, shoulders, back, and neck."

"In addition, some Gypsy Witches are experts and specialize in prognostication or predicting the future of an individual by reading tea leaves, hand-palms, and tarot cards. I had my palm read and the results were rather accurate and scary."

And he laughed. His buddies did not know whether to laugh or not. So only a couple of snickers, and then on with the show.

"I talked to a Lady Syeira, a gypsy witch, the adopted daughter and senior associate of a 100+ year old Princess Luminatsa. This Princess has the reputation of being the greatest witch in the region. She has the reputation of accomplishing the impossible witchcraft happenings. Unfortunately, she took sick the night before our appointment, so I spent my learning time with the senior associate of the Princess. However, I was assured that if had a major problem, just let her know as she felt her resting place was not far away and she needed one more major 'happening' to go happily."

"So, to summarize my witchcraft research. I am optimistic that we can recruit the help of the Romanian Gypsy Witches in our war efforts. We need but to identify a target and communicate with them," Mo'ata concluded.

There were a few moments of silence as the growing and rapidly maturing young men were digesting all this new information. Maybe this idea of using witchcraft to fight high technology might become more than a dream.

Na'via was getting anxious and said, "May I tell about my witchcraft research? I had a really good experience too. In fact, my experience was so good I just might make it my future profession."

There were suddenly collective expressions of surprise on three computer screens. Na'via's buddies simply thought he was playing with them.

So, he continued; "I spent several weeks in Haiti at the Black Queen Cleopatra's Humfo studying Voodoo Witchcraft. I met some very real people and learned a completely new way of life."

"First, a humfo is a place for solving people's physical and spiritual problems. And it is also a school for educating and training Voodoo Priests, male and female. Senior priests and their high-level adepts perform healing services and teach. All of this is accomplished in a small village like atmosphere, somewhat like a college campus with everyone working at a specific job. The center of the area contains a large open, but thatch covered temple surrounded by several buildings. The temple is the largest structure and used for most rituals and ceremonies. It is used in both a spiritual and physical healing sense. Surrounding it are buildings for health clinics and a small hospital, library and classrooms, housing for senior staff, students, certain workers, and several administration buildings. Nearby villagers provide much support such as farming/culinary, buildings/grounds maintenance, and laundry/cleaning support. It is a large and very well-organized school of Voodoo; perhaps a couple hundred people. I was much impressed."

"The Voodoo Priests use many LOA or gods which originated from past male and female spirits. People die, but their spirits do not. And most spirits are available to communicate with if you know how to do so. Voodoo Priests know how to do this and how to ask the spirits for help in solving problems. It is by use of this supernatural assistance which can be called upon, through certain ceremonies containing rituals with ancient language, music, dancing, and a variety of physical and written symbols. Often more than fifty people may be directly involved in one ceremony. And yes, animal sacrifices/blood, is frequently used. In addition to solving problems, the priests of a humfo re-interpret past events, predict future events, identify people who will affect certain future lives or other people or events, see into the minds of select people, and change the observation/interpretation of one's life events. All in all, in the hands of a skilled and powerful Voodoo Priest, voodoo can be a powerful weapon. After I finish high school, I am thinking of studying to become a voodoo priest."

Mo'ata asked, "You talk about physical healing, where do the priests get their drugs, from clinics or hospitals?"

"No. Similar to your gypsies, the humfo prepares his own drugs from local plants and other 'substances' such as bones, teeth, fingernails, or ashes."

Next Ey'tuka asked, "Do you think that the Voodoo Priests would help us in our war efforts?"

"Most definitely—I did not talk to Queen Cleopatra. But I do have two good friends as senior level adepts, and I talked to all three of Queen Cleopatra's daughters. I am sure they would seriously consider a problem target if we provided them with one."

Tsu'tey had started searching in China for a form of witchcraft which they might appeal to for help in their endeavor, but it was too early to report on his efforts. He simply said, "I am not ready to report."

This seemed to satisfy all the Four Musketeers. So, they decided to look for possible problem targets and continue learning about their selected witchcrafts.

"I can only give you a brief summary of several candidates," said Ey'tuka. "These are the candidates for whom the 'Committee' has solid evidence, and who are directly involved with one or more specific nanotech homicides. I promised Uncle Dagda that there would be no stored e-mails or typed info concerning this data. You may take hand-written notes, but as usual you must continue destroying these conversations anyway. So, if you want additional data or info later, we will have to talk privately—the old need to know concept. I will start with the strongest candidate."

"Dr. Franz Gunter, nanotech scientist in Munich, produces, sells, and ships nanotech products to the Middle East and to China. There is strong evidence, via international customs and passport control check points, that he provided the nanotech system used in the Istanbul Ciragan Palace massacre. Mo'ata, if you want more info let me know and we will talk later."

"Dr. James Walters, nanotech scientist in Ottawa, had a student who is the son of a Columbian drug lord. This young scientist regularly consults with his mentor. There are no established nanotech homicides in Columbia or neighboring countries."

"Dr. Mario Kemps, nanotech scientist in Buenos Aires, produces, sells, and ships his nanotech products to several places in the world, especially South America and Africa. There is strong evidence, again via international customs and passport control points, that he provided the nanotech system used in the South African diamond mine massacre. Na'via, if you want more info let me know and we can talk later."

Mr. Faustino Mariniti, international businessman in Rome, imports and exports cosmetics, vitamins, and drugs in and out of Italy. He also collaborates with Italian nanotech scientists by selling and shipping nanotech systems to Africa and China. He is a man of no scruples. There are several suspicious collaborators working around him, most of them are associated with newly developing African countries. Nanotech homicides have been found in these countries; the 'Committee' suspects the businessman is a key player here. He is being carefully watched."

"Dr. Anneka Anderson, nanotech scientist in Stockholm, teaches, performs nanotech research, but does not produce nanotech products for sale. However, she has several African male students from northwest Africa. During the past year, in the neighboring home villages of several of these students, a variety of macabre killings occurred, probably nanotech systems. This combination of Swedish-African 'civil war' is very possible in several of these less than totally democratic countries."

"Dr. Albert Langdon, nanotech scientist in London, teaches, designs, and produces nanotech products and is attempting to mass test his new products in various underdeveloped countries, particularly in Brazil. Recently there have been several macabre killings near Manaus, Brazil, on the Amazon River. A close friend of his, importer-exporter businessman, Mr. Gregory McCorland, routinely trades in this part of the Amazon. During the past two years, three packages of nanodrug products have been shipped from Dr. Langdon's laboratories via Mr. McCorland's company. They each disappeared within the jungle before they could be seized and evaluated. Now, another close watch situation."

"Several other nanotech scientists and international businessmen are being watched by the 'Committee'. I outlined for you the most suspect. So, what do you think?"

There were no negative comments from his buddies.

Mo'ata spoke up, "I would like to explore the possibility of what my gypsy friends could or would suggest doing to neutralize Dr. Gunter in Munich. It would allow my soul to rest easier if this scientist were no longer producing nanotech killing machines. If there is no disagreement, I will tell my gypsy friends about this scientist and his probable involvement in the Istanbul massacre."

No one spoke up.

Then Na'via said, "I think I would like to do something about this Dr. Kemps in Buenos Aires. During my several weeks in Haiti I developed several strong friendships, plus my mother's hungan said he could be helpful if we identified a 'disease that needs to be cured'. I think we have a target mind that needs curing, If you agree I will talk to my friends and ask their advice about Voodoo cures. I could even try to talk with Queen Cleopatra. And yes, I am certainly thinking about revenge for my father, bless his soul."

Ey'tuka added, "I fully support each of you. I will explore this Dr. Langdon in London. There may not be strong evidence that he is directly involved in any specific group of homicides, but it seems to me it will probably be only a matter of time. If there are no objections, I will talk with my Irish Ms. O'Keefe about this scientist."

Only Tsu'tye had nothing to say. He was still recovering from the killing of his uncles by his father who subsequently committed suicide. An even though he had been reading about Asian/Chinese Witchcraft, he had not yet gone to China to see these forms of witchcraft for himself. He decided that later this summer would be a good time to become involved. Besides, he still needed to take ownership of and check out his family's nanotech factories in Yangtzhou and Jincheng City. He planned to continue in the university next year, so he needed to take care of his in-China responsibilities as soon as possible.

No one said anything for a short time. Then Ey'tuka commented, "If there are no more suggestions or questions opinions or comments, let us close off. It would be wise that we not routinely update each other of our efforts until something positive or negative occurs with the 'targeted mind."

Four young men will soon learn that converting their thoughts and ideas into actions is not so easy.

12

WORLD WITCHES CONCLAVE

High Priestess of Irish Witchcraft, Ms. Banthnaid O'Keeffe, checked over her computerized notes concerning the World Witches Conclave which would take place, tomorrow, in one of her forest classrooms, near Rosecommon, Ireland. It was held for one day, every few years, at a different outdoor location somewhere in the world. The last meeting was held in a secret lofty butte cave, near the top of the Killdeer Mountain in North Dakota, USA. It had been organized and presided over by Chippewa Chief Byiansuwa, Chief Medicine Cloud. All such 'witch' meetings were kept secret and away from media limelight. Many people still thought that witches were offspring of the devil. And over the past several years they did have much success in eliminating 'problems' in their parts of the world. Therefore, the location, topics, and participants were known only to the six members of the Conclave who would be attending the one-day analysis of world-local affairs and share their common problems.

Ms. O'Keeffe had assigned one of her five students to each of the attendees. Each leader of one of the six forms of witchcraft had made his own hotel/motel/camping accommodations and would bring with him/her a maximum of two associates. Each would contact the Irish Priestess when they arrived and give the location of their two-night accommodations. Tomorrow each of the Priestess's students would serve as a host/hostess for the meeting, drive a one-day rental car, go to each of those locations, pick up their assigned group at 6:00 AM, and take them to the meeting location. It would be a twenty-thirty-minute drive and twenty-thirty-minute walk into the forest, a location where none of the foreign participants had ever been. So, hopefully a secluded and secure place. The Irish Priestess would have her flock of ravens up and about providing maximum security.

As the Irish Priestess walked around the meeting site, she made one last check to be certain that there were adequate garden chairs and small tables for everyone, six Leaders of World Witchcraft and possibly two associates with each one, all arranged in a small circle. And she thought through the participants and the possible problems they would bring to the meeting.

Her first thoughts focused: '**Chief Biyansuwa**, Chief Shaman of the native Indian peoples in the central and northern regions of North America, slim, windblown brown, gentle, intelligent and crafty; then there was **Queen Cleopatra**, Voodoo Queen of the Caribbean and Christian Africa, tall, slim, beautiful, dark black, plus one of her identical triplet daughters-for education purposes; next **Priest Wu Xian**, High Shaman or WU Master of Shamanism of China, small, very oriental features, specialist in mysticism and superstitions; and **Princess Luminitsa**, Centenarian Witch of the European Gypsies, face and body of age, mind of youth, influences/controls many of her well trained Gypsy oriented witches; **Priest Quetzalcoatl Totec Tlamacazqui**, High Priest of the Aztecs, one blue and one green eye, eagle's nose, bent back, and with super intellect in people sciences, millions of followers in Mexico, Central and South America; and then there was herself-**High Priestess** of Irish Witchcraft who was focusing on Western Europe'.

She thought to herself, 'this is a very excellent group with tremendous world-wide witch knowledge, numerous followers, who are capable of creating positive action in many places where there is currently much negative action. It will be fascinating to hear about their living/social problems, what they are doing to solve them, and what kind of success they have been having over the past couple of years. I am certain that they will be open to helping with the recent growing international nanotech homicide problem.'

At seven o'clock the next morning, again the Irish Priestess was standing in the center of a now completely formed ring of chairs, each filled with a member of the World Witches Conclave. They were the Leaders of the major types of witchcraft from large areas in the world, and would share this one day every two years discussing local/international problems that they were trying to minimize.

The Priestess began, "Welcome to my little forest nest in Ireland. We have been here trying to help solve human social problems for more than twenty years. And we have had some successes and some failures. After we each share our 'curative' efforts in our regions, describing successes and failures, I will introduce a new social international problem that you do not yet recognize as a problem."

"Did everyone successfully travel and accommodate by using our new clandestine arrangements? If not please let me know. And look around, you will see more than 100 bird-guards flying above us. They are our police-ravens. And they can be mean if we need them for security purposes."

And she smiled and looked around to take analysis of each senior participant. She saw many serious-smiles. It would be a good learning-for—all meeting.

"High Priest Totec from Mexico City requested an opportunity to speak first. If there are no objections or current comments, let us begin. And please let us remember that our meeting format is limited to 30-45 minutes per speaker, including short questions. Three speakers, twenty-minute break, and three more speakers; then a 'local' lunch. After lunch we can return to any speaker or topic, or form small groups for need-to-know exchange information."

As all speakers would do, High Priest Totec spoke from his chair and within the circle of Leaders. The circle was small enough that microphones were not necessary. "Thank you for these special arrangements for our bi-annual meeting. Travels went well for us. And my people always benefit from new ideas and concepts that we learn at these meetings. So, I look forward to sharing our social problems with you and learning how you are trying to solve your human/social voids."

"As the Americans say, 'Let's get down to it. So, I will try to summarize 100 years of work in trying to help my people live better."

And he winked at Princess Luminitsa, as the two of them were always trying to show who was the oldest of the two. The Princess just frowned in return.

"Many of our problems have increased during the past few years. This is especially true in two areas: ONE-Social-good education and job opportunity, political bribery and corruption, narco-traffic by violent cartels, grossly inequal income distribution; TWO-Health-infectious diseases such as hepatitis A, HIV/AIDS, rabies, parasites, dengue fever, yellow fever, leishmaniases, cholera, onchocerciasis, malaria."

But over the many years his people had brought birth control, nutrition education, hygiene concepts, electric/electronic 'machines', and fresh water into most homes. So, he continued talking about his problem-solving efforts within the framework of the family and home. He and his people did not get involved in the political corruption or drug cartels; but they did assist in the national and international efforts in disease prevention and health care.

The next speaker was the Voodoo Queen Cleopatra from Haiti. She nodded to the other Leaders and spoke.

"I also want to thank the lovely Irish Priestess for providing this beautiful and secure setting for sharing and exchange of possible solutions for our many social problems. We consider that we have two groups of people due to the living land that we walk on and surrounding seas from which we drink. So, let me describe the two sets of social problems before the world islanders that we face, islanders and landers."

"Our major social problems are chronic and impossible to cure, only to palliate and decrease in personal and group pain levels. First allow me to talk about the islanders included in all islands in the Caribbean area and the coastal areas of Central and South America."

"We have high unemployment, overpopulation, malnutrition, poverty with unequal income distribution; inadequate education and health care causing chronic diseases such as Hepatitis A, malaria, leptospirosis, Ebola, syphilis, debilitating diarrhea, HIV/AIDS. Add to this hard crime such as drug trafficking with violent drug gangs and professional assassinations, many corrupt politicians and businessmen, and decreased foreign investment because of the increase in coastal sea levels."

"If one looks at the social problems in Christian Africa you will see some of the same; however, there is also air and water pollution, plus very rapid urbanization with de-forestation, and ethnic and political insurgent movements within and between countries. With similar reasoning we try to solve the problems related to diseases and home/ women/children. We have had several voodoo adepts assassinated by becoming too political. But many curative efforts have produced limited and very positive successes."

And the Queen of Voodoo continued talking about their voodoo training program and how it had been successfully integrated into the life-system of surrounding regions. She suggested that the witchcraft regions which have many similar problems could meet privately in the afternoon and exchange ideas and 'curative' methodologies.

The third speaker for the morning was Priest Wu Xian of Beijing. Because the Priest was the world's best hypnotist, he always began a presentation among friends by promising them he would be on his good behavior and not use hypnotic phrases nor ancient Chinese contextures. They were safe in his presence, and he smiled with open/closed? eyes.

As he began his talk, many of the police-ravens flew into the air and around. It was as if they were clarifying his introduction. "Beautiful ravens are always welcome in my efforts to describe our life's work. And I will do my best to make them all happy."

And for the next half an hour Priest Wu Xian described their curative efforts for his Chinese people.

"Many of our problems have increased in quantity and variety over the past few years. Let me start with decreased education, job opportunities, healthy food, and clean water. Rapid urbanization has caused increased pollution of air-water-soil from acid rain and extensive soil erosion. A positive foreign trade balance has resulted from increased factories manufacturing electronic and metal consuming products hence dangerous pollution. Decreases in the youth populations and increases in the aged populations will soon lead to retirement problems. Continuous ethnic and political tensions, drug and mafia criminal activities, and corruption in politics and the business world has acerbated existing problems and produced new problems. So, where did we begin? Well we began with better education, jobs, food, and clean water for everyone. Fortunately, health and diseases are not the major problem for us."

And he continued for a little while longer. As many sitting tails were being over-used, it was time that the walking legs got their turns. Seasoned speakers like Priest Wu Xian can recognize this in his audience, and simply thanked everyone for listening and suggested that their suggestions be placed into the suggestion box on the big oak tree near his chair. He pointed. They looked. A small burst of laughter and people got the message. There was no tree.

They stand up, walk around, nibble fruits and nuts, drink fruit juices or teas, chat, and acknowledgement of the call from nature began. Each young Irish host/hostess had arranged nearby relief locations and directed/took her/his specific guests in that direction. After a short time, the tails were ready to return to the work for which they were designed, and everyone returned to their seats to sit and listen to the last three Leaders as they continued to describe their social problems and how they were approaching potential curatives.

The first speaker after the break was Princess Luminitsa of the Gypsy world. She stood up, bowed to Priest Totec of the Aztec world (as if to say, see how some older people can easily both stand and sit), winked, smiled, sat back down, and began her summary analysis of the problems of the past 100 years of eastern Europe. The two of them were the only 100-year-olds in the group, and they were still teasing/courting/flirting. Everyone thought it fascinating to watch. Maybe hormones never die.

She began by looking around the chairs and found one 'associate' who was reading from his cell phone. So, she sat there and stared at the 'child', embarrassed him until his attention was obtained, then spoke up, "Now that I have everyone's small and non-large minds, I will educate you."

"Much of what I will tell you about eastern Europe is similar in central Asia (especially Russia). Major problems include tax evasion, private and government corruption, and who will pay for the self-created welfare states of health, education, and the new pension plans. Much of these difficulties arise from conversion of socialism (communism) to capitalism (democracy). Eastern Europe has better economy than western Asia, hence there is massive immigration/migration from east to west. Illicit/injection/inhalation of drugs are a very major problem. And that includes cannabis, cocaine, amphetamines, heroin, and many opiates. A major source of these drugs is the red poppy which is still commonly grown in central-south Asia. High levels of drug consumption have led to high levels of HIV/AIDS throughout these regions. And add continuous ethnic tension, mafia, plus terrorism to the list of social problems, and you have a variety of starting points to try to raise the standards for my people."

"We have been focusing on family and youth education concerning drug consumption and viable job opportunities. It has been difficult to distract the youth away from drug (poppy) growth, manufacture, and out of area sales. This 'job' can be a very excellent source of income for uneducated males at any age."

And she continued discussing their approaches to minimize the drug culture which she saw as one major cause of the low economic life in this part of the world.

The next Leader of Witches to report his efforts to try to help his people in central and northern regions of North America was Chief Biyansuwa from Ontario.

He had such a soft voice and everyone became silent such that they would be able to hear everything. After all, he was going to report on the USA, whose social problems should be minimal, and certainly the ideal social model to develop, minimize, and maintain with the lowest social problems; or would it?

He began, "Thank you for listening to me, I hope you will hear me, physically and psychologically. The 'wealthy' or 'high income' upper North America has the highest living conditions physically, but also has many difficult problems. Let me try to explain."

"The concept of one house per family and one car for every family member is a target that many citizens of this region do achieve. Now here is the price they are paying."

"Because of high living standards, immigration/migration of peoples from every place in the world to the USA is high, continuous, and not always legal. A wall is being built between the USA and Mexico in attempts to stop immigration/migration from the southern Americas. And each year more restrictive laws are developed to control all forms of legal and illegal entry. The trade deficiency is very high. The national debt is huge. And some administrations cause previous agreements and treaties to no longer properly function. Hence, anti-immigration, anti-trade, anti-Europe, and anti-ethnic long-term friendships are unraveling and re-raveling."

"There is a continuous growing income generation divide. The lack of income sharing by the wealthy and the tax evasion of certain professions and organizations continue to grow. The problems of all American-Canadians include: cybersecurity crimes (hacking, fraud and abuse). While the health problems do not involve infectious diseases, instead they include non-infectious diseases such as obesity, diabetes, cancer, heart disease, stroke, respiratory diseases, Alzheimer's disease, and a variety of drugs such as cannabis, cocaine, heroin, and opiates."

"So even wealthy individuals, families, groups, and social system areas have their share of 'social problems'. With our large and heavily populated regions we try to subdivide our efforts on specific problem—areas diet education for obesity, access to doctor/nurse care and financial assistance for diabetes, nicotine treatment for cigarette smokers and vapers, special clinics for heavy drug users of heroin and opiates."

"As with many of our colleagues here today, we sort of shy away from politics and big business. We too have lost several 'workers' over the years."

And Chief Biyansuwa continued talking about their efforts to help his people; some successes and some non-successes. Best is just to not give up.

The Irish Priestess and Hostess of today's Conclave began her presentation with an apology. "Today, I am sorry but I will not describe our many years of efforts in trying to directly help our people. East

Europe has a very high-level standard of living, similar to North America and Western Europe, and indeed the problems we face are similar to those recently discussed by Chief Biyansuwa and Princess Luminitsa."

"Instead, I want to introduce a new and rapidly growing social problem involving a new science called nano-technology. New nanotech drug products are being converted from a cure to a kill mode. This is a new science in which nanotech scientists construct molecules/substances in the laboratory which can cure diseases (many cancers and other select cell/tissue diseases). These substances are indeed molecules (similar to vitamins, hormones, and foods). However, the substances are being modified to inhibit the functioning of certain body organs (brain, heart, and lungs) or destroy/dissolve body units (blood vessels and nerve cells). In other words, from nano-cure substances to nano-kill substances. The latter are somewhat similar to very powerful reptile or insect venoms. And they can be constructed to target or home-in on various cells, tissues, or body parts. Therefore, most deaths are very gruesome and macabre, and they can have a delayed (several hours) action. Cause of death cannot be determined with a normal doctor's analysis. And the person initiating the killing is almost impossible to determine when he is assassinating one person at a time or even killing in groups. More than 500 people have been macabre-killed in the past 5-6 years."

"The United States has established a government level Division of High Technology. This Division has a new Committee of Nanotechnology Control which is composed of several international experts in many fields of science, law, business, trade, transportation, and more. This Committee has identified several possible candidates who are highly suspect of constructing and/or initiating nano-deaths. I have access to their work and a list of these candidates. I cannot openly share them with you. But many of these deaths have occurred in your world regions with your peoples. So, this afternoon, let us talk one on one, and I will give to you the necessary information to identify those nano-kill candidates identified by this Committee. I can try to answer questions concerning this rapidly expanding 'social' problem that has already been identified in all areas of the world. Let me try to answer some questions now. But keep in mind I am not a scientist so my answers will be limited."

And the Irish Priestess attempted to answer the flood of questions. The area of nanotechnology was new to most of the attendees. Many of the older students and adepts knew more about this concept of **'death by nano'** as the young ones had begun calling it. So, the questions and lack of good answers, because of the lack of science people, was to be expected. They struggled and went directly on-line to learn more. They sort of agreed to temporarily settle for a very powerful poison substance that, with a time delay, could kill a person, and could not be detected; hence it was almost impossible to detect the substance or the 'killing person'. It was used by 'bad' guys to kill 'good' guys. Indeed, it had gotten the attention of these witches serving as social scientists for their people, and would probably receive early attentions in their work. But she warned everyone, whatever you do in the future, remember the **Witches Oath**:

HOMOCIDE – NO SUICIDE – OK

As time approached noon, the Irish Priestess picked up on a growing restlessness among the participants. So, she suggested they break for lunch. She pointed to several additional tables in an area just outside the meeting circle, suggested that they should again make nature happy, help themselves to food and drink, move their chairs as they like for general conversations, and return to reform the circle and begin the afternoon meeting around one o'clock. Everyone was ready for a breath of fresh air and readily complied.

The tables contained:

1) Uncooked – carrots, broccoli, cauliflower, mushrooms, red onions
2) Cooked – salmon, green-brown beans, lean beef, red potatoes, brown rice, plus onion/garlic and flax/chia stirred in,
3) Drinks – water, white or green or fruit teas, fruit juices, iced brown tea
4) Desserts – apples, peaches, cherry, avocado, blueberry, pomegranate, mango, pineapple,
5) Specific Nuts – walnuts, pecans, almonds, flax seeds, chia, peanuts, pumpkin seeds, brazil nuts, cedar nuts, pine nuts...

13

VOODOO WITCHCRAFT IN MOTION

THE DRUMBEATS GREW LOUDER and faster in celebration of the cult of the LOA or Voodoo God. Ten groups of rada drums, the manman, segond, and bula, varying in size from one half to one meter tall, were getting hot as they had been continuously beaten for the past two hours. The muscular male drummers were indeed sweating profusely. No more so than the fifty male and female dancers, who were dressed only in loin cloths and ankle bracelets, and who had been dancing throughout that time in the open-air Temple in the Humfo of the Voodoo Queen Cleopatra. The dancers revolved not in particular formation, but anti-clockwise around the central poteau-mitan. Each danced as the whim took him without regard for his neighboring dancers. Various types of dances were being performed, especially the yanvalu-dosbas and the naga-chaud, dances to appeal to the snake/serpent and warrior/soldier spirits. The ritual was orchestrated by the resident senior mambo to contact all LOA-Racine ancestral spirits in the targeted area of the spiritual family of Dr. Mario Kemps.

A couple of weeks previously, Kef had a long private conversation with Queen Cleopatra and her daughters. He reviewed the information that he knew about the American government committee, nanotech systems, and the group of people who were believed to be prime candidates in causing the nanotech-deaths of many innocents. He revealed the possible role of Dr. Mario Kemps and the killing of his father and diamond mine working friends several years earlier. Queen Cleopatra had recently heard much of this information from the Irish Priestess.

As the dancers became exhausted, they would drop out, drink more of the special ritual wines, and after resting for a few minutes, return to the earthen dance floor. A couple of hundred watchers had been singing a variety of songs to attract all 'interested' spirits of the dead. They also had been indulging in consuming large quantities of the special wines and swaying to the rhythms of the drums and music. The air was filled with a variety of intoxicating vapors, and numerous mysterious objects hung down from above. Most of those objects were parts of recently sacrificed animals.

Suddenly the music stopped, the dancers dropped to the floor, and on each side of the stage area, two meters tall monster drums began to utter a new and different rhythm. Four muscular young men, standing on short tables, were changing the atmosphere by beating out a new and haunting music designed just for the LOA-Racine of the spirits that were now in the specific region of the target. The three young daughters of Queen Cleopatra, coal black bodies, lovely, naked, gleaming with very strongly perfumed oil, entered the Temple from three different directions. The exhausted dancers moved to sit along the sides of the floor. As the three young mambos swirled their bodies, dipped their heads, rotated their shoulders, and raised their arms to the sky, they began their special dance. This new frenzied dancing continued for one half an hour. It finally reached a peak of passion when their heads started rotating, their eyes turned back into their heads, their mouths gave spittle as their throats uttered strange sounds, and they each collapsed into a trance. They were carried from the temple.

Soon after the conversation with Kef, and a second conversation with the Irish Princess, Queen Cleo sent her three daughters to Buenos Aires, capital, and largest city of Argentina. The city is located on the western shore of the estuary of the Rio de la Plata on the southeastern coast of South America. It was established in the 16th century in two regions—city and port inhabitants of the water area are called Portenos, land inhabitants of the surrounding region are called Bonaerenes.

Dr. Mario Kemps was a German descendent whose father was a World War II Nazi who escaped to Argentina in 1941. Father brought with him a lot of stolen gold, so the Kemps family purchased land in both regions, and lived very well.

Mario received his MD at the University of California and advanced training in nanotechnology at the California Institute of Technology. Father had strong political connections (and money) so a new nanotechnology division was established at the University of Buenos Aires. With total control of his research he produced whatever nanotech system he wanted, used it locally or sold it abroad.

The three Haitian ladies, twenties, beautiful, identically alluring, arrived in Buenos Aires, were met by mother's Haitian immigrants who housed them and had prepared certain advanced plans. The next night they were 'attractively undressed', taken to a purchased 'set up' at the Buenos Aires Hyatt Regency Hotel-Club. They were introduced to Dr. Kemps, danced, and played the evening away, and then they all went to the same king size bed on the top floor, the Kings Suite. He was properly serviced. And they took certain of his personal belongings, left him to sleep away the night while they flew away the night back to Haiti.

The three highly trained daughters returned with four vials containing—fresh sperm, groin hair cuttings, toenails, and inside the cheek cellular scrapings, all directly from the target.

A few minutes later a small group of people entered the Voodoo Temple and approached a cauldron which was sitting on the top of a bright yellow blazing fire in front of an alter in the center of the stage area. From the group, two young ladies placed four vials on the altar. The vials contained the four substances recently brought from Buenos Aires. Three young men each carried a reve, which are tall wooden boards painted with many different ritual symbols. And they placed these around the area, enclosing the altar. Five other young men carried long pendulant flags, displaying sacred symbols of various LOA, which were placed just outside the altar area. Last of the group was a tall, regal barefooted black woman dressed in a long red and green gown and wearing her dark hair in a honey cone spiral on her head. She had a long face, heavy red and orange make up on her face, hands, and arms, no eyebrows but long eye lashes and jade blue eyes. Even though she was in her sixties, she looked twenty-five years old. She carried her Damballah, or sacred candelabra, in her right hand, and frequently waved it over the crowd.

All eyes had turned to her and everyone started chanting—Voodoo—Voodoo—Voodoo. She climbed onto the stage area and positioned herself near and directly behind the altar. She raised her arms in a gesture to her LOA and her people. Everyone stood up, raised their arms, and started shouting 'Queen Cleo—Queen Cleo—Queen Cleo'. After a few minutes, all again went quiet. A few minutes later all things and people in the area went deadly quiet. Her LOA had arrived. They could feel it.

Silently Queen Cleo walked up to the altar. One by one she picked up each vial and placed them on the altar. She then began chanting in an ancient Haitian dialect.

'Atibo-Legba, l'uvi baye pu mwe pu, agoe!
Papa-Legba, l' uvi baye pu mwe
Pu mwe pase
Lo m'a tune, m'salie loa-yo
Vodu Legba, l'uvri baye pu mwe
Pu mwe sa
Lo m'a tune m'a remesye loa-yo, Abobo

[Atibon-Legba, remove the barrier for me, agoe!],
Papa Legba, remove the barrier.
So that I may pass through
When I come back, I will salute the loa
Voodoo Legba, remove the barrier for me
So that I may come back
When I come back, I will thank the loa, Abobo.]

The Voodoo Queen continued her chanting in a second ancient Haitian dialect for more than one hour. But not one eye closed nor did one head fall among her followers in the audience, including Kefentse Legoase, during this 'time of communications with the spirits'. Some individuals stood and engaged in silent conversation with their ancestral spirits. Others fell to the floor in hypnotic trances or psychotic fits. A few jumped up screaming and ran from the temple in fear of hallucinations and devil visions. Several even died or committed suicide when they encountered hostile family spirits and were carried outside.

Eventually, Queen Cleo ceased chanting. She reached forth and took the vials, one at a time and threw them into the caldron on the fire. Each vial exploded in a rainbow of colors and disappeared. She then began a series of Black Magic quotations. Each quotation took much from her because after each quote she seemed to shrink to a smaller statue. After eight such quotations she fell into a heavy sweat. Her eyes rolled into her head. She began uttering incoherent expressions and began to shake; muscle spasms shook her extremities. Falling to the floor she began frothing at the nose and mouth, rolling, and beating her head on the floor. Eventually she entered a hypnotic trance and passed out.

Her followers in the audience all stood as one and shouted—'Queen Cleo's LOA—Queen Cleo's LOA—Queen Cleo's LOA—until four of the males near the altar wrapped her in a cloak and carried her out of the Temple. Everyone knew that somewhere someone felt the fear of Queen Cleo's LOA. They had faith in this. And they believed correctly.

Dr. Mario Kemps awoke at noon two days later. He was somewhat dazed but remembered a lovely night having slept, he so thought, with three of his five teenage black girls in his oceanfront mansion, the Villa Rodrigo Bueno. None of them were yet awake so he knew he must have done some things well. As he thought about the night, he smiled. He left the bed and headed toward the marble bathroom. He felt lighter as he walked. As he passed one of the tall mirrors, he glanced at himself. His doctor friends had been telling him that five consorts were too many. And he had only laughed at them. Over his sixty-seven years he only had four wives, nine children, and about fifteen consorts. Not too many.

He stopped and turned to the mirror. Something was wrong. His groin was empty. His testis and penis were missing. He looked like a woman. But he had no pain, no blood, no surgical scars. How could this happen? Suddenly black and white mirages filled all the walls. They were filled with the faces and images of the African diamond miners that his nanosubstance had killed a couple of years ago. And they were screaming. He put his hands over his ears and closed his eyes. The visions continued within his eyes and the screaming continued within his ears. He opened his mouth and let out a shattering scream of his own, grabbed his head, turned, and fell in a faint to the floor. And this was to continue until either true death came or maybe just… forever.

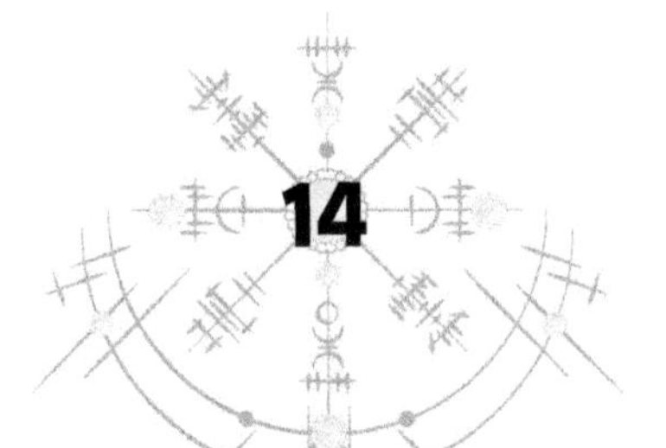

14

GYPSY WITCHCRAFT IN MOTION

Aykut, with his new dog Amber riding in the back seat of the convertible with his head in the wind, had returned to the Romanian gypsy village of Karacakoy near the Black Sea just north of Istanbul. It was February cool, but the sea mists moderated the temperature enough that both boy and dog enjoyed the fresh air. They had returned to talk with the one-hundred-year old plus Princess Luminitsa and her daughter-acolyte, Aysha. As he drove through the village and up the side of the heavily forested mountain side to the aged Princess's cottage, he hoped that the Princess would accept his proposition to consider 'taking out of action' Dr. Franz Gunter, a nanotech killer candidate in Munich.

As they pulled up to the old cottage and stopped, Amber jumped out of the car, gave a big woof, and ran to and stood up to kiss and say hello to Aysha. Amber was now somewhere near 2 years and 170 pounds, and standing on his hind feet he could reach up and kiss her on the nose. She loved this.

Aysha had been waiting on the front porch with her two adult cats. The three 4 legged ones greeted each other and took off chasing across the yard. They knew each other from past visits to the village. The two 2 legged ones walked past the porch, skirted around the house where Princess Luminitsa was sitting in a 'comfortable' patio chair, sunning herself. Aykut hugged her, kissing both cheeks, and gave his best smile. He said, "Good morning to the Bright Shine of the Black Sea sun.

I hope you are feeling well, as I am sure you already know why I am here today. Yes—I have very important information to consider."

The Princess held up her hand as if to say stop-wait. Aysha then came forward to pour three glasses of hot steaming rabbit-blood-red tea. To each glass she added one black 'tea' leaf. They stirred their teas, very slowly drank, as they would have to wait several minutes until the atmosphere had become appropriate for 'serious' discussions. First the three of them must drink, close their eyes, relax-concentrate, allow the forest birds and animals to vocalize for several minutes, and the plants to resonate their odiferous contributions to the cottage area.

Princess Luminitsa had previously spoken with the Priestess of Irish Witchcraft during the recent World Witches Conclave. She already understood that Aykut would tell her that his information came from the highest international authority investigating nanotechnology homicides all over the world. And that one Dr. Hans Gunter had synthesized a nanotech substance that dissolved/digested human bones, sent it to an international conference in Istanbul, and killed over 300 high technology scientists and their financial supporters. Aykut's father was one of those killed.

Dr. Gunter lived and worked in Munich, Germany. He had been seeing Sorceress Chavali, a 'trained' and 'experienced' student of Princess Luminitsa, every few months for the past several years. Sorceress Chavali had been giving him very favorable readings of the tarot cards, her special expertise. He paid very well. And he now relied upon her and her reading to make all his future and professional decisions. However, he had only come to her for his 'reading' one time since the Istanbul massacre, over two years ago. It was thought that Dr. Gunter was feeling guilty and had become very depressed with the mass murder on his conscience. Uncle Dagda and his ISAAT team, who were monitoring Dr. Gunter, had suggested to Jamie who suggested to Aykut who was now talking to Princess Luminitsa that Dr. Gunter would be returning for a reading with Sorceress Chavali in the next few days. Maybe an international cure could be identified.

And it was early 2035, when Dr. Gunter went to visit Sorceress Chavali in the Munich suburb of Vaterstetten, a short distance metro ride from his laboratories. He had requested in advance his usual, a 'maximum' tarot card reading.

He walked up to and rang a bell on the ground floor condo of a multi floor apartment building which had been neatly renovated after the War bombings many forgotten years ago. A pretty young gypsy female, Melvi, let him in and led him to a second floor 'reading' room. The Sorceress, with her long red hair, in her bright red and green dress, green and blue head scarf, was sitting at her small table in the center of her tarot card room which had red walls filled with yellow half-moons. She had three different rooms on this floor, one for each of her specialties—tarot card reading, palm reading, and mental/physical sickness analysis/therapy. She knew that authorities were probably watching her and so she would be careful—strike some fear in her long-term client, but not too much.

Over the past several years she had gotten to know Dr. Gunter well enough to recognize that he frequently tried to hide a deep-seated fear of the spiritual unknown. He had always cringed when a card related to negative spirits became a significant part of his reading. This was probably why he came to her often, to try to appease these negative spirits that he seemed to hear. And as the recent message from her teacher-elder Princess Luminitsa explained, he may be in a high stressed state due to a recent mass killing that he had played a major part in. He entered the room with only one table and took the only empty chair, directly facing the Sorceress, his back to the entry door. Soft-gentle strange music filled the air. They awkwardly shook hands across the table. She saw he was already sweating, and the room was cool winter.

The Sorceress spoke first, "Welcome. I am happy that you have returned to me. I have not seen you for a couple of years. I have missed our conservations. You look good. Are things going well?"

But she thought to herself. 'In all reality he does not look good. He has aged ten years in the past two years. Now he seems almost bald, skin is bland white, large cheek droppings, nose redder than normal, eyes rather bloodshot, and a much more bent stature. Indeed, there is a real problem here.'

Dr. Gunter responded, "A couple of years ago I started having trouble sleeping at night, and recently I have developed an acid stomach. My stomach is so painful that one of my doctor friends at the university gave me a potent anti-acid solution which contained a pain killer. Without this drug I would not be able to sleep at all. But my work continues, and my nanotech sell very well. So, life both good and bad. That is why I need you to tell me about my tomorrows."

"All right. How do you want your reading session today? You requested a maximum. Do you mean a total mixture—Major and Minor Arcana with Court Cards, all suits of wands, cups, swords, and pentacles, seven time shuffled, laid out in a nine card Celtic Cross, four perpendiculars by five verticals, the central card to be observed last, all other cards turned over at your choice and read immediately. Do you want to maintain this same pattern? It is wise to do this."

"Ye…es," he slowly answered. "I know that I do need a continuum, but a new continuum. My mind has not been working all that well lately either. So, yes, let us use the nine card Celtic cross. And please let it be a good reading."

He was beginning to sweat even more as the Sorceress began shuffling the cards. His mind could not leave the stupidity of his choice. He had accepted five hundred million euros, designed, and provided a potent nano-molecule drug which could dissolve/digest human bodies. The drug even had a nano-digestion component and a several hours delay molecular attachment. He did not know the buyer. He thought, he paid up front so his name was not important. But when the news splashed across the newspapers and TV, he knew it was his design. More than 300 scientist colleagues killed in an Istanbul massacre. Newspapers of bloated bodies raining down from the sky! It was now his nightly nightmare. He badly needed a positive card reading. The Sorceress would save him.

"All right," and she motioned for Melvi to serve her tea. Sorceress Chavali always served a 'spiked' tea to her clients during the readings. She had been aware of Dr. Gunter's stomach problems so he had prepared a mixture that would both sooth his stomach and yet provide a 'susceptibility' to new thoughts in his mind over the next couple of hours.

After a few minutes of drinking the tea and discussing minor things, Dr. Gunter asked to begin. Even with the tea he was very anxious, but his color was better and he had stopped sweating. So, the Sorceress began shuffling the deck for the standard seven times. The entire deck of 78 cards, was laid out with each fifth card in the formation of the nine card Celtic Cross, face down with the medieval figures facing her client.

Then she looked up at him and noticed his hesitation for continuing. He had started to sweat again and his nose was becoming redder. It began to run. He moved his chair back a little as if trying to rise and maybe flee. He started looking all around in every direction. He groaned loudly and closed his eyes.

After several moments, he finally opened his eyes again and said in a weak voice, "Let us begin, but I am not certain that I will be able to finish this session."

The Sorceress spoke quietly for a few minutes and again calmed him down. What if he should leave in the middle of the reading and their 'neutralization' plans would have to be postponed or discarded? She would have to go more slowly in her interpretations of the cards as they were turned over. But Princess Luminitsa had anticipated this and had told her how to handle such problems for over-anxious people who did not really want to hear what their future might entail. So, she was ready.

The first card that Dr. Gunter chose was the first card horizontal; he always chose this card first. He knew that the first card represented how he felt about himself that day. She turned the card over. It was the nine of swords.

Sorceress Chavali began her interpretations. "This card expresses your mental anguish and upset mind due to recent violence. You have developed despair over your recent greedy and incorrect decisions, and you are now in a bout of guilt and depression."

As she looked him in the eye it appeared that his eyes were not seeing her; he was looking somewhere far away. He was already blanking out what he did not want to hear. Not unusual in clients in such depressed state.

Dr. Gunter's second choice was number five horizontal, which was the nine of cups. "This card represents what you want in life, now. It says that you seek a warm nest to inhabit, to lie down in, to become comfortable and happy, with maybe some good wine and food."

His eyes did acknowledge this comment, and he even smiled a little.

The third choice was the second card vertical. "This card represents your current fears. The ace of cups expresses that the current calm may turn into a storm in the pool that you now find yourself floating. You are seeking rescue boats, but looking in every direction there are none. You must continue seeking a means of rescue. Never give up as there is a rescue built into every disaster."

He was not really hearing her but he quickly chose the next card from the bottom of the cross. His fourth selection which represented what was currently going in his favor was number five vertical. He picked it up and handed it to the Sorceress.

She turned it over. "Your choice represents that recent wealth has reached your favor. This wealth should make you very happy, but appears to not have done this. You now need to block out the world in order to be able to keep and enjoy this wealth. You need to hide away the wealth and use it at a better time."

Dr. Gunter let out a shout, stood up, and stomped around the table speaking rapidly in German. After several minutes, he let out a curse, looked at the door of the room, finally turned around again, and sat back down. His face and eyes were now bright red; his nose was running. He was very flustered and breathing heavily. However, he took a deep breath, quickly reached over the table, and selected another card. It was card number five from four horizontal. He picked it up and gave it to the gypsy witch.

Sorceress Chavali could see the very deep distress of her client and reminded herself to be more careful, and gentle with her interpretations. She turned the card over and said, "This choice of a Moon card shows your current psychic state. Your psychic energy is low. Just as the moon controls the ocean tides, it also influences the daily rhythmic cycles of our bodies. You need to re-match the currents toward a more favorable direction in order to re-route future directional movements. This may require using illusions and magic. Such is possible and available to you. Your psychic energy must be increased."

He closed up for a few seconds; whether he heard her or not she could not tell. Seemingly lost in thought, he chose card number six from one vertical.

"The Hermit card proposes one to use isolation and self-guidance in times of trouble and despair. Not journeying but remaining in a place of comfort, listening to available-trustful wisdoms, analyzing all pluses and minuses in view, and carefully choosing a new and different path to follow, even if the end of the path is unknown."

For the first time Dr. Gunter looked his 'trusted' Sorceress in the eye. She smiled at him, but he only shook his head. He looked at the last three cards and knew that if he got up and walked out now, all recent predictions would not happen. Reaching for the center card and then stopping, that card could only be turned over last. So, he pointed at card four vertical. The card was the King of Swords.

Sorceress Chavali looked at the card, swallowed, picked it up, looked at her client, and began a long interpretation of this difficult-complicated card.

"Your seventh choice represents who is negative and who is positive for you. The King of Swords is the king of psychological battles and wars. It symbolizes air and control of air. Today most military engagements are fought only after the air above the war zone is won. Wars cannot be won until the air above the battle ground is controlled. This choice number, seven, represents who is yet negative for you. It implies that your recent great victory is unfinished as the air is still cold and unfeeling. It has not yet become warm with solid comfort, so the victory is not complete. Such may require more time and effort."

He automatically looked up, expecting to see some form of danger descending from above. The air above was both positive and negative. He needed to make it positive. Again, he hesitated for several seconds, looked around the room, finally choosing his eighth card, two horizontal and turned it over.

"This card is the one you have been waiting for. It is the Empress of Venus who rules love, emotions, forgiveness, productivity, and happiness. It promotes a form of living that we all deserve to have, but not all of us are so lucky. It also provides a path to help find this love, whether never present or present and lost. But it is not automatic. Love must be earned. Sacrifices must be made and the true values of human nature must be allowed to surface."

Dr. Gunter groaned. His mind immediately saw the families of the many scientists who died because of his 'great' research efforts. He had developed several nanodrugs that had cured more than forty-seven cancer patients, but the last of his nanodrugs for killing had been super successful—more than 300 homicides. The latter families could never forgive him and love him—nor could he, never.

He had begun to turn red and hyperventilate. Again, his nose started running as he began to shake. He stood up, prepared to leave, but decided to finish what he had started. It could not get worse. He desperately needed to know his future. And the last card was the critical one. So, he reached down and turned over the central card, card number nine. It was the Devil.

Both he and the Sorceress just sat there and looked at the card. Dr. Gunter did not want to know more, but she had to interpret this card which represented his future.

She began, "The devil implies excess vanity, selfishness, and egotistical emotions which often result in loss of control, darkness, and perpetual chains. It does not represent death, but instead portrays a form of endless excess emotional existence. The only way forward is to...

Dr. Gunter screamed, jumped up, threw over the table scattering the cards onto the floor, ran out the door and down into the street. He kept running and screaming, his eyes seeing nothing, and his mouth frothing, as he ran against traffic down the middle of the heavily traveled street. He stripped off his coat and threw it. Then his shirt and shoes went into the air, bouncing off of cars. Cars and trucks stopped while trying to avoid him. Pedestrians tried to catch or stop this crazed old man. Three blocks further he turned and ran down the up escalator and into the local metro station. A train was coming in and it did not stop. The cards said he had to conquer the air; so, he opened his arms to make his wings maximal and leaped into the front of the train and met it face to face.

In the same general time frame in the garden on the Black Sea, Aykut finished telling Princess Luminitsa about Dr. Gunter and the Istanbul massacre, most of which she already knew because she had previously learned about it from the Irish Priestess. Aysha served another round of tea. As they stirred and sipped the rabbit red blood tea, there were noises at the corner of the house. Aykut jumped up to investigate. It was Amber and the cats. Routinely the cats would kill field mice, hide/bury them, and the dog's super nose would find them. Finding them was alright. But digging them up and running away with their winter hidden foods was not alright. So, a local animal battle was in motion fun to watch, but noisy. And if the kill was recent, it could be a bit wet-red-smelly.

15

LI AND ORIENTAL RELIGIONS/WITCHCRAFT

JIANG LI IN CHINESE, or Li Jiang, English version, was the son of Chi Jiang who assassinated his two brothers, Jun and Cho, at their General Grandfather Mei Jiang's old castle in Shijiazhuang, China in 2033 and then committed suicide. Li was now on his way to his other home, China. Li inherited from his father and uncles the Jiang Nanotechnology International Company (JNI) in Silicone Ledge, near Los Angeles, its Chinese headquarters in Nanking, and its two factories in the Seven Dragon Gangs Parlors in Yangzhou and at the Ancient Ming Castle Cluster in Jincheng City. The two uncles also used secret facilities at the Citadel of Masyaf in northern Syria for the testing of nanotech weapons on humans. This citadel was the ancient home of the Federation of the Assassins, known internationally as the assassins who used heroin and poisons to help perform their deeds. Li did not know if he was owner of this latter 'hell of a hole' or not. He must check into all of these components of the JNI. He was now legally owner, President, and CEO of the JNI in Los Angeles, but was not sure about the ownership restrictions in China or Syria.

Li had lived part of his younger life with his Uncle Cho in Nanking, was both a Chinese and American citizen, had just turned nineteen, and carried with him documents that declared that he was indeed legal owner of JNI. He was not certain just how the Chinese government would view this situation. He also did not know who was currently in control of the foreign factories of JNI and just what types of nanotechnology systems they were producing and to whom or to where they were being sold. Attempts to contact the administrative offices of JNI in both Chinese cities had not been successful during the past months. There was no available information on the facility in Syria. His father had an excellent support staff at the JNI in Los Angeles, so Li kept most of that staff in place and the research/ production facilities in action. He had then decided that before his last year in high school he would spend some time in China, personally checking out his company's status and also exploring Chinese witchcraft.

Before he left the USA, he had contacted some of his personal Chinese friends from his past for possible security assistance. Li, himself was a black belt in Wushu/Kung Fu and specialized in the Five Animals. He feared he just might need some of his friends as he did not want to disappear somewhere into western China and not return. His friends would meet him in Nanjing. But first he had an appointment with the JNI lawyer, Wi Jong, a life long friend of his father, in Hong Kong.

His Cathay Pacific jetliner from Los Angeles to Hong Kong was in the last hour of its thirteen-hour flight. Soon they would be serving the second meal on the flight. But he had enough food—sitting down. As this was a business trip Li had much seat space, so he took out his written research paper about Chinese Witchcraft. He had just woken from a long two-hour nap and wanted to finish re-reading his work. His mind was ready to re-absorb his research essay on the 5,000-year old spiritual beliefs in folk religion and mythology which began in the Chinese villages and still very strongly live there today. And he began to relax and started reading.

"There are numerous myths throughout the several thousand years of Chinese unwritten and written history. After reading many of these myths, I conclude that they would be of little use to us in our quest to identify and neutralize the nanotech killers,'

'Folk religion, however, is currently a major player in the lives of many villagers in Asia, including most of China. It is composed of various forms of magic and sorcery, the worship of many gods, personalized spirits, ghosts of ancestors, and involves a wide variety of rituals and ceremonies by *holy men*. For many Chinese, Confucianism and Buddhism do not provide adequate answers about afterlife; but Taoism incorporates many elements of Chinese folk religion and the supernatural. The holy men, and women, are called Shamans and the practice is referred to as Shamanism.'

'Shamans are people who have visions, perform their magic while in a trance, and are believed to have the power to communicate and control spirits in and out of the body. They usually perform their rituals and ceremonies on mountain tops, shrines, or in a person's home. The rituals are used to cure both physical and spiritual problems. It is believed that they can leave everyday existence and travel to other worlds. Occasionally animals such as snakes/dragons are employed in the curing efforts. In this world, today, Shaman means an agitated or frenzied person.

'In general, Shamans are very poor and come from the lower classes of society. Sometimes their spiritual power is viewed as being so great that they need to live separated from society. Hundreds of years ago every village had a Shaman living in its vicinity who served the village. They served as priest and doctor. Many were a special caste who passed this tradition from generation to generation. Most Shamans were afraid to reveal their historical secrets to anyone other than close family members. It was believed that if they lost or someone stole the secrets necessary to communicate with the spirits, they would die a very bad death. Today, only a few such Shamans still exist, most of them reside in remote villages, and many are very honorable.

'The Wu-Shamans are a special type of Shaman who are thought also be able to cast harmful or negative spells. The word wu is used to refer to sorcerer/sorceress, wizard, witch, or immortal shaman. Apparently, the Wu-Shamans can communicate with both positive and negative spirits, and employ their assistance when needed.'

Now this was something that Li would have to inquire about when he visited some of the villages. But the stewardess was waiting with the next hot meal, so he put his research away. He would eat a little and return to his report later. Company business in Hong Kong first, then a trip north to his 'old' home.

The limousine of the Jong, Tsing, Choi and Associates International Law Firm picked him up from the Hong Kong International Airport and took him to the Royal Gardens Plaza near the Tsiui Sha Tsip Center at the tip of the Kowloon Peninsula. Ko Jong, Wi Jong's son, met Li at the door of the building, welcomed him to Hong Kong, and escorted him up to the fourteen-room suite of law offices on the twentieth floor. Ko was twenty years old, studying law at the University of Hong Kong, looked very much like Li, tall, handsome, and very Chinese. They could easily pass as brothers; it was thought that the Chiang and Jong families might be linked through common great grandmothers. Over the next few weeks they would become close friends as they saw many similar world problems and solutions in common.

While waiting in his father's office waiting room, Ko continued telling Li about the law firm's legal area involving business. "We have many national and international clients, especially in international trade areas. As you know, the USA imports more products from China than from any other group of countries. And this includes Japan, the EU, and the SEA Little Tigers. The USA is always pressing China to import more American products. As politicians and treaties change, the laws between the two countries also regularly change. Then new tariffs get involved. Currently we are expanding into the trade area of high technology between China and all other countries that are high tech oriented, especially the USA. This area is becoming more complex as new laws monitor and restrict international movement. Many high-tech products are now labeled terrorist commodities—special attention."

Li responded, "Yes, this is an area that we are struggling with at the moment. We are having difficulty with the shipping of certain of our high-tech products, especially our nanotechnology systems. I must discuss this problem with your father, and maybe send our American legal counselors here to discuss future potential legal solutions before we have any major lawsuits facing us"

Li planned to follow in his father's footsteps and become a nanotech scientist; but already being the owner of a nanotech company, he must also face the additional challenges of manufacturing, selling, importing and exporting both domestically and internationally. So now was as good time as any to learn, learn, learn.

Suddenly, Mr. Wi Jong appeared at the door, and invited Li and his son into his large bamboo paneled office overlooking the South China Sea, They sat in large comfortable arm chairs in the conversation corner of the room and tea was immediately served by a white coated-gloved servant. Mr. Jong immediately expressed his feelings, "Welcome to Hong Kong and China, and to our humble work areas. I am extremely sorry for your father. We were childhood friends but separated in middle school when he went abroad for his future education in the medical sciences. When he established the Jiang Nanotechnology International, I became his legal counsel in China. Part of my responsibility was to monitor the JNI factories here in China, and 'to keep an eye on you during your educative years in Nanjing. Therefore, I know in detail about the JNI operations in China and your early life here with your uncle."

Mr. Jong was tall and slim, balding dark hair (dyed), dark mustache and goatee (dyed), minimum of facial wrinkles (botox) for a sixty-plus year old, dressed in a silk custom gray suit, the epitome of a wealthy Chinese top-of the line lawyer. He was a long term, very loyal friend of the Jiang family, and a special friend of Li's father. Li will need him.

"I don't think you remember, but you and Ko met one time many years ago. You were only six years old and he was eight. It was at your great grandfather's castle near Shijiazhuang. Ko remembers. But you were both so enthralled with the mountains and castle, and there were several young boys at this weekend affair. I think you do not remember."

Li responded, "You are right. I remember the big old scary castle and a fun bunch of boys, but I have forgotten names and faces. Of course, Ko's face has probably changed a little since then."

Ko nodded and they all laughed. He was the proper Chinese son and would basically listen and rarely speak. And Li imbibed the great uncle relationship that was being established for him. He knew that he would need a lot of help solving the company's problems, and learning something useful about Chinese witchcraft.

Mr. Jong spoke up. "Let me tell you of the situation of the two Chinese JNI operations. After your father and his brothers 'died', there were many problems at both locations. I know that several years ago you went to both places, so you are aware that the factory in Yangzhou is in the middle of the Seven Dragon Gangs Parlors, and that the factory in Jinching City is in the Yu Tower in Guoyu Town, next to the Heshan Tower; the Heshan Tower is the regional headquarters of the Seven Dragon Gangs, which is a branch of the Triad, the monstrous Chinese mafia. I also know that you barely escaped from the Yu Tower and Jinching City that time."

"To make a long story short, the Chinese mafia took control of both factories and brought into the Yangzhou factory a couple of nanotechnology scientists from Beijing University. Just what they are producing and to whom they are selling are not reported to any government or regulatory agency, Chinese or international. I would not want to get legally involved with these people unless we had some very solid reasons to do so. And when you go there you must be extremely careful. Please recruit some of your Kung Fu friends to travel with you. In addition, if you will allow, Ko wishes to go with you. He has a law school friend who lives in the area. This friend might be of assistance, especially if you want to learn something about Chinese witchcraft."

Li was stunned. How did Mr. Jong learn about this?

Upon seeing the puzzled expression on Li's face, Mr. Jong added, "You must be more careful while here in China. During the last hour of your flight one of my people was sitting very close to you on the plane. He said that you were intently studying a report about Chinese folk religion, witchcraft, and shamans. When Ko and I discussed this, he remembered a law school friend who is from a village southwest of Beijing. He called his friend and asked if he was going home for the school break. This friend would be visiting his family during the next couple of months. And he would be happy to have Ko and his 'cousin' visit with him. Today, Shamanism is the village religion in most of China. Now is there any other way that I can help you?"

Li just grinned from ear to ear; and Ko and his father were elated that they could assist this parentless very bright young man. Mr. Jong knew that a solid brother-brother relationship would result from this common venture with Li and Ko. And a grand-uncle-nephew bond also might be established. He was pleased, but he knew that the legal road may not be the only nor the correct road to travel at this point in time. They would need something more.

Another hour of discussing a possible travel program, and Li began nodding off. So, Mr. Jong told Ko to take Li to the Hong Kong Marriott Resort and put him to bed such that he could get caught up on his sleep. He would arrange the travel specifics to the Nanjing area. And they would talk again tomorrow afternoon, and begin their adventure the following morning.

The two boys left in Ko's Mercedes convertible to the HKHR Resort. After checking in, they were both too excited about their coming quest so they went to the upper Seagulls Eye terrace restaurant, had two Chinese Dog beers. Then suddenly, completely relaxed, Li just went to sleep. Ko recruited two assistants to carry him to his room. Once there, Ko left him on the bed, asleep in his clothes, and left the hotel laughing to himself.

He commented, "We better go slowly during these next few days. Li just might need his Kung Fu reflexes earlier than anticipated."

And Li dreamed about Shamanism all night.

Before Li arrived, Mr. Jong had filed a legal challenge to the ownership to the two JNI factories now in question. But any judicial decision concerning this lawsuit might be months in the future. So, Li decided to put a hold on the JNI problem and focus on witchcraft and Shamanism, for now.

Li, Ko Jong, and three 'security' people (high black belted Kung Fu) flew by private jet out to Zhengzhou. They went to visit with a famous Wu Master on Ghost Day during the Ghost Month which was the seventh month of the lunar calendar. This was the time when ghosts and spirits, especially family spirits (souls) come up from the lower realm. They will attend an elaborate celebration including a large vegetarian feast with many empty seats available for select spirits to join in. In the evening there will be a performance of a famous Chinese opera entitled the 'Night Without Death.' Li declared that he may or may not remain for the opera, depending upon how the meeting goes with the Wu Master. Ko was disappointed as he wanted to see everything.

Upon landing, a Hongqi limosine picked up the two young men while the escort personnel followed in a Jiangling SUV. They went to the La Ka Shuk Temple to meet with Wu Xian. The Shaman's acolytes met them at the front door of the temple. The temple was moderate in size and contained many ancestral family altars. Strong believers in Shamanism lived near their family spirits/souls and had home altars. The wealthy also paid rent for family altars within the temples, a major source of income for the temple. In this way the family spirits were honored every day by the priests.

The acolytes met them at the door and graciously took them inside and directly to the wizard's private meeting room. Because they only wanted information about Shamanism, not to study the sorcery/religion, not to become a follower, or not to retrieve data on their ancestors, they would go no further within the temple.

High Shaman Wu Xian, Master of Shamanism of China, was sitting at a small round table, wore a ritualist red robe with black head-dress, and was surrounded by red-gold draperies and wall hangings which were all covered with numerous small and large blue-green dragons. He was small, bald, had a long grey goatee, heavily wrinkled typical Chinese face, with bright shiny amber eyes that immediately noticed everything around him. He invited his two young guests forward and bid them sit at the other two chairs at the table.

"Welcome to Enlightenment."

Li responded. "Thank you, my name is Li Jiang and my friend's name is Ko Jong. We are here to learn about Shamanism. We know it is several hundred years old and is the religion of the Chinese people and has changed much over the years."

Wu Xian gruffly coughed. He gave both 'boys' a very negative 'hard stare',

"Shamanism is more than a religion. It is the dominant form of life, death, and after death of the Chinese people. It has always been and will always be."

The old Shaman's voice was gravelly and he spoke with a slight Manchurian accent, so the fellows had some difficulty understanding him.

"I will tell you briefly what you should have learned as children, and later my acolytes will answer any questions you may have."

"Shamanism controls the lives of its people and protects the spirits of its people forever. We Priests are the bridge between all Chinese communities and the Chinese spiritual world. We accomplish this through mind reading, visions, spirit control, and extended experiences. When necessary we travel/fly to other worlds to seek answers for our people. All problems can be solved through spiritual consultation, especially with problem makers. Occasionally we use animate or non-animate actions such as with recently passed ancestors. We can and do predict the future. We can and do read minds."

"One very critical component of Shamanism is the need to maintain a supreme comfort with one's ancestors. Unhappy ancestors will lead to a terrible current life pattern such as heavy sickness, harsh accidents, sudden deaths, loss of loved ones, backwards of forward movements…We can communicate with one's deceased ancestors and readily do so. And we create numerous spells such as good/bad luck, physical and mental cures/sickness, remembering/forgetting, power/weakness, love/hate, increased/decreased skills…"

"And we use numerous rituals and ancient languages to enter various worlds always seeking and solving spiritual problems. Solving spiritual problems solves physical problems."

"For now, that is all you need to know. My senior-most acolyte, Wan Fu, will now introduce you to our temple and answer any questions you have."

And High Shaman Wu Xian stood up, slightly bowed, and walked out of the small chamber. A young man, probably near 30 years old entered, and asked them to follow him. He led them out of the temple and to the front, again. Now it appeared that they would re-start their religious venture with a knowledgeable and well-trained Shaman close to their age. Li understood, future contacts to the High Shaman would be through a highly trained man their age.

But they were still in a state of shock when Wan Fu led them back into the temple. They had just been 'briefed' on a 2000+ year religion in fifteen minutes. Yet they seemed to understand and accept this Chinese guiding light which they had taken for granted all of their lives. Amazing.

Wan Fu led them around the interior and explained/described the various areas, how and for what they were used during various rituals and celebratory events. In most Chinese temples one can worship Shamanism, Buddhism, Taoism, Confucianism, and private ancestor worshiping.

"If you compare the houses of worship in the East versus the West you will notice one major difference. Eastern holy houses are very similar because the many religions did not carry out numerous killing wars with each other. While the houses of religion in the West are very different because Catholicism, Eastern Orthodoxy, Protestantism, and Islam had many centuries of killing wars. Today, they still do not agree."

Outside they strolled along and Wan Fu continued describing the religious buildings in China and the far East. Li had sort of lost interest and had begun focusing on his own problems. Were his father's Jiang factories here in China now his or did they belong to the Triads? Would the High Shaman Wu Xian help them against the nanotech killers? It would appear he needed advice and assistance whichever way he turned. Ko's father seemed the logical place to begin. It was good that he had already decided to not stay for the festival or opera. Maybe Chinese religion/witchcraft was not the way, for now. So, he decided to ask for advice.

"If wanted to see ancient or old Chinese villages where would I visit?"

"That is good," Wan Fu replied. "Working with High Shaman Wu Xian for several years has allowed me to travel through much of China. I can give to you good advice about Chinese villages and villagers' life style 2 to 3000 years ago."

"Is it all right if we sit here in this tea house and drink some hummingbird tea? And I can give you some ideas. You can take notes if you want."

Li turned to Ko and inquired, "Is that good for you? Maybe a half an hour?"

Ko nodded in agreement.

Wan Pu began to recall several of the famous ancient sites and villages which were still alive, had not changed architecturally, and where the villagers lived in an 'ancient' fashion.

"Six thousand years ago the bronze age settlement called Banpo village was the first established village in west-north-central China. In 139 BC it had become Xian or Sian, the capital of the Han Dynasty, the first of 13 dynasties over the next 2000 years. In 150 BC Emperor Wudi sent the first ambassador west through Central Asia and into Europe and began the Great Silk Road. Today Xian is called the Fountainhead or Birthplace of Chinese Civilization. It is most famous as the capital of the Ming Dynasty and houses the Tang Palace surrounded by a

10-meter tall undefeated city wall. Less than half an hour drive from the old village walls, stored for 1000 years underground, is the 7000-man sized Terracotta Army of Qin Bingmayong Bowugan Warriors and Soldiers. Unfortunately, the restored old village inside the walls and the perfectly preserved Army have become so internationally popular that Xian is now a city of nine million people and thrives on tourism. Ancient Chinese culture has been greatly diminished. It is now an ancient-modern, but certainly famous, city."

"At least we can say Shaman Xian was born and raised there, greatly expanded Shamanism in the entire region. He probably has several million followers in west-north-central China. The older and smaller villages have his strongest believers."

"Plus, there are many Chinese villages which are yet ancient Chinese. Examples include Pingyao Ancient City, Wuzhen Water Town, Shexian, Langzhong, Lotradzg, and more. I will brief you on several of them."

"Pingyao Ancient City is located in the middle Shanxi Province in north China. It is more than three thousand years old. For hundreds of years it was the home of a powerful trading family which allowed the village to develop into a nation-wide business. It became the major economic center of north feudal China and was enclosed by a 6-meter high stone wall, still solid today. The village can be traced back to the Han Dynasty. Most of Pingyao is still composed of typical Chinese courtyard dwellings; some families have occupied their family house for hundreds of years. These buildings are built of stone and brick/masonry, cool in the summer and warm in the winter, vaulted ceilings, numerous intricate wood carved doors, windows, floors, and false ceilings, most of which are hundreds of years old. Pingyao was added to the UNESCO world heritage list in 1997. The famous Shuanglin Temple contains more than 2000 terracotta figurines of various sizes dating back to the Song and Yuan Dynasties. The Rishenchang Exchange Shop/Bank was the first (1643) and is still the most famous Bank in China. While most villagers wear past era clothing, ride animal drawn or electric carts, and drive/walk on 5-meter wide sidewalk/roads."

"Shexian is located at the base of famous Mt. Huangshan (Yellow Mountain). It was designed and built in the Ming (1368 – 1644) and

Qing (1644 – 1911) Dynasties. Within the village are three ancient wonders—Ancestral Temples, Ancient Residential Houses, and the Town of Arch. The village was built and has been maintained as a living museum of Classical Chinese Architecture—preserved from Ming and Qing eras. Most of the many classical structures are office buildings and shops, houses, bridges, towers, roads, fountains, walls, wells, archways, massivegates are hundreds of years old. Most families share continuous life styles similar to their ancestors."

"Langzhong is 2300 years old as it was the capital of the old Ba Kingdom in the south-west region of the Sichuan Province. In the middle of the mountains, it was titled the 'biggest Fen Shui Ancient Town' from the Tang to Quing Dynasties. Built into the side of the mountains it has many cliffside living facilities, the famous Yaintai Taoist Temple, and several other classical Chinese architectural wonders. It was the political, economic, military, and culture center of the entire region for more than 1000 years. Today most villagers live a half ancient versus half modern, older generations versus younger generations, life styles."

"Wuzhen Water Town is one of the four Grand Ancient Towns of the Yangtze River. It is called the home of fish and rice. It has little changed in the past 1500 years. It has maintained an exquisite blend of nature and water geography, streams, rivers, canals, and lakes, all built by the Qing Dynasty. It resembles the Chinese version of Venice, Italy."

"And there are many other ancient villages such as Lijiang, Dali, Hongcun Village, Fenghuang, and on, that have changed very little over the years. If you want to ask questions about the past from direct descendants of the past, this can be easily done. Almost any dynasty can be probed from its current living lineage. Shamanism originated in these ancient villages, and today still lives there."

Li commented, "Thank you for the information and advice. We will seriously consider asking you to help us identify components of our religion if it becomes necessary. And I hope that you will help us stay in touch with the High Shaman Wu Xian. I feel that there is some way he will be helping us in the near future."

Li and Ko got up, again expressed their appreciation and headed back to their body guards and automobiles. Was this the best they could do?

16

CORNERING THE MARKET

THE NEW CORPORATION, CALLED Equus Transport International (ETT), did not hold a conference for several months. They had all been too successfully busy. So, the London meeting was overdue. They were still living as three little rich boys when they were at Trinity College in Cambridge University, riding their horses on week days, womanizing on weekend nights, trying not to grow up, dreaming of successful business ventures initiated with venture capital from their families, and starting 'small' import-export companies. They were now evolving into an international pharmaceutical manufacturing-export-sales corporation. The heart of their new business was going to be nanotechnology.

Over the past couple of years, various ideas of marketing this new science, for curing or killing, allowed the formulation of a corporate plan to materialize. They talked with several nanotech scientists in Europe and the USA, who had less than high ethics, to seek one or two who would design and produce selected nano-molecular systems. And they recruited several international transport and market company CEOs who had world wide client/export bases. The three of them would be Senior Directors and the major shareholders.

Equus Transport International Board of Directors

Senior Directors – Charles Somersham, Ali Abdel Aal, and Quaid Gang Hu Design, Produce, Manufacture

Dr. Albert Langdon (London)
Dr. Anneka Andersson (Stockholm)
Dr. Edward Kline (New York City)

Shipping, Distributors, Sales -

Gregory Mc Corland – London to South America
Jackson White – London to USA to Canada
Faustino Mariniti – Stockholm and Rome to Africa
Ali Abel Aal – London to Middle East
Quaid Gang Hu – London to China and Southeast Asia

Several weeks before the Equus Transport International became a legally official corporation, Mr. Charles Somersham and Dr. Albert Langdon met in Mr. Somersham's special business office at #601 in the Daycott Hotel on Daycott Street in downtown London. Earlier they had agreed to work together to establish an international system to produce and market nano-molecular-systems to selected buyers. Dr. Langdon would be responsible for design and production and Mr. Somersham would supervise the marketing. They would each begin with administration salaries of one million euros. One hundred million euros had been obtained from a venture capitalist.

It had already been agreed that the senior directors and major shareholders of the ETI would each have 10% shares, while the minor shareholders would each have 5% shares. And of course, each shareholder's company would reap the profits from his net sales. All officers including the President and Central Executive Officer, Executive Secretary, and Financial Officer, would be selected by the Board. Physical location of offices and clerical personnel were to be determined.

Sitting in the only two comfortable arm chairs in the small one desk-one desk chair office, Mr. Somersham began, "I hope you had no trouble finding this rather out-of-the-way location. I use it as a special office for special problem solving."

"No," Dr. Langdon replied. "I have lived in London for more than thirty years. I could probably find you anywhere in this city."

"I think all three areas of the nano-systems, that we are currently using, are necessary to be able to corner the marketplace."

"Level A – multi-systems with the organic nano-trigger mechanism, MoAB homing protein component for select tissues/organs, stomach digestion blocker, delayed self-destruct component—must be introduced into the body via digestion system—must be stored frozen in liquid nitrogen and dry ice—directly targets large body organs.

"Level B – multi-systems with the organic nano-trigger mechanism, MoAB homing protein component for select brain regions, delayed self-destruct component must be introduced into the body via spinal cord must be stored frozen in liquid nitrogen and dry ice directly targets regions in brain.

"Level C – single-system with cellulose nano-trigger mechanism must be introduced into the body via digestion system can be stored, shipped, and consumed at room temperature."

"I like to call the systems in Level C by a code name, Nano-Bottoms." As he laughed, he said. "Do you have any questions?"

Charles responded, "I am familiar with the Levels A and B. As you said these nano-technical-systems are being employed at the cure level in hospitals and also in the villages or in the streets at the kill level. But Level C is new to me!"

"Of course, it is only found in my research laboratory. It has not yet been thoroughly tested in humans. We have only completed tests in mice. But it will be safely available for sales to human systems, very soon."

Dr. Langdon continued. "Let me explain it this way. This new system is still unproven. It is my set of ideas and I would rather not talk about it until we have made several designs and tested them in humans. Some early tests work well in mice, but have not yet been tested in other animals. We are optimistic. And if any of the molecular models work extremely well, we will have a cheap, environmentally stable nanotech molecular system which will make us a lot of money. It should be easier to store, package, and ship. And it is based upon the digestive system related to human diarrhea. It will indeed make for a very smelly way to go. Do you understand what I am not saying?"

Charles was stunned. 'He did not know whether to cringe, smile, laugh, or what. Would such a product be marketable? Probably very much so. What a way to get rid of your enemies and leave a very harsh message. And with simple room temperature storage capacity, it could be used as minor/major war type battle weapons. Normal weapons training would not be necessary. The cost of military would be greatly reduced, almost non-existent. And we would out-sell these guys that sell bomb-bomb weapons. HA. We would be super competition for the USA and European weapons manufacturers. If administered in food or drinks, it would not need syringes and needles. It could possibly be placed in the drinking water or fresh foods of one person or a target group population. WOW!'

"In terms of prices, that would depend upon the Level and variation with each nano-system within that Level. Except Level C, my Nano-Bottoms, here minor changes would not be needed. We will soon have the cellulose trigger systems functional and reliable. Then, for example, multiple capsules of 100 to 500 could be priced cheaper per capsule than capsules of 10 to 50. You could accommodate various quantities of 'customer' need by various warring factions in areas of unrest in developing countries. And I am sure that we could easily out price the gun/bomb competition boys."

Charles spoke out. "This Nano-Bottom system could indeed be a scary weapon. If you just threatened my family with such, I would immediately surrender. I would not even think about it. Oh! Oh! Oh!"

And they both suddenly realized what they were saying, and changed the subject.

"The best that I can do is to try to determine what our 'customers' want and/or need, contact you and let you decide which nano-system to provide, and any possible time frame that may be involved. We will have to work together on the price for custom designed systems. Perhaps in the near future we can set a standard price on the Nano-Bottoms. Are you in agreement with these ideas?"

Albert responded, "Yes. The key is the self-destruction of the nano-system. If it self-destructs, and there is no evidence of a weapon or remnants of a weapon, for example a bullet, then the person is not killed, he just died. An there is no killer."

"This is a good place to consider talking about prices with our marketing partners."

And they continued covering communications, money management, advertising and other components in the establishment of a new multi-national corporation.

Charles' family limousine had picked up his senior Director—Cambridge buddies from the International Heathrow Airport. Gang Hu and Ali Aal always enjoyed the lovely English countryside from London to Colchester to Somersham Meadows 200 acres estate. The long entry driveway up to the lovely English manor house situated on a knoll was lined with a beautiful three rail fencing. And much of the land was so sectioned into pasture areas for breeding Irish racing horses and long horned Scottish cattle, or planted in soybeans or winter wheat—animal feed. There were three out-buildings for horses, for cattle, and for farming. The mansion had three floors, four master windows, two tall turrets, stone and large wooden framing outside. Inside it had 11 bedrooms, 2 kitchens, several comfortable living areas, two large patios, and an attached green-house for growing flowers and vegetables. Five local villagers were daily employed to maintain the numerous work areas. Everything was well organized and it was a beautiful setting. Not even remotely similar to Shanghai or Cairo.

Whenever the three 'little boys' came together in England, they always reconnoitered at Charles' family estate, Somersham Meadows, to go horseback riding all day, and to their favorite tavern, the Boars Head Inn, and womanize all night. Only after a couple of days of such relaxation did they settle down to discuss their new ETI.

And their timing for the 'visit' was to be able spend tomorrow at the Royal Ascot thoroughbred race. Gang Hu had the list of entries for all races and already chosen his winners where he would definitely do his betting. Much of his life was spent on the racecourses, so he anticipated some celebrating tomorrow night; however, a couple of classes higher than the Boars' Head Inn.

It was early on a beautiful summer evening and sitting on the large patio overlooking many acres of emerald green pasture, one fence enclosed area close to the house that was filled with his father's famous crimson colored Irish racing horses, the fellows sat, inhaled the sweet oxygen rich air, drank their scotch, and nibbled boiled soft crab legs and ate pretzeled crackers.

Charles began discussion in the direction of the ETI. "I want to hear from each of you how things are going in your part of the world, where we are good and where we are bad. Who wants to go first?"

Gang Hu, the Tiger, was never one to follow others so he came on strong and first. "In general, not bad. Various Levels A and B are selling a little, and Level C is testing out in villages in western China. However, it is not happening as you said it would. I guess we need more time."

"As you will remember my family have lived from Shanghai and up the Yangtze River, for several generations. They still control most trade, legal and not so legal on most of the rivers in the area. However, the other large cities and major rivers in the mid-coastal region of China are controlled by the Chinese Triads. They are a vicious and deadly group of gangs who do not tolerate competition. Recently they have begun to produce nanotech systems, and of course market them throughout central China. So, I am going very slowly in trying to establish a market and not create major problems with them. They are brutal and if I step on their toes very hard, one of your partners and Senior Directors might disappear."

"Otherwise, we are currently testing the Level C systems or Nano-Bottoms in several villages in the western mountains of China up near the Mongolian border. First reports say that they worked as proposed most of the time. So that is very positive. But not equally to everyone all the time. And that is negative."

Charles agreed, "This is very important. We need to establish the legitimacy of this new type of nanotech system if we are to make it a good sales product."

Charles and Gang Hu looked at Ali; so, Ali finished his scotch, poured another, and began his report.

"We have no competition in the major cities of the Middle East, such as in Cairo, Alexandria, Damascus, Bagdad, Beirut, Tripoli, Tunis, and others. In fact, there is a lot of money which can be used to 'neutralize, your competitor or enemy. And if the weapon which is used leaves no evidence and is cheaper than guns, which also requires the training of many soldiers, why not give it a try. Cheaper and easier to eliminate your competition. And if carefully used it can minimize collateral damage. Yes, we are starting to enter this centuries-old marketplace with a new weapon system. Many people are interested. This could go big time for ETL."

"There is much interest for the Level A and Level B nano-systems with the wealthy oil people. They like the idea of selecting how to neutralize their enemy; with gentleness or harshness. And we now use the word neutralize, not kill. It sounds better and the 'clients' approve. They are not killing. They are neutralizing. Neat?"

"But back country areas in several regions of developing counties where politics is still being solved with guns, our Nano-Bottoms are getting second looks, depending upon prices. There is possibly a big growing market as every year there are more African countries dividing into two or three sub-countries. For them, Nano-Bottoms can be cheaper, easier to use, more specific with less neutralizing children and families, and a scary way to die."

Charles commented, "I never thought about it in those ways. But if not by bullets or bombs, then why not by a nano-system? Which is best? We can advertise it as a NONOTECH KILLER. Neat—Huh?"

The evening dinner bell rang for the second time calling the dozen family members and guests who were going to share an all seafood meal. The table was set, cold white wine was ready, and hot clam chowder was steaming away. And the last three gentlemen temporarily forgot the ETT and joined the rest of the group. New people and new subjects were welcome. And true success in business was just around the corner. And they planned to be there.

17

SHAMANISM WITCHCRAFT IN MOTION

High Shaman Wu Xian is the conduit for life, death, and post death to thousands of villagers in the Nanjing-Shanghai region north of Beijing. Recently several of his villagers suffered a variety of medically unexplainable sudden deaths of their inhabitants. This was similar to what the Irish Priestess had explained to Wu Xian during the recent World Witches Conclave in Ireland. So, the nanotech 'disease' had arrived and struck down some of his people on his grounds. He must respond immediately. And he had his suspicions—the West Branch of the Triads.

He needed certain information to confirm this. So he called in several of his highly trusted senior acolytes and sent them out to gather select data from the 'contaminated' villages, how the Triads were organized today, state of the Ming Tombs and tomb complexes, heroin/nanodrug manufacture and distribution, and exactly who is Mr. Kai-Do Luawan, the organizer and head of the Central Branch of the Triads; they controlled the entire region from Beijing to Shanghai and west.

And he stressed they needed to be extremely careful because the Triads were vicious killers.

While waiting for this information, a couple of nights later he contacted an old 'friend' who had worked as an assassin for the Triads for forty years, but 'retired' five years ago. Kong Mon was famous for 'killing' more than 250 men, women, and children. Soon after blowing up a school bus with 35 children, he left the Triads. Kai-Do Luawan and he struck a deal that he would receive five million USA dollars, in return he would not 'kill' Kai-Do Luawan's two sons, five grandsons, nor his pride and joy great grand-son. Besides, there were fears worse than that of death, and his 'colleagues' knew that he knew all of them.

But with such a life, Kong Mon's soul was in jeopardy. He appealed to Wu Xian to save his soul. An agreement was made. The High Shaman would maintain his soul in a special high place for a minimum of ten years. But this required that Kong Mon never kill again and assist with special 'handling' of select souls.

The two of them would meet that night in Wu Xian's under the temple-library study. Only Wu Xian had a key to this very private 'study'. At 8:00 PM Kong Mon came to Wu Xian's regular office on the first floor of the temple. They looked each other in the eyes, but did not touch. Wu Xian considered Kong Mon's soul contaminated, but had promised to save him/it. He wanted/needed some information about the Triads and Kai-Do Luawan. He knew that Kong Mon would readily provide anything he wanted. They went down the five levels, entered the study, sat at a small table in desk chairs, and began a difficult and short conversation.

All walls of the small room were filled with old books and ancient paraphernalia. Strange religious items and amulets hung from the ceiling. Kong Mon had cold shivers as the room was strange, cold, and felt close to the lower world. He remembered that the High Shaman controlled his soul for a minimum of ten years, this was year eight. Should he be nervous? Probably. But he could only do what was asked of him. Shamanism was an open concept with only upper, middle, and lower levels. He felt that he was now in the middle level, and hoped he could return to the upper world, soon. The air smelled of fresh hypnotic mint.

High Shaman Wu Xia began, "I need to learn about the Central Branch of the Triads. You worked for them for many years. Please tell me about them."

Kong Mon was struck—he panicked—must he chose between Shamanism and the Triads? He knew he had to answer with truths. He was afraid to lie.

He stuttered, "Years ago, there were several Chinese criminal groups in China, South East Asia, Europe and the USA. It was a secret transnational crime organization which was independent, but did occasionally communicate within itself. There were four major such groups here in the East—Hong Kong, Macau, Taiwan, and mainland groups. Two general types existed—dark forces were loosely organized gangs—black societies obtained control of local politics, police and many legal and illegal markets."

"In the 18th century, these crime organizations melted into one large secret criminal club called Heaven and Earth Society. In the 19th century the Hong Kong British battled groups called Triads on opium trade from India. In the 20th century after World War II many new criminal gangs/groups established several gangster societies and formulated—Wo Hop To, Rung, Sun -Do-On, Rung, Luen, Chuen, 14K, Tung, and others. Today there are several Triads in mainland China".

"I always worked for the Triad called Wo Shing. Mr. Kai Luawan became Head Master more than 40 years ago. I always worked directly for him for 35 years. Frequently I was 'loaned' out to various action groups which required 'wet' work. But I always returned to his command, and payroll."

"Wo Shing worked or controlled 'trade' in most of north-central-east China. There were many pockets where they also controlled politicians, police, and sometimes the military. Their most successful activities involved drug trafficking of heroin, opium came from the Golden Triangle and was refined here for methamphetamines for the USA, and ecstasy for Europe. Now they have started producing a new drug called nanotechnical substance. Other areas where they have had much success include counterfeiting US dollars and euros, copying video entertainment as VCDs and CVDs, duplicating famous women's apparel, casino gambling, sports betting, grand theft, hacking and cyber-electronics."

"Wo Shing has a standard criminal/military organization. There are rankings/number-codes which depicts who directs the various action divisions. These divisions include terrorism, cyber gangs, heavy crimes, political crimes, street gangs, youth gangs, professional criminals, and spy councils."

"Mr. Luawan, as Head Master, makes all first decisions and the Action Heads are then responsible for positively carrying out these decisions. All of my 'killing' orders came directly from him. He is a very difficult person.

If I remember correctly, I think there was a regular change of all Action Heads every few years. But the two of us became like big and little brother. It made him happy when I performed well. And bonuses were substantial and often. He trusted me such that I frequently attended his family on vacation trips, without him, to boost security to a higher maximum, as he liked to say. So, our relationship was good."

Wu Xian thought to himself for a few moments. 'If this assassin and his master are good friends, I should ask no questions or I might tip him off as to what I must do in the near future.'

Instead he just said, "Thank you." He rang a hidden bell. Two guards came from two separate hidden doors. They helped Kong Mon stand and marched him out of the room. The two 'gentlemen' did not see each other again.

Six months later, High Shaman Wu Xian called his acolytes to him, one by one, to receive their reports about the Triads and their leaders.

1) "Five small villages, just north of Ming City, each with 50 to 100 villagers, including children, were found by neighboring villagers at different times over a period of three months. Many villagers were dead. Some had been dead for two or three days when first found. All had bled from the mouth, nose, ears, and eyes. And autopsies revealed that each victim's head was filled with coagulated blood. No cause for these deaths was identified. This was true of men, women, and children, but no village animals were so affected. A very unexplainable macabre form of death. Local authorities still do not understand."

2) "The Triads are considered similar to the various mafia that exists in many western countries. It certainly is the major crime organization in China and has branches in the immigrant Chinese populations in many cities throughout the world. Basically, it

is composed of more than one million members of numerous criminal gangs of various sizes and criminal tastes. The gangs use codes to distinguish ranks, levels, and positions of the gangs and gang leaders, such as Dragon Head, Chief Head, Assistant Head, Street Gang Leader. They are involved in terrorism, armed robbery, racketeering, smuggling, narcotics, prostitution, people trafficking, contract murders, and on and on. They do not hesitate to kill off competition and competitor's families."

3) "Kai-Do Luawan is the seventy-five years old Dragon Head of the Central Branch of the Triads which controls the region from Beijing to Shanghai and West. He claims to be a central descendent of the Ming Dynasty. The Ming and Qing Dynasties left more than twenty tombs and tomb complexes which have now been discovered and many have been renovated. Several are listed on UNESCO's World Heritage Sites. Emperor Qing's Tomb and several family tombs are now a major tourist attraction and are open and available to viewers six days a week. It is a government owned and controlled area. Nearby, about five hundred meters away, are grouped several ancient buildings which Kai-Do purchased. He also purchased fifty acres of the area and partially renovated and walled off the ancient buildings area. These old buildings are now out of view from the major tourism tomb area. These renovated buildings provide parking garages to the housing of the Triad management complex below; a reverse skyscraper office building complex."

4) "During the renovation period, 2000 to 2016, Kai-Do, using his heritage, Triad monies, and numerous 'connections, renovated several of the smaller tombs. He converted some 'tomb-caves' and several associated above ground buildings into major office facilities for his Central Branch Headquarters. He also has a very deluxe underground living facilities with extensive electronic security and communication systems, again for private and personal uses. His major above ground city headquarters is in Nanjing, where his wife and children live. Kai-Do is famous for having cut the throat of more than 50 of his past competitors and all their family members."

5) "The Ming tomb complex, contains the bodies of several past emperors and their families. The first Ming emperor, Zhu Yuanzhang, built the Ming Xiaoling Tomb as several large underground tombs and a complex of thirty-four buildings with numerous smaller tombs. On the northeast corner of the complex, specifically the Jingling, Yongling, and Deling tombs, are under a 100-year lease from the Chinese government by Kai-Do. He closed them off from the other tombs and connected smaller select tombs by tunnel to nearby coal mines, which he owns. The entry to the coal mines lies two kilometers away and passes under the Knaul mountain."

6) "For controlled entry to his Triad 'tomb-caves', one entry to the complex requires a two-kilometers underground train ride, and the other is a set of very secure elevator rides from the above ground car parking to the below ground offices and labs (reverse skyscraper). The first five levels below ground are the bookkeeping and general management offices (for many of the Triad 'companies and gangs.)' Levels six and seven below contain the second home and offices for Kai-Do and his seven Chief Heads. One of Dragon Head's living and office facilities are on this floor. He does not trust anyone, so he lives and works in the same space. His people, the underlings, come to him."

7) "In addition, several of the side 'tomb-caves' have been converted to drug manufacturing laboratories. The science employees, including at least a dozen high technology scientists and laboratory staff, all of whom had western training, can use the car/elevator route or exclusively the lab train, if they so desire. The train provides the major supply entry and product exit mode for the laboratories. Just what those laboratories are producing in addition to heroin, we do not really know. Monitoring the incoming supplies to the complex reveals much of it is from the USA, is high tech and very top secret."

8) "The Central Branch of the Triads has specialized in the illegal drug world for many years, both manufacturing and distribution. First it was growing the poppy for opium and refining for heroin. Then it became a synthetic world of converting meth

into methamphetamines. Now it appears that a new synthetic drug may have caught the attention of these Triads. It is called nanotech-molecules. It is being produced from something other than poppy. I was not able to find out more."

High Shaman Wu Xian carefully thanked each, and told them not to speak about this to anyone, and to completely forget what they had learned. He next went into a one week of seclusion to review everything he had just learned. The Central Branch of Triads and its Dragon Head, Kai-Do Luawan, were powerful, dangerous, and unscrupulous people. His own acolytes/associates and their families must not be involved with any type of revenge, but this type of abnormal killing must be stopped immediately.

During his seclusion he went, alone, to Kai-Do's family cemetery near Ming City, At the grave site of Kai-Do's father he performed three different rituals using three different ancient languages on three different successive full moon nights. He managed acute communication with several of Kai-Do's family spirits, explained the life style of their current live offspring, and agreed to participate in a 'correction' procedure with them.

Eleven days later, beginning with the next new moon, Kai-Do, and his ever-present bodyguard, were walking, using flashlights, through the corridors between two of the 'tomb-caves' deep underground. He had been informed that they needed more lab space for expansion of nanotech molecular system production. And he always made the first and last decisions for important matters. He thought this nanotech stuff was going to be a big winner.

They walked for more than an hour, looking into several tomb areas, but he was not happy with what he saw. One of his lab assistants, who knew just what the Master wanted, and could use a bonus or two, led him in a different direction. Fifteen minutes later they entered a long zig zag tunnel. It was cold and wet. And the group had to form a train like arrangement to get through the tunnel. One guard took the lead, Kai-Do was second, the others followed.

Suddenly, a moderate sized earthquake occurred, common in this area. The corridor ceiling and walls collapsed around the first members of the group. The lead body guard was immediately killed. Kai-Do was caught in only a part of the rock slide, but it trapped both of his legs. Most of the followers were either killed or isolated in the corridor on the other side of the rock fall. He could not move. He shouted for help, but only echoes and shouts came back in the darkness.

Then he heard some noises coming from the open end of the corridor. It was a slithering-liquid sound. He turned on his flashlight. Directly in front of him and rapidly coming toward him was one of the giant pythons/dragons which had inhabited these caves for thousands of years. This one looked to be 5 to 6 meters long and probably more than one half meter in diameter. It was pale yellow-brown in color and had bright gold-yellow eyes. Kai-Do did not know what to do. He froze and could not even scream for help. Suddenly the beast opened its mouth, and Kai-Do felt a very hot breath on his face. Then there were the slimy digestive juices dripping down on his head and face and puddled on the floor. Next darkness swallowed first, then dragon swallowed second, and Kai-Do partially screamed. But he was swallowed third and last.

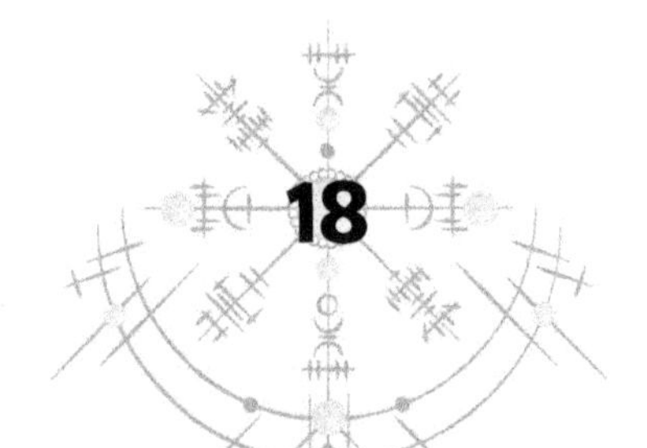

18

COMMITTEE OF NANOTECHNOLOGY CONTROL III

At 9:00 AM on the first Monday of February 2036, the Committee of Nanotechnology Control meeting in the Federal Trade Center Building on the Constitution Avenue in Washington, DC, settled in. Mr. John Reasoner, Committee Chairman, looked around, counted heads from seven different countries, all committee members were present, so he called the meeting to order.

Mr. Reasoner began, "Welcome to Washington, DC. We have much new information and data to present to you today, and several key decisions to make. We have managed to keep much of this 'news' out of the 'news'. It helps that much of this recent news began in several developing countries so it travels slower and is easier to banket. Yes, we are talking about many new medically unexplainable sudden deaths—MUSDs. First, Mr. Dagda Murphy will present some old data and we can then compare it with this new data."

"I wish to thank you for giving of your time and efforts in trying to solve this international nanotech 'plague'," Mr. Murphy opened his presentations. "These nanotech molecules can be designed for curing and for killing humans. And we have plenty of data showing it has cured a variety of diseases, especially single cell diseases such as cancer. But our current focus is on the killing aspect of the nanotech molecular system."

"To remind you of the past killings, which began in 2028:

- 2028 – 6 deaths
- 2029 – 6 deaths
- 2030 – 24 deaths
- 2031 – 24 deaths
- 2032 – 356 deaths
- 2033 – 2 deaths
- 2034 – 5 deaths+
- 2035 – 11 deaths+

"During these years the nanotech molecular systems have become more and more sophisticated: from a one simple organic trigger molecule; to several nanotech molecules bound to each other and working as a unit: for example—organic trigger molecule + MoAB homing molecule + stomach digestion blocker molecule + special time release component + self-destruct component. In the beginning, the nano systems targeted specific areas of the brain via the spinal cord. Next, any single body cell or tissue or organ could be targeted via the blood. And soon, later this morning, I will tell you about the most recent development, a new digest-activatable cellulose nanotech trigger molecular system which apparently causes a very macabre form of death."

Dr. Lawrence Batly politely inquired, "Were the types of MUSDs different over the years or just different for each system?" "Alright, let me first compare the old and new systems, and then I can tell you what we know about this most recent cellulose nanotech molecular system."

Dr. Joseph Barkly asked, "Do you see this increase in sophistication a result of several different laboratories under a central control, or several laboratories spontaneously following their noses?"

"We really do not know, nor do we think we have the necessary info/data to try to make such decisions. We do think there is a general over-all controller called a Korrectorizer—sort of like a symphony conductor.

But whether he has control of one or more orchestras or laboratories, that would be just a guess."

Mr. Murphy continued, "I will give you my logic. If you will remember during the years immediately before the Istanbul massacres, we received several rather macabre notes based upon who was just killed. There was a death pattern which 'he' used relationships of certain days of the month and the first letter of the victim's name. Let me remind you with a couple of examples:

NO – HI – TECH – STOP

OPEN – THE – BRAIN

"We still believe our enemy is a group of international conservative industrialists trying to suppress/eliminate their major competitions."

Nanotech System Killings in Developing Countries

"These death patterns have continued, but several changes have occurred during the past 2-3 years. After the Istanbul massacre of more than 350 high technology scientists and their financial supporters, there was a lull in MUSDs. For two or three years, only a few high-tech scientists were targeted by using the three or four component organic nanotech systems. But lately, the targeting has shifted to high-tech scientists from developing countries. Most of these countries are trying to become high tech oriented. They are developing their own high technology to compete in the worldwide science marketplace. Many of these scientists were trained in the USA or Europe, education financed by their own countries, returned home after advanced training, started their own laboratories, began training their own people, and were then killed in their own home cities by someone."

"Two high-tech scientists were killed in 2033. However, we could not connect them with any organization."

"In 2034, there were five MUSDs who were high-tech scientists working in the following areas: 1) chips or monoliths integrated circuits; 2) multiple electronic routing systems; 3) automated-integrated software computer programing; 4) new forms of Bluetooth Technology; 5) modified cyber-security programing.

"Each was located in his home city/country—Indonesia, Brazil, Lebanon, Estonia, and Morocco. They were each given needle injections somewhere in their skeletal muscles—arm, leg, or buttocks—while walking down the street in a bazar or shopping area. The 'assassin' just walked away among the resulting turmoil. Within 10-12 hours the targets' red blood cell factories in his bone marrow started to shut down. Production of new red cells stopped. A couple hours later he died of asphyxiation."

"And yes, each was injected on the first Wednesday evening on each of the first five months of 2034 while routinely shopping—no witnesses from a crowd of possible witnesses—dead while asleep."

"The names of the young scientists were Dr. Setiawan Gozali, Dr. Antonio Sontoro, Dr. Mohamoud Haddad, Dr. Nikolla Rebane, and Dr. Razzaak Kachloul."

Dr. Batly asked, "How did you identify the deaths of such a diverse but collective group of high-tech scientists? They lived very far from each other."

Responding Mr. Reasoner, "Dr. Stronger can best answer that question. Dr. Stronger, Chairman of Nanotechnology at MIT in Boston, please."

Dr. Stronger replied, "Two ways—these five young doctors were all students at MIT in the Division of High Technology. They routinely associated with my students in Nanotechnology. Even bright young scientists know how to gossip. Plus, the World Health Organization out of Geneva is always directly notifying us whenever there is a MUSD anywhere in the world."

"Frequently we try to send a small forensic team to the death location in an attempt to obtain a sample of the nanotech system which was used. With each of these cases we sent a team which included a nanotech forensic specialist. No luck. But we did confirm the type of death. Asphyxiation by way of non-functioning red blood cell factories—no red blood cells in the body."

Dr. Stronger added, "There is one interesting relationship. The three Muslims were good friends and routinely attended the Friday mosque. They also frequently partied with the two Christians. The group had similar computer related research in common. So, it was only natural that they knew each other rather well."

"Why were they each killed in the same way during the same time frame? There are many possibilities. There were rumors that they were trying to set up a new joint research company. After the newly trained young doctors had trained others, the university did not need an English language speaking nanotech teacher in house—so they were replaced. Some of the new trainees were now superior in status compared with their teachers—so they were eliminated. This sequential nanotech provides supplies to a company to make money—their 'home' bosses did not agree. Methodology was a major experiment by the nanotech molecular system producers. I could go on just guessing. We really do not know."

Mr. Murphy spoke up, "I prefer the double rationale, making a test run sequential trial effort, and eliminating overly qualified young faculty personnel—bigger than the boss (political). It is really just a guess."

After several questions, answers, and discussion, Mr. Reasoner suggested that they continue with the facts, return later if necessary.

He began. "In 2035, a similar but different pattern occurred. Eleven young 'developing country' scientists in advanced training in various high-tech laboratories in the USA, Canada, and Europe were nano tech killed. Each was from a different country. Each country was trying to become scientific modern. Each trainee was sponsored by his country. And the focus was solar-energy. All were African. The names and countries are as follows:

Dr. Amazigh – Berber in Northern Africa—trained in USA
Dr. Haile – Ethiopia—trained in USA
Dr. Abubakar – Egypt—trained in Sweden
Dr. Khalid – Morocco—trained in Sweden
Dr. Yassa – North-Central Africa—trained in USA
Dr. Yannik – Ivory Coast—trained in Canada
Dr. Mamadou – Congo Republic—trained in Canada
Dr. Nkwabi – South Africa—trained in England
Dr. Chidiebere – Nigeria—trained in USA
Dr. Mtumwa – Somali—trained in France
Dr. Faisal – Sudan—trained in Sweden

"The patterns for this group of young high technology scientists are similar to the previous group which I just described. Each one was shopping in a store in his own country in the late afternoon when attacked. Death was received due to a small needle injection in a skeletal muscle. Ten to twelve hours later the red blood cell factories in the bone marrow closed down—asphyxiation. This time the nanotech molecular system was the same; and the pattern to the timing of the various deaths, one death every first and third Wednesday evenings, was very similar."

"What did they expect to learn when studying abroad?" asked Mr. Reasoner. "What new technology would they bring back to their people? I hoped it would be advanced solar energy knowledge. I assumed they studied solar modules, solar high-tech panels, multi-solar systems, direct current to alternating current theories, and solar photovoltaic technology for cars, trucks, buses, and metros/trains. I checked this out. And yes, those were some of the many components of solar technology that these young men were studying and teaching in their countries."

"I would imagine that the killing of those scientists will now destroy or certainly delay the efforts of these countries to develop solar technology systems," said Dr. Dorthy Lawess. "It seems to me a good way to strike fear into other developing countries—a message to their high-tech scientists in solar technology."

Mr. Bradimer said. "It seems to me that hiring a group of assassins and letting them do their killing at random of unarmed civilians would be easier and cheaper. There has to be some special nanotech reason for this mode of interfering with the attempt of solar energy knowledge transfer to the African continent. And they used a not yet fully tested positive nanotech molecular system. Looking at the countries of these young scientists one sees a lot of sunshine. Solar would be an excellent science to import and produce. But the killing methodology, I do not understand."

Mr. Reasoner suggested they take a long coffee/tea plus sugar break. Then they could look at previous and new potential nanotech scientists who are/were candidates for MUSD homicides. Some of them are no longer with the living world.

Update of Candidates as Nanotech Assassins/Killers

Half an hour later Mr. Murphy began by updating the committee members concerning the previous list of nanotech killer candidates.

"Some of them are still with us. Some of them are no longer with us," he began.

"If you will remember, most recently our number one candidate was **Dr. Mario Kemps**, brilliant nanotech scientist from Buenos Aries. He was an extremely active man, professionally and personally. He developed several nano tech systems, shared all of his wives and his employee's wives, had several children, horses, a cattle ranch, and maintained a harem of black teenage girls. He is now in permanent retirement from all of this due to sudden physical changes in his reproductive system. In fact, his bathroom is his daily physical/psychological challenge."

"Because of our original 'need to know' agreement, I cannot explain in detail how or what happened. Suffice it to say, he is no longer a macho man."

And that drew a round of smiles and comments from these educated-mature professionals, but there were no 'outspoken' comments.

Our number two candidate was **Dr. Franz Gunter** of Munich. He was another brilliant nanotech scientist who had developed several very sophisticated nanotech molecular systems which could cure and/or kill. He lost a battle with cards; then he had an accident when he ran head-on into an underground metro train that had started to brake, unfortunately not fast enough. Dr. Gunter lost the head to head encounter. He is now permanently out of business. We have simply listed him as 'neutralized'."

Again, there were many variations in facial expressions by committee members, looks around the table, but no words seemed to come forth. They were all aware of the clandestine assistance of witches—who, where, how, was not important.

The next candidate I wish to speak about is **Dr. James Walter** of Ottawa. He has Columbian connections with a previous graduate student, who is now a nanotech scientist, and the son of the head of a Columbian drug cartel. Dr. Walters remains in contact with his nano-trained student-doctor and even sends to him, occasionally, 'forbidden' supplies. We think they are making nanotech killer type systems in Bogota, possibly testing and/or using them in the villages there. But the government is not cooperative in our efforts to monitor this 'important' high technology government laboratory. So? Not much we can do except watch from a distance."

"Turning to a brilliant female nanotech scientist, **Dr. Anneka Andersson** of Stockholm, who has moved up on our list of nanotech killer candidates, also because of her younger trainees. She is a well-respected Professor at the Karolinska Institute and has developed several nanotech systems which can be used for cure or kill. There are several black African male doctor trainees working with her in the labs. Three of them rent bedrooms in her house. We are watching them. Why?"

"The trainees routinely go home on vacation once or twice a year. Their home village chiefs have been noted to have found nearby MUSDs while they were there, or perhaps discovered in nearby areas after they had returned to school. So, we believe they are either stealing the systems from the labs, or are given permission to select and take a few samples home to test in humans."

Dr. Joseph Barkley asked, "Were any of these African victims tested with a forensic team that had a nanotech specialist? In other words, did all victims have similar death symptoms? Was the same nanotech system used?"

"No," responded Mr. Murphy. "At least three of four different systems were used. And each system had a self-destruct component. So probably there was some experimentation or drug testing in motion."

"Another candidate, who now is more important for us to carefully monitor, is **Mr. Faustino Mariniti** of Rome and Milan. Remember, he is a wealthy playboy-businessman who controls a shipping empire between Europe and Africa. Several times his ships have been caught with illegal-major contraband cargo. This includes weapons, terrorist's supplies, and critical technology for bomb making, as well as transporting illegal immigrants. His companies routinely carry merchandise back and forth to most African countries that border the Mediterranean Sea and the African side of the Atlantic Ocean. In several of these countries, Egypt, Lebanon, Libya, and Morocco,

WHO has several reports of MUSDs observed in outlying villages. We think this sequence of events occurs via a nanotech science laboratory in Milan, a shadow business partner of Mr. Mariniti. Nanotech molecular systems are custom ordered, designed, synthesized, shipped, and delivered to a buyer in select African sea ports."

"Mr. Mariniti has been shipping in the Med Sea for many years, such that when one of his ships is caught, he has a string of lawyers and 'assistants' in various Med Sea ports who 'correct' the illegal seizure of his ship and/or merchandise. He brags that his delivery percentage is near 98%, regardless of the 'empty' or 'falsely loaded' cargo containers."

"In summary, we have developed a new list of candidates which include the above discussed scientists and businessman. And we will add six new candidates to keep our work list at ten. Again, we consider this to be a maximum workload based on our annual budget. We will give you that list and spend time describing each candidate, her/his professional and personal background, and discuss what brought her/him to our attention, later this afternoon."

Mr. Reasoner took over, "We have programed enough time this afternoon for questions and answers concerning our methods of monitoring, and following up on any new sudden massacres, which I feel we must be ready for in the near future. But first Mr. Murphy needs to explain about a possible new cellulose nanotech molecular system that is currently being tested in several African villages, we think. If so, it could be used for mass killing."

A New International Nanotech Marketing Corporation

Mr. Murphy began, "I would like to now give to you some special information about **Dr. Albert Langdon**, who works in London, but would be far happier if the world had been created for him, instead of against him. He has always been at the bottom of our list, but we have never really focused on him. That was a mistake."

"He is an excellent nanotech scientist, has won several international prizes, trained many students, but recently quit the university system and turned to commerce to make money."

"Dr. Langdon joined a group of businessmen and established a new corporation, Equus Transport International, ETI, which is designing, producing, manufacturing, freight/shipping, distributing, and market/selling a variety of nanotech molecular systems for cure of kill. We are certain that this corporation is taking custom orders as well as selling to the highest bidder. To our knowledge, this is the first business organization which is trying to attempt to corner the market in nanotechnology. ETI has several production and marketing partners. For example, a friend, Mr. McCorland routinely ships industrial goods from Europe to Africa and Brazil. We have data following one of Mr. McCorland's ships into certain seaports in northwestern Africa and northern South America, especially up the Amazon River. Several villages along the Amazon have reported MUSDs over the past couple of years."

"Ten years ago, when Dr. Langdon left the university, he established his own Langdon High Tech (read it as Nano-System) College. He now custom designs his own nano systems and has trained more than fifty foreign pre-doctoral laboratory technicians from developing countries. The fees of the foreign technicians are paid by their countries, so they return home after two years of courses and lab training. Dr. Langdon regularly visits each country and helps them establish nanotechnological laboratories for their governments. For a substantial fee he initiates research and production of whichever nanotech system they wish to develop."

"The reason we left Dr. Langdon to the last will now be explained."

"Dr. Stronger, will you please come forward and explain the science."

1) "We have learned from his foreign students, with appropriate financial inducement, that Dr. Langdon has apparently produced a new cellulose active nano-trigger, instead of the usual organic active nano-trigger, for a newly designed cellulose nanotech molecular system. The organic nano-trigger system requires a typical medical biopsy Styrofoam packaging, with dry ice and liquid nitrogen frozen vial(s) of tissue/liquid, for transportation. If we are correct,most of the past assassinations/killings were accomplished with this mode of transportation. Apparently, this new cellulose system is stable at room temperatures. So, transportation of the new system

eliminates the need for the freezing process during shipping and handling. This would make a much easier and a better system to work with. This is a major improvement, especially in outlying areas, anywhere away from city dry ice availability."

2) "We followed a shipment of a couple of small packages, each containing a nanotech system, via one of McCMetals ships down the Amazon. We noted the villages they were unloaded, and watched them disappear into the wilderness. We tried to have the packages followed. No such luck. And because the packages did not require refrigeration, they disappeared quickly and easily. And yes, within one week several villagers in nearby villages were found dead—MUSDs. Reporting it to the police did no good."

"So, if we had to guess, this cellulose trigger system appears to be stable at ambient temperatures, must be ingested, probably goes through the first part of the digestion process intact, and then the bacterial cellulase activates it when it enters the colonic bacterial milieu several hours later. Result is internal-external diarrhea, and a miserable death."

There was collective sigh among the committee members. No verbal comments were forthcoming. What can you say about such a macabre form of death?

After a few moments of silence, Mr. Reasoner spoke. "I understand that there is a bad winter storm headed into Washington later today. Therefore, it is possible some of you may have difficulty with flights, especially going toward Europe. I have taken the liberty of having a hot meal delivered to us here in this room. I am passing a short menu for you to chose from. We will order your choice, which will be delivered to us in one half an hour, at 12:00 noon. If this is inconvenient, please speak up. For now, we can continue discussing the current candidate information and data. Or if there are specific pertinent questions to explore, we should not wait until later to discuss. We will open the doors on the new potential candidates after lunch."

"Oh yes. I must remind you of our 'need to know' restrictions.

Remember there are no witches on our payroll."

Dr. Batly gently asked, "Do you have any laboratory mice which we can use to first test our mice with our meals?"

It was not a funny joke!

19

IRISH WITCHCRAFT IN MOTION – I

Saint Patrick was a fifth-century Roman-British Christian missionary and bishop in Ireland. He became known as the 'Apostle of Ireland'. And today he is the primary 'Saint of Ireland'.

Born as Maewyn Succat in Rome in 386 AD. His father, Calphurnis, was a decan from a Roman family of high social standing. His mother, Conchessa, was a close relative of the Patron St. Martin of Tours. However, Patrick was not educated.

As a boy he was captured by pirates, taken to Ireland, and sold into slavery. Because he was young, he spent his time in the fields tending sheep. His master was Milchu, a high Priest of Druidism, which was the dominant religion in Ireland at that time.

During these early years he did not accept Paganism and began to believe his enslavement was a test of the true God and became devoted to Christianity.

When, finally a free man, he returned to Rome, joined the Church, and went to France to study priesthood under St. Germain. Patrick became a deacon in 418 AD and a bishop in 432 AD. Under Pope Celestine I, he was sent back to Ireland to support the struggling Christian groups living there.

As a missionary and knowing Irish Druidism, he set out to combine the two ideologies. He performed many pagan rituals and

Christian baptism together and introduced a Celtic cross which could be used for native sun-worship as well as for the Jesus God.

Bishop Patrick supported both Druidism and Christianity with councils, monasteries, and the creation throughout Ireland, and was very successful at blending the two modes of thinking and worshiping.

Throughout his 30 years of Irish preaching, many legends were created about him. Such as; he drove all the snakes out of Ireland; the three leafed shamrock represents Druidism and the Christian Trinity; and there was his famous autobiography 'Confessio'.

Saint Patrick died in 461 AD and was buried in Downpatrick, County Down, Ireland. He is annually honored with the celebration of Saint Patrick's Day on March 17, Irish families, world-wide attend church and eat special meals of cabbage and Irish bacon on that day.

Because Patrick is the Patron Saint of Ireland it is not surprising that the earlier Celtic mythology is sometimes considered the beginning of the amalgamation of Irish mythology-Druidism-Christianity.

In the fall Jamie had returned home after a great summer in Ireland. He had studied Irish mythology/witchcraft with Ms. Banthnaid O'Keefe, High Priestess of Irish Witchcraft. He had selected Dagda, the High God or Great Father of the Irish, and was getting to learn the necessary Celtic dialect and understand the appropriate spiritual connections. The High Priestess's spirit mate, Morrigan, was the Great Queen of the Irish. It was a common arrangement because Dagda and Morrigan regularly fought together in most battles. This could be useful in the future.

The Irish Priestess assigned one of her trained witchcraft students living in Boston to continue to work with him, while he and his musketeer buddies finished their last year in high school and began college. Also, he maintained regular communications with Ms. O'Keefe in exploring an opportunity to identify the appropriate targets for their soul mates to help them in neutralizing. They both 'felt' that action was near, perhaps next year.

Jamie wanted to enter Harvard University Pre-Law Program. So, he had taken the SAT and Harvard University entrance exams. His father, Theodore O'Reilly, assassinated Czar of High Technology, and his father's two non-identical triplet brothers, Johnathan O'Reilly, former President of the USA, and Jackson O'Reilly, former-Attorney General of the USA, had all graduated from Harvard. If he wanted to follow all of his male role models into law, he needed to study hard and score high on those exams. He planned to do just exactly that.

He lay there in bed, half asleep and half awake, while snow filled the air and ground. This was thinking weather, one could not travel from the house anyway. Schools closed. Businesses closed. Roads closed. But he loved being locked into a thinking mode. So, his mind, as it often did, started drifting on its own.

Jamie thought back to his last pre-teenage year. 'It all began when my father was assassinated by some kind of a nanotech molecular system. And I still do not understand this system that is now killing all these people in such a sadistic way. Why was my dad the first? Why did they then have to kill my best-ever school mates? And next my three foreign buddies' fathers were killed. Even my uncles and the United States Commission, led by my Uncle Dagda, had no success in identifying who they were, let alone catching and punishing them.'

'When my modified avatar speaking buddies joined to help, we found many things about those so called 'molecules' and nanotech killers, but it was not enough. I guess that is why I have to follow my father and uncles into law, and maybe do a little investigator/detective work using the assistance of Irish witchcraft. I feel comfortable with both warm/solid Uncle Dagda and cool/mystic King Dagda. With both of their protection I am sure I can help eliminate the nanotech killers and avenge my father.'

'I remember feeling how lucky I was to meet Li, Aykut, and Kef at the summer camp in Switzerland. And when they immediately and unanimously agreed to help me find my father's killer, I knew I had found cool lifelong friends. And what happens? Kef's father gets nano-killed in the Saatfordam Diamond Mines in Bloemfountain, South Africa. Then Aykut's father gets nano-killed, along with 300 plus others, in a giant macabre massacre in Istanbul. And last, Li's father, founder and president of his nanotechnological company, learned that his brothers were stealing their brother's ideas and illegally producing and selling nano-tech weapons. He invites his brothers to their grandfather's Shijiazhuang mountain castle, removes their heads and buries the heads in their childhood mountain play caves, and then he commits nano-tech suicide.'

'What a teenage-hood I had. I was overtaken by a new macabre 'disease' that killed my father, friends and friends' fathers. I must try to remove this 'disease' from the world. Lawyer/detective/mystic—that will be me someday. I will do it. Nothing can stop me.'

As the snow blanketed the sky, Jamie drifted off to sleep.

Jamie was very successful in his college entrance exams and was now studying pre-law-social sciences at Carroll College on the Cambridge campus at Harvard University in downtown Boston. Jamie still lived in Dorchester, south Boston, so he drove his hybrid electric Lexus CT to school, and used a student reserved parking place near campus. He was conservation oriented so the hybrid was his logical choice. With his mother and one older sister, he was living in his birth house, so of course it was special. And now he had taken over and was comfortable in his father's den/study room. It took several years before he could accept that his father was physically not present, but spiritually very present. Spirits do have a place in the world, so he had learned.

This particular Saturday morning he had his bi-monthly special visitor and substitute father, Uncle Dagda. They were sitting in the only two arm chairs in the office and were chatting away.

Uncle Dagda continued, "You tell me that your studies are going OK. With all you have been through, am I supposed to believe you?"

Jamie replied, "I am doing my best. But you know my uncles had high grades and were writers and editors of the various law school journals. I will get there someday. I am still spending study time learning ancient Cyrillic and Irish witchcraft communications. Priestess O' Keefe and I both feel that something is going to happen very soon. Have you talked to her recently?"

"I talk with her regularly. And yes, she has expressed similar feelings during our recent conversations."

"Then you must see how my excitement is not yet with the law school professors. I want a shot at the people who killed my father, first."

Uncle Dagda said, "OK. Later this morning, 11:00 AM our time, is 4:00 PM her time in Ireland. We can put in an EVCJ communication with our encrypted skype and talk to her directly."

Jamie said, "That would be good because your codes work better and faster than mine. I'm using my Uncle Jonathan's ex-Presidential codes, and these seem to be no longer popular."

And he gave his big winning smile. Uncle Dagda was pleased he had recovered some of his sense of humor. There were several years when he did not even smile, let alone joke.

"So, really, how are your grades? Are you avoiding studying? Do you need some tutor assistance?"

"No. I just need to get past the nanotech weapon action which is coming up. Great King Dagda, Great Queen Morrigan, and Priestess O'Keefe all agree that it will happen soon and suddenly."

"Well I sure hope it happens soon so you can concentrate on law school," replied Uncle Dagda. "And I do have some new information that I wish to tell you and the Priestess this morning."

"Please tell me now!"

"No, not now. I will inform both the Priestess and you when we talk skype. First, I want you to tell me about the family: your older sister, your mother, the house, working part time, etc."

So, Jamie slowed down, retrieved a cup of fresh hot tea for Uncle Dagda, and began describing recent past and current happenings within the fatherless family unit. It was just too early to think about a law specialty; and GIRLS—NO; No time yet.

Finally, Uncle Dagda spoke out, "It is near 11:00. Let me initiate that encrypted skytype to the Priestess Banthnaid O'Keefe. Let me notify my secretary at the Committee Office."

Five minutes later both his and Jamie's cell phones rang and they opened them, simultaneously.

Uncle Dagda began, "Hello Banthnaid. How are you today?"

The three of them were all genetically related, and had been working on this nanotech problem for several years, so each knew each other and what the call was all about.

Banthnaid answered, "Hello Dagda and Jamie. How are the both of you?" Jamie spoke up, "We are very good, thank you. And we are ready to go!"

She answered, "When are you not ready to go? Be patient. You inherited your father's non-patience. All will happen when the time is ripe. I feel it coming."

Jamie said, "Do you hear what she said. That is what I said that she said."

Uncle Dagda responded, "I hope all is well with you and your work. If you will allow, let me give to you both some new information. And we are usually limited to three minutes on these special phone calls. So, I will be brief. Turn on your recorders. A one-time through."

"This is all new data and info from the past two weeks inflow. We have identified a newly established English corporation entitled Equus Transport International – ETI. It specializes in producing and marketing nanotech systems, and sells them custom designed or in quantity to 'anyone'. In tracing some of the systems in their sales we think many of them are the killer type systems. Key members of the Board of Directors and various sub-companies include three nanotech scientists and six or seven transport/marketers who go to more than twenty different countries, mostly located in Africa, Middle East, and South America. One of their scientists is Dr. Langdon who has been high on our candidate list for a long time."

"Initial data indicates that they may have produced a new type of cellulose nano-killer system which is stable at room temperature. If this is true it could be treated more like army ammunition or bullets. It would be cheaper, and probably easier to use. But we do not understand how it is dispersed. Several villagers in four or five countries have been discovered as macabre MUSDs. And there are no exterior wounds on the outside of the bodies. Plus, ETI products had been delivered to these areas, prior to the death discoveries."

Priestess O'Keefe asked, "When did this ETI become active with production, shipping, and deliveries?"

"Uncle Dagda answered, "We began to monitor their production and marketing about one year ago. We found the MUSDs in villages only in the past few weeks in Africa. We are certain of the London to African country routing. But beyond this we are not certain. Currently we have sent nano-specialized forensic teams in three of the African villages trying to learn more, assuming it may be a source for this possible cellulose nano-system."

He continued, "In addition, three of the senior people of this ETI are ethnic Celtic/Irish."

"Now that is very interesting," she responded. "Then we will only use illusions."

Over the next few weeks, the Priestess and Jamie each communicated with their spiritual sister and brother. Several times they exchanged ideas and plans to neutralize the ETI group. The two of them then compared their plans with Uncle Dagda. Finally, a good plan was formulated, organized, and implemented for the next St. Patrick's Day.

As March 17 approached, Charles Somersham and his Irish-Scottish buddy, Gregory McCorland, had grown closer. Charles sold his company and became President and CEO of ETI. Gregory maintained his company but also accepted the new role of Associate CEO. Charles began working more closely with Dr. Langdon, Dr. Andersson, and Dr. Kline. He was seeking new nano-tech designs from 'his' nano-tech scientists and he would perform initial marketing evaluations. When one turned out positive, he would communicate with 'his' marketers and get their opinion. Gregory took up the role of travel and visiting/checking 'their active sites' to evaluate mode of action. He would look for the simplicity and effectiveness of use. He and Charles would then talk about the pluses and minuses of various designs and sites.

So, they were meeting regularly in the out-of-the-way office in the Daycott Hotel in the center of London, Gregory's home company headquarters was already in London, so these meetings were easily kept confidential. Ali Abdel Aal and Quaid Gang Hu, the other two senior directors, had their own home company's headquarters in Alexandria, Egypt, and Shanghai, China respectively, so they were not available for often nor for rapid decision making.

As the two of them sat in the two small armchairs in the Daycott Hotel office, Charles spoke up, "Do you mind the extra travel in trying to combine your company's business with the ETI's business?"

Gregory replied, "No, not at all. I love the extra travel; and the action of this new cellulose nanotech system is something that you must see for yourself someday. It is really amazing. In the water or fresh fruits, as long as it enters through the stomach, it does what Dr. Langdon says it will do. diarrhea. Both inside and outside at the same time. And the smell. Wow!"

"Oh don't," exclaimed Charles. Please do not give me details about the action of the cellulose nano-system. I could never go near a village with such an active site in it. My stomach would never take it. I take your word that there are terrible odors present."

"Say. Have you been meeting regularly with our three nano-tech scientists?" asked Gregory.

Head shake affirmative.

Gregory continued, "Do any of them propose to construct additional nanotech systems that will have similar stability at ambient temperatures? This is much easier to ship from laboratory to victim. The dry ice packaging is expensive and difficult to hide from authorities during transit, internationally and within most countries. And you are right. This is not killing or murder, it is beyond that."

"The next time I talk with them I will try to impress upon them the advantages of an ambient temperature stable nano-system."

'In addition," said Gregory, "We have never had a shareholder's meeting. When we began two years ago, you and I went around talking to various qualified people about joining us as both a participant and shareholder, no money up front. We could not afford, and therefore, did not have an official shareholder's meeting. Our corporate members should get to know each other. Maybe they will bring in some new group ideas. Sales are very good. Profits are very good. We are slightly behind on orders. But that is good. I think it would be a very good time to have an ETI Corporation business meeting. Such meetings need not be annual or even semi-annual. They could be called when needed or requested by shareholders."

Charles added, "We might even attach a neat party-affair to the meeting. I am a Chivas Regal Scotch Whiskey and an Irish Guinness Draught Stout Beer person. How about you?"

"That sounds about right. Agreed."

"In this regard," Charles continued. "Twice in the past month I have had dreams of a fabulous yacht meeting/party somewhere off the Ireland-Wales-England coast in the Irish Sea on St. Patrick's Day. Two little leprechauns told me just how to arrange it, and informed me that we would win some kind of an Irish prize which would pay for everything. What do you think of that?"

Responded Gregory, "I'll tell you what. If you have a similar dream for a third time, or I have a dream like that, let's do it. The first official ETI business meeting would be truly unforgettable."

And the two of them broke down laughing. Charles reached into the bottom drawer of his desk, withdrew a bottle of Chivas Regal Scotch Whiskey and two glasses, poured each glass half full, gave one to Gregory, took the other for himself, and they raised them to the sky. They saluted the ETI and their future.

'Two weeks later both Charles and Gregory had essentially the same dream on the same night: a yacht trip with three business/tourist days, April 16, 17, and 18, catered by a group of Irish leprechauns, and enjoyed by all of the ETI shareholders—both business and pleasure. The dream told them to meet in Dublin, Ireland on the afternoon of April 16, at 2:00 o'clock, board a 2030 Shamrock 148 motor yacht, accommodations for ten, and cruise up and down the Irish coast in the Irish Sea near the Isle of Man. Later they could celebrate at the St. Patrick's Isle Castle on the Isle of Man. They would be accompanied and catered by a team of leprechauns. All expenses paid. How could they refuse?

But what exactly are leprechauns doing these days in our modern world, Charles asked himself. He turned to the computer and some Irish friends who lived in London. He needed to know. Here is what he learned.

'Leprechauns are Irish fairies that originated in the Aos Si Irish folklore. Most are little people near three foot tall. They wear predominately green clothing. There are several colonies of leprechauns living in the numerous green forests in Ireland today. These colonies are usually composed of several families, thirty to fifty members including grandparents, mothers,fathers, and children. They have their own closed lifestyle system so are rarely seen. Some colonies are more open and raise goats to produce goat cheeses, goat skin shoes and clothing. Some also perform at big people's festivals by singing and dancing to ancient Celtic and Irish music. They sometimes also cater to big people's special events such as weddings and anniversaries. Leprechaun women prepare special Irish foods and the men serve the tables.'

After Charles had digested all of this, he declared this was indeed a gold mine,

"Let's go," he declared! And so notified Gregory.

{What Charles did not know is that the leader of the group of leprechauns who will guide them is a family elder, Peter, who is a very close friend and past student of the Priestess of Irish Witchcraft. He is the highest ranked male Irish witch in Ireland. And he and the Priestess had already talked about this voyage.}

20

IRISH WITCHCRAFT IN MOTION – II

A COUPLE OF WEEKS AFTER the dreams, Charles received an award notice from the Irish International Honorary Foundation. It stated just what the dreams had portrayed. They would provide a two full-day yachting vacation in the Irish Sea in honor of the success of the new 'Irish' corporation, ETI. The award had his name as the senior awardee. All expenses would be paid in advance. It should begin and end in Dublin on March 15 and 18, respectively. Additional details would arrive in one week,

On April 15, Charles Somersham arrived at the Dublin International Airport and went by taxi directly to the Dublin O'Kiber Yacht Harbor. He wanted to be early and check everything out. He was still a little suspicious of the gift, but he could not say no to such a gift. He immediately spotted the white Shamrock 148 motor yacht, boarded her, and began looking around. The captain, Tim Landry saw him, came over, introduced himself, and started to introduce him to the boat.

Charles said, "You have a beautiful creature here, Capt. Tim."

"Yes," Capt. Tim answered. "It has been well maintained as it is rented almost every week during tourism season. I am the senior pilot for this and two other yachts in season. So, if you want to return in the future, don't forget me and Shamrock. You are lucky to get it out of season and at a nice discount price."

Charles agreed, even though he did not know any of the details he could not let this young captain know such things. He was the President of the corporation which was in charge. This Tim was a simple licensed-experienced Irish boat pilot with a nice yellow and growing white beard. Enough. He had no need to know any details.

The yacht was luxury service for ten guests in five state rooms, and an area for one pilot and three crew members. Capt. Kim would show Charles around. So, they slowly climbed up the gang plank and entered the Shamrock.

The aft entry was through an open deck with several deck chairs, swim platform, and jacuzzi. They continued strolling into a large salon sporting a cocktail bar with a large viewable television within a large circular seating arrangement, three double sofas and six armchairs. All walls, carpets, furniture, drapery, and décor colors were white, emerald green, light rainy sky blue, and occasional yellows and browns. The third room was a moderate sized dining room with elaborate seating arrangements for ten guests. And the last major room on the middle level was a very well-equipped gallery. Beyond was a corridor which led to a small living area for the captain and crew. The entire entry level was surrounded by windows and an outdoors narrow ledge walk-way.

Between the large salon and the dining area were two semicircular stairs. One led down to the five bedrooms, each having two double beds and a full bath. The other went up and led to the pilot house and an aft open sky lounge with six lounge chairs and small bar.

After the tour, Charles asked, "Thank you. Everything seems perfect. What do you expect for weather for the next four days?'

"Excellent," answered Capt. Tim. "The weather for the entire Irish Sea will be perfect for the next several days. This is not always common in March. You really are living in a streak of good luck."

"Will we be able to cruise up the coast to Dundalk? When I was a boy, I once visited my uncle and swam the beaches off the Castle Bellingham. I would like to see them again," asked Charles.

Capt. Tim responded, "I think so. If we leave on time, we can cruise the Irish coastline and probably have dinner off Dundalk if you like."

And almost if on cue three small heads came from the crew bedroom corridor. Tim introduced them to Charles.

Mr. Somersham, "These are our crew and caterers for the voyage: Peter, Jon, and Luk. They all have excellent English. We have worked together before. And I am certain you will be very satisfied."

Each leprechaun shook Charles's hand. They were wearing their typical green clothes required by management to emphasize the Irish effect. Also, Peter had some experience as a boat pilot, so he would assist Capt. Tim in emergencies. All systems seemed ready to go.

And over the next couple of hours the 'guests' began arriving, That morning he had received an e-mail from Dr. Andersson that she would not be able to join them on the company yacht trip. She would wait for any report of possible procedural or program changes within the corporation. So, it apparently was going to be an all-male business-party.

Charles arranged the bedroom assignments: Mr. McCorland and himself in #1; Dr. Albert Langdon and Dr. Edward Kline in #2; Mr. Ali Abel Aal and Mr. Quaid Gang Hu (Tiger) in #3; Mr. Faustino Mariniti in #4 as he **preferred** a single room if possible; and it worked out well as Mr. Jackson White in #5 could be.

Each member of the Board of Directors of the Equus Transport International arrived on time such that they cast off near 3:00 PM. After settling in, all met in the large salon, gave their drink requests to Peter, took a sofa or chair and started a couple of days into relaxation Irish heaven style, Peter brought the drinks, Jon prepared snacks for nibbling, and Luk began dinner preparations. No one was concerned about trying to develop serious new plans for ETI. It was doing well and was too young to make major changes. But a general discussion as to direction for continued expansion was a very good thing to do at this point in time.

As everyone became comfortable in a soft chair or sofa with a drink in one hand and a reverse cracker-pretzel with dip in the other hand, Charles began the conversation. "Welcome to our first official

ETI Corporation meeting. Past mini meetings don't count. Most of you know each other. Mr. Jackson White from London is about the only unfamiliar face among us."

Mt. Jackson spoke up, "Thank you. I am honored to be a member of your new ETI. And to receive special rewards before I even do anything yet."

Charles laughed, "We will try to make up for that."

"We hope to use this excursion to relax, get to know one another better, and talk about the plus and the minus factors concerning our manufacturing and marketing efforts. If changes are necessary or could enhance our bottom line, profits, then now is the time to bring up new ideas and make suggestions. No final decisions will be made during these two full days, but I would love to have some good positive ideas to think about and pursue. So please speak up. First ideas are often the best!"

Tiger was one never to hold back so he spoke out. "I have a major problem. I am marketing nanotech systems in China along the Yellow River region. But I have the problem of dealing with the Chinese mafia, the Triads. They are not currently marketing nanotech systems, but they are developing a laboratory with nanotech scientists to produce and sell their own such systems. Do I confront them? Do I make a partnership arrangement to share the market? What do you suggest?"

Faustino Mariniti suggested, "I have had much experience with mafia types in Italy. I confronted them and yet I am still here with several companies and several ships. I suggest begin by cutting a deal for the market but develop your own 'independent' system. Then in time, push the Triads out by changing your products or your territory. China does have a few billion people -HA- a very large market. Your market is larger than my market which is only all of northern Africa. Go for it. But if you cannot deal with them, you have territory and territory and territory."

"Any other suggestions?" asked Charles. "Anyone else have experience with mafias? Maybe now is a good time to give you a brief orientation of our last year laboratory production and marketing sales around the world. Let me hand out a copy of last year's data, which is not yet final. Please look through the numbers."

And he handed out a photocopy to everyone present.

Nanotech Sales

	G.I. Intro	Blood Intro	Spinal Ch Intro	Total
Northern Africa	104	56	18	178
Middle East	130	100	43	273
Asia-China	32	26	12	70
South America	26	36	2	54
Canada-USA	0	32	52	84

"Interesting! Middle East is doing exceptionally well. What do you say Ali?"

Ali answered, "I say it is good. But if you look carefully, we have high sales by the GI introduction method. Most of this is the cellulose nanotech molecular system. Sales are good. But profits are smaller, because this system is cheaper to sell. We have many political mini wars in eastern and central Africa and western Asia. Hence the demand for smaller, simpler, and less expensive weapons is high. Also, part of this region has oil money. The oil rich can afford more expensive-sophisticated weapons. Hence, we have a reasonable amount of these weapon sales also. We expect to continue to increase our sales base as there is a lot of violent disorder in this part of the world. Military weapons, guns, tanks, missiles, helicopters, and airplanes are expensive and require many trained personnel. The cellulose nanotech weapons are easier to transport, store, and later to deny usage because of the delay in action. But they do not consistently work. Otherwise, I would say that all other nanotechnology is working very good for us."

Tiger spoke up, "Yes. The major problem is this new cellulose nanotech weapon does not affect everyone equally or the same. It needs more testing in humans."

Dr. Langdon responded, "OK. I hear you. It was my idea several years ago to build this set of systems, but I could not find any venture capitalist to fund me. I was super happy when Charles and ETI came along. The success that you are having, proves my brain is still functioning at any age. Now you need to guide me into a more potent and/or an easier to administer type of nanotech system."

"And I will work out the flaw in the cellulose system."

Peter whispered in Charles ear, "Dinner will be ready in ten minutes."

So, Charles announced, "A lobster-shrimp dinner will be served in fifteen minutes. Let us continue tomorrow. Anyone needing to touch their make-up, you had better hurry."

They were hungry from a long day of travel and time changes. They did not need a second notice for good food.

The next day, Charles was happy that he could look west and see one of his childhood playgrounds, Castle Bellingham. It had not changed. But it was too cold for swimming. This morning the beaches were empty. He would have to come back another time.

Everyone had breakfast and took their second cups of coffee into the large salon to relax into the comfortable sofas and chairs. They began a few hours of analyzing just where the ETI was in the business world, where it should go in the next few years, and how each of them could be involved. As they talked and thought and talked Capt. Tim slowly moved the yacht across the Irish Sea toward the Isle of Man.

Charles had prepared a program which would now be put into play for most of the rest of the day. He hoped they might finish a little early such that they could socialize a little more. He had designed this to be a business-party. He started the business.

The conversation was carried out in a casual business atmosphere. They had not been together long enough to have created personal nor business related problems. And they would all be operating in different parts of the world, so there should be no future competition, perhaps some teamwork. Areas discussed included:

- How the various nanotech molecular systems worked Dr. Langdon gave a layman's level of explanation of action of the three general types of systems, and the differences between simple versus complex as in 2-3 component systems.
- Difficulties of packing and shipping the different types of systems.
- Difficulties of re-packing and short vs long term storage.
- Difficulties in re-assembly of components when shipped separately.

- Methods of administering the systems; bottled water, fresh fruit and vegetables, intra-venous, intra-muscle, intra-spinal cord, other.
- How to use the time lapse between administering system and its action
- In an emergency, how to destroy the system when not used for a period of time.

[all of this is true for nanotech molecular systems that cure or kill]

They had lunch at 12:30, and would restart the business discussions at 2:00. After lunch but before the restart of the afternoon session, Charles, Tiger, Ali, and Gregory went up to the upper deck open sky lounge. Charles smoked his pipe. The others lit up cigarettes.

As Charles stood and looked at the beautiful Irish Sea, he saw some very large animals. He asked Capt. Tim, "What are those creatures over there?"

Capt. Tim responded, "Those are blue sharks. They are the second largest shark in the world, 200 to 300 kilos. And much more dangerous than the larger great white shark. Why? Because they swim in families/teams and they collect their food near the surface. And we are directly over the largest blue shark breeding grounds in the world. Do not swim here!"

Charles said, "That is all right. I did not bring my swimming trunks," And they both laughed.

He then went over to the 'smoking' brothers and explained to them what they were now passing over. They all stood up and started counting the water wonders. Beautiful but scary.

Near 2:00, they went down to the large deck and continued the business discussions until all was satisfied that they wished to proceed in developing the corporation in the direction of nano molecular systems. So far, it was a very successful effort. They now deserved a little relaxation-vacation. Tomorrow they would explore the Isle of Man.

That night they had special Irish stewed lamb, baby carrots, and red onion as the main course for dinner. Shortly after dinner Charles called

Capt. Tim and Peter to conference with him in the small meeting room. Charles began, "I want to explain how I want the final timing of our excellent journey. Get some paper and pencil and take notes."

The two Irish men looked at each other, and did as told.

"You both know the area so I hold you both responsible for carrying out my commands. We should all be awake for breakfast around 7:00 AM. Call the Island's dual limousine service station, sea and land. Order a sea maxi-taxi pick up from the Shamrock at 8:00 to take us to the main pier in the capital, Douglas. There will be eight of us. We should be met by a normal land taxi and a land maxi-taxi. The normal land taxi will go to the Isle of Man Airport and drop off three of our Board Members."

"Dr. Edward Kline needs to return via Etihad to New York on an afternoon flight. Mr. Jackson White will catch a London Air morning plane to London. And Mr. Faustino Mariniti needs to go home to Rome via Italia on a morning flight. Because we have finished our business, they each have found work for which they must return, skip the day of vacation! So, their lives?"

"The rest of us will use the land maxi-taxi and go across the island to St. Patrick's Isle Castle near Peel. We are going to the St. Patrick's Day Music Festival on the Castle grounds. Later in the afternoon, say 5:00 PM, a land maxi-taxi should pick us up and take us back to the main pier in Douglas. A sea maxi-taxi must be waiting for us at 5:30, and we want to immediately return to the Shamrock. The yacht should be ready to cast off at 6:00. I know it is a ten to twelve-hour journey from the Isle to Dublin. I want all of us back in Dublin by 6:00 AM. All of us have morning flights from the Dublin International Airport. So, several regular taxis will be necessary from the pier to the airport at the time."

"Do you have these numbers? As you can see, we have several air flights to catch at the end of this 'chase', so don't let me down. I am very good at tips."

Both Capt. Tim and Peter smiled and declared they understood. There were no questions. They all said good-night. And Charles went up to the aft open sky lounge to smoke his pipe and join his smaller circle of confidants and their cigarettes.

The next morning after breakfast the remaining eight shareholders were aboard the sea maxi-taxi speeding toward Douglas. Charles had settled in the front shotgun seat next to the Taxi Captain to ask him some questions.

Charles began, "You have a lovely sea taxi here. Have you been driving it long?"

The Captain answered, "Yes, sixteen years. As you probably know, we maxi-land and maxi-sea captains are also trained in tourism information, because we usually have ten plus riders and a nice audio speaker system. Do you have any questions about the Isle of Man?"

Tiger was the first to speak up. "Describe the island in five minutes or less."

"The island is called the Jewel of the Irish Sea," he began. "It was first occupied in the Bronze Age, conquered by the Vikings in the 8th century, and then ruled sequentially by Norway, Scotland, England, Wales, and Ireland. Today we are a self-governing British Crown territory. The land is near 30 to 50 kilometers, shaped like an oblong pearl, reasonably flat, few trees but large grasslands and rocks, one large 600-meter mountain, and from the top you can see five countries. We are near 100,000 people."

"Now I understand that you are going to the St. Patrick's Isle Castle. That is on the other side of the island. It is more of a tear drop shaped projection north-west away from the west side of the big island. Occupying the wide part of the little isle is the renovated red-grey stone castle. It is very nice and it is now decorated for this afternoon music festival. I assume that is where you are going?"

Charles responded, "Yes. What other old castles and famous old buildings are there on the Isle of Man?"

"The most famous and most tourism popular are the Castle Rushen, Port Soderich Glen, and the Old House of Keys. Museums to see include the Natural Trail via the Heritage Electric Railway, Manx Aviation and Military Museum, House of Manannan, and the Ramsey Heritage Center. And, the best hotels are Resort Los Cabos and The Forge. Excellent restaurants are everywhere."

And the chatting of questions continued as they pulled up to the dock at the main pier. They all climbed out, said goodbye to the three who entered the normal land taxi and headed to the airplanes, home, and work. The remaining five entered the land maxi-taxi and it followed the cross-island route to St. Johns and on to Peel. Exiting at Peel, they walked a couple hundred meters down a long entryway onto the isle and then up into the St. Patrick's Isle Castle which was about 100 meters above sea level.

Ali and Gregory slowed their walking to look at the many tent covered booths which were filled with numerous Irish and Manx culture exhibits. All of the fellows found many things of interest in the various booths containing Irish arts and crafts, textiles, ceramics, wood and metal statues and sculptures, leather and straw-rush clothing, Irish clothes and shoes, wine tasting and whisky tasting, and Irish curios of all varieties. There was even one large tent covered booth exhibiting Celtic versus Irish culture, courtesy of the Manx Culture Society.

And after a couple hours of shopping, they found themselves at a large open food pavilion with more than 50 tables and chairs for open ended dining. They were tired, and ready for some stomach satisfying action and nicotine. The eating area was on a slight incline facing the beautiful blue-green sea. On the up-hill-castle wall side were several food serving tables. The various tables offered: lamb or chicken kababs, and smoked salmon; pitta bread and colcannon mashed—potatoes mixed with cabbage and bacon, boxty—potato pancakes; Irish soda bread; Barmbrack bread, meatless vegetable stew; Irish porter cake (special for St. Patrick's Day), soda bread pudding, carrageen moss pudding, and Irish whiskey truffle.

After a five-minute sweep of the offerings of the food tables there was unanimous agreement that they would have to sample everything and that would probably take a couple of hours of the beautiful sunshine; and they would probably not finish until 1:00 PM show time. So, one does what one has to do in life. Today, Charles, Albert, Gregory, Tiger, and Ali were ready to make-Sacrifices-Sacrifices-Sacrifices. The business partners were even becoming friends.

For the next two hours they each averaged half a dozen plates of food and 2-3 cigarettes. Charles and Albert stoked their pipes. They were content and ready for some good old Celtic and Irish music and folklore dancing.

The St. Patrick's Day Music Program in the outdoor theater of the Castle on St. Patrick's Isle on the Isle of Man was fantastic.

I. Lord of Dance – 8-10 dancers, light and heavy shoes, acapella, traditional and contemporary music.
II. Coig – fiery Celtic high energy and non-traditional music with fiddles, piano, guitars, banjo, mandolin, whistles, and bouzouki.
III. Poehemia – singing and playing traditional Celtic, Irish, and Celt inspired originals with electric and acoustic instruments.
IV. Laurence Nugent – world and all Irish champion on flute and tin whistle in playing traditional Irish music and story-telling.
V. Cos Ceol – three world famous ladies playing traditional Celtic music with harp, violin, fiddle, and piano.

It was an outstanding program. If you did not like Celtic/Irish music before this afternoon, you would certainly now have a new warm spot in your heart. If you already loved Celtic/Irish music, you had an afternoon of continuous pleasure.

They were a half hour late by the time they got back to the Shamrock. But all was ready. They quickly settled in, pulled anchor and headed back toward Dublin. An hour later the five of them met upstairs on the aft open sky lounge. Each relaxed in his lounge chair. His evening cocktail in one hand, his cigarette or pipe in the other hand, laid back and watched the beautiful star-studded sea sky. And each was content that the future was going to profitable. And that they would have a profitable part of that future.

Peter had provided everyone with their favorite drink, and then joined the rest of the crew below. Charles had told the crew they wanted to have a closed going away conference, and wanted to be left alone.

Captain Tim remained behind the wheel in the pilot house, no automatic pilot tonight as the distance was too far, when Charles asked him, "What is the weather going to be for tonight?"

The response, "Cool and possibly patches of fog. All should be OK."

Charles turned to his key ETI team members and said to Dr. Langdon. "If you want you can tell us about your ideas for an ambient stable nanotech molecule system that can be inhaled, enter into the lungs, and stay there for several hours, and then act, please do."

Dr. Langdon answered, "First, I will make a couple of design changes to the cellulose system, and then... Yes, I have been studying this other new system for some time. It would possibly work something like this."

Suddenly they entered a thick fog bank. It was too thick for the fellows to even see each other. And just as suddenly a gigantic blast of warning sirens from a nearby oil tanker blasted out near the right front corner of the yacht. Everyone panicked. Capt. Tim hit his sirens, turned the steering wheel far to the left, threw the gears into reverse, and pushed the accelerator lever to maximum speed backward. The boat bucked and jerked to the right and all occupants on the open sky lounge flew over the side and landed directly in the water. Capt. Tim felt them go overboard but the fog was still too thick to see anything. After a few minutes he got the boat under control, had missed the oil tanker, and radioed down to the leprechauns to come to the rescue.

The four Irishmen searched all night, but in the absence of vision due to the thick fog it was not possible to even see anyone in the water. It was also not possible to get the small scot boat into the water. Capt. Tim radioed for help, but they were a couple hours off the coast of the Isle of Man. And this was an area directly over the blue shark breeding grounds. They stayed in the area all night. The fog broke toward morning. Rescue boats and one rescue helicopter arrived at dawn. But too late. No signs of human life. Apparently, most of the ETI Board of Directors had provided excellent food for the baby blue sharks.

The following day the London Times second page headlines read 'Irish Sea Accident'—five businessmen missing from leisure yacht semi-upset in a heavy fog when a large set of maverick waves hit the boat in early evening hours. Because the fog lasted all night rescue operations were delayed until sunrise, but it was too late. No bodies nor body parts were found. The businessmen were board members of a new corporation entitled...

If one checked the passage of oil tankers through the Irish Sea on St. Patrick's Day-night, there were none. And if one examined...

For some unknown reason, the emergency SOS was late in responding.

21

THE REAL FIRST TEAM II

In 2037, the four genetically linked Irish males, Jonathan and Jackson, fraternal twin brothers and brother of Jamie's deceased father, Theodore, Dagda uncle, and Dr. William, cousin, were having a late afternoon tea on the top floor of the O'Reilly Building in downtown Boston. They were closely monitoring the nanotech war, or newly, a nanotech—witchcraft war.

Jonathan commented, "The idea of encouraging the Four Musketeers to pursue witchcraft to battle Korrectorizer was a super idea. Don't you agree Dagda?"

"These days, anything that works and works well is super," replied Dagda. "Yes. I think you are very right. All of the data and info received by the Committee of Nanotechnology Control and the Priestess of Irish Witchcraft support this current conclusion. I have some of the numbers with me. We can take a look at them shortly."

He continued, "With the potential of a new US President being elected next year, there is a good possibility next year that I might not be re-appointed again to head up the Committee's work. During the past eight years, I have not been very successful. Actually, my helping the boys gave more success. However, I still want to learn everything and try to make more progress identifying and neutralizing the nanotech killers. Because I might not be in this investigative role soon, I want to pass all that I learn on to you guys. Plus, I will soon be 'walking' toward the 80-ville. Retirement?"

And they all smiled because they knew "Uncle Dagda' had military commando training and continued many of those exercise routines. He was in much better physical condition than most lawyers and scientists, including those present in this room right now.

"Because I have been directly responsible for finding and neutralizing this group of conservative industrialists from day one, you cannot hold yourself to blame. In fact, all four of us have been involved. You provided me with the guns and ammo, I aimed, shot, and missed. More than 500 innocents have been killed in a variety of very macabre fashion."

Jonathan continued, "Most of these high-tech scientists each had 14 – 15 years of college level training. That is more than 800 years of wasted advanced education, most of it in the USA. And now what is happening, the killings have shifted into illiterate peoples in developing countries. Can it be the same assassins? If so, why? What a tremendous waste of knowledge and human lives. And now where are they going? I cannot give up or retire until I catch Korrectorizer and his major associates."

Then he added, "And we also owe it to the first one he killed, our younger brother, Theodore."

"Yes, we do" replied Dagda. "The person is an American male, living in Washington, DC. He is in his late sixties. And he has had working experience or working knowledge in the international legal field, the American Congress, Federal Bureau of Investigation, and the National Security Agency. He is a very clever, a politically well-connected lobbyist. Plus, he has at least one close associate currently with MI6 or with MI6 training in London who also has international transport connections."

"His Committee of World Conservative Industrialists, as we previously thought, do have members from major industries such as petrochemicals, heavy metals, silicon chips-based industries, hoofed meat industries, non-organic agriculture, and possibly others we have not yet identified. Each major industry has one voting member in selecting nanotech targets. Every year they meet in a nondisclosed location and select five targets. Each target can be a single person or a single group of people. Korrectorizer then negotiates the nanotech molecular system to be used. The general date is selected. Then he selects a general location, offers a price. If all is go, he secretly selects the nanotechnologist and the 'hitman', and the target will be hit as the committee has determined."

"We know this has been his routine for the past three-four years. Unless we can somehow stimulate a change, he will probably continue with this pattern. We also know that he has several nanotech scientists producing his nanotech molecular systems. Plus, the scientists are not informed who the target is, nor where the hit will be made. Just like a gun manufacturer. He makes the system that can kill, is paid via a negotiated contract, gives and gets."

"And I will get him, or die trying."

Dagda suddenly got up, went over to the side table, and took a third cup of tea. He rarely took more than two cups because of caffeine risk. Suddenly all of that was forgotten. He walked over to the office window facing his favorite waters, the Charles River. He looked down and already knew the result of his sudden declaration. Whatever was necessary would be.

Dr. William cousin commented, "Do you have any specific plans to try to catch this guy?"

Dagda answered, "Yes." But he said no more.

Jonathan, sensing the gravel in the air, spoke out. "If you have some of the Commission's info and data handy, could you please share some of it with us? Maybe we might have some new ideas or a different approach which you would find useful."

"OK," replied Dagda.

He went over to his briefcase, took out his I-pad and a large packet. "I am not sure how to start. This is five-six years of data that I recently summarized. It will be available if I should not be here in the near future."

Jackson reached over and offered Dagda a big chocolate cookie and said, "First have a piece of energy. I know just how short your summaries are." Dagda smiled, took a big one, sat down, relaxed and slowly ate the cookie. He then began sifting through his memory.

"All of you remember the first major massacre in the Saatfordam Diamond Mines in Bloemfontein, South Africa, that killed more than 200 diamond miners. We have traced the nanotech molecular system that caused these deaths as coming ship by ship transfer from

Buenos Aires, Argentina, laboratory of Dr. Mario Kemps. Dr. Kemps is now reduced to one half a crazy man for life. He has no gonads and continuous nightmares of black dead diamond miners laughing and dancing in circles around him."

"And then there are the two massacres in Istanbul, Turkey. First a killing of a family of Syrian immigrants in Haydarpasha. And the High Technology and Entrepreneurs Congress at the Ciragan Palace in which more than 300 international high-tech scientists were killed in a very macabre way body bones dissolved and the remaining skin shell full of pink blood, all while they were sleeping."

"We have the nanotech molecular system shipping route from Munich, Germany, Dr. Franz Gunter. It traveled via a combination of trucks and ships from Germany to Russia to the Black Sea down to Istanbul. Dr. Gunter is now dead. He accidently ran head on into a metro train in his home town."

"Several years ago, you will remember that the Committee of Nanotechnology Control developed a candidate list of possible nanotech killers. Both Dr. Kemps and Dr. Gunter were on that list. Others on that list we have little new data to discuss."

"However, nearly two years ago a new nanotech marketing corporation, entitled Equus Transport International, became functional and is composed of a group of nanotech scientists and businessmen. They are apparently manufacturing and selling a variety of nanotech molecular systems. Recently, this ETI was involved in a major boating accident in which five key members of the Board of Directors, CEO, Chief of nanotech design and production, and three major shippers/marketers were killed by sharks in the Irish Sea. Two of them were on the Committee's candidate list Dr. Albert Langdon and Mr. Gregory McCorland."

"Two members on the Committee's list that were also on the ETI Board of Directors were not on the ship Dr. Anneka Andersson and Mr. Faustino Mariniti, so they are still alive. They will now be included on the new list."

"Several nanotech killer candidates and few others, including Gunter, Kemps, Somersham, McCorland, Langdon, Abel Aal, Gand Hu, and Kai-Do Luawan, have been eliminated due to combinations of witchcraft in different locations. No one has ever been eliminated by legal government actions. I do not know nor understand any of the methods or mechanisms involved. I only understand the results—elimination. I know the boys were involved. Again, I do not know how; and I am sort of trying to not find out by how or by whom. And I am trying, sort of trying, to not find out. That knowledge could get into legal problems for me, for us, for them and for their friends. And since they were successful in working with these witchcraft friends, I hope these arrangements can be useful again in the not too distant future. I am asking no direct questions. But I will supply them with info if they ask me. I hope you will all do the same."

There was a quick agreement among the 'Irish clan'.

"What does this do in terms reducing the size of the candidate list?" asked Jonathan.

Dagda answered, "You are right because several on the list are no longer with us, but several are still there, including: Dr. Walters—Ottawa, Dr. Andersson—Stockholm, Mr. Mariniti—Rome. And there are four others who were only recently added and are still there: Dr. Kline—New York, Mr. White—London, Dr. Jose—Madrid, Mrs. Jersey—Los Angeles. I'm certain more will be added."

Jackson said, "A few down and always more to go! How?"

"You have to remember," said Dr. William, "in our modern age, our international systems created heroin, khat, temazepam, ketamine, LSD, ecstasy, amphetamines, mescaline, cocaine, cannabis, methamphetamine, cigarette/cigar smoking, and vaporized E-cigarettes (vaping). Add to that nanotech molecular systems by accident. And the world will probably create more."

"Now this is when a person X kills a person X (himself)."

"If you want to compare person X killing person Y (someone else), then you can also include poisons, nanotech molecular systems, knives, guns of all calibers, sizes, mobility, and control mechanisms, plus multi-powered and sizes of rockets, guided missiles, and more."

"Many of these have been with us for hundreds of years and are still here, probably for many hundreds of more years."

"Therefore, should we expect that we suddenly can control or make disappear the nanotech molecular systems? I think not!"

Jackson spoke up, "Is it really so dangerous out there? We sit in our comfortable offices and read about it. Talk about it. It makes good cocktail talk for those of us who can afford cocktails. And we do nothing about it, unless it directly effects a loved one. And then we run around in circles because we do not know what, where, or how we can do anything."

As the room was suddenly quiet. There was not much left to say. Too many known diseases with not enough known cures. Yes or No!

Finally, Dagda said, "My immediate task is to focus on the nanotech molecular systems. If I can help cure the world of this growing disease, I will be content and maybe even a little happy."

"Uncle Dagda," commented Jackson. "The Committee has info that this man, Korrectorizer, is in Washington, DC. Can you give us any such info? Where did he come from? What background would he need to coordinate an international 'hit squad"?

"The answer to that has taken a lot of my thinking," answered Dagda. "This person must be a politically oriented male who probably began in Washington, DC as a lawyer and a Congressional Aide, most likely with a Senator. He next used his new knowledge and influence to obtain a position in the Central Intelligence Agency and then on to the National Security Agency. He slowly retired from the government and became a registered lobbyist. Now Washington would expand his connections and make friends with Presidents and Chief Executive Officers of major industrial corporations. He identified the politically conservative ones who had the necessary thinking to move forward to protect their 'in risk' scientific marketing base. He would bounce ideas off of those who would support eliminating competition by 'whatever means seemed necessary'. This would take a few years. And he could set up a system which would protect his clients by developing an underground management network, identifying a new scientific medical weapon which would be scientifically complex but exciting, and establishing the-for-gamblers-to-cash-only-system."

Jonathan spoke up, "Excellent. Yes. That is a very good background. I lived through life as a lawyer, Congressional Aide, Senator, President, and now lawyer and retired President. I probably know more Washington lobbyists than I do Washington lawyers, which is the most common species in DC anyway. And yes. If I so desired, I could build such a clandestine organization. I would simply call it the President's XXX Foundation. It could target industrial groups and individuals, or select scientists. It could be established to maintain a continuous lid on the system to protect the 'clients', and make a lot of non-taxable monies. I would only need someone like Dr. William cousin here to develop the necessary biological weapons, which can be secretly controlled, and that provide excitement and leave a new special fear."

And again, everyone was quiet. Were they really talking about creating or purchasing mass murder?

Conversation dropped to zero for a couple of minutes.

Finally, Jonathan spoke up. "The last time we met for our afternoon tea meeting I mentioned that I would try to find a Professor at Harvard U. to teach us about Witchcraft. I was successful. He will join us shortly. Maybe we can outlearn the boys concerning witchcraft knowledge."

Dagda commented, "Want to bet?"

And they all laughed.

22

ARE WITCHES REALLY SCIENTISTS?

As the afternoon tea meeting wore down, Jonathan announced the surprise visitor would arrive for a pre-dinner presentation about white versus black witchcraft. Jonathan and Dr. William had invited Dr. Drake Mathuson, Chairman and Professor of the Department of Paganism and Pre-History, Harvard University. The small group were just chatting about their 'boys' when Dr. Mathuson arrived. The secretary showed him to the office-meeting room; Jonathan introduced him to his family; the secretary delivered a new pot of tea and cups for the group; Jonathan poured tea for everyone and passed around a tray of pastries; Dr. Mathuson and Dr. Jonathan were both on the Editorial Board of the Journal of Harvard Social Review, so they started the how is the world doing thing. But Dagda had to leave shortly; so, Jonathan asked to start their education to inform them about witchcraft—and to start at the zero-knowledge level. They confessed to knowing nothing.

Dr. Mathuson smiled and sort of began, "Let me be sure. You are dealing with a group that is committing international macabre homicides, one at a time or in groups. And you are having limited success. So, you have recently decided to use witchcraft to assist you in identifying and capturing these people. Is that a reasonable summary of the problem?"

Jonathan nodded, "And elimination of problems if necessary and if possible."

"The reason I ask is because when witches exert positive efforts, it is called white witchcraft," Dr. Mathuson began. "When they exert negative efforts, it is called black witchcraft. In other words, the same witch can do either. OK?"

Jonathan asked, "OK. If you will allow us to ask questions as you move along. This is an area where we are all very ignorant, and we do have an immediate need to learn much and fast."

"Then I will continue rapid-slowly. Today, scientists could be designated as modern witches. However, witchcraft is not likely to be called scientific. But many of today's scientific ideas probably evolved from witchcraft. You will soon realize that you know much more than you thought."

"Faery/fairy traditions involve nature-science linkages. This relationship enthuses the deities that personify biological existence, life forms, fertility, death and rebirth. However, there is no known standard secret book of shadows in witchcraft."

"Most early religions worshiped a sun 'GOD' or gods. In ancient Persia, Zoroastrianism was the religion of fire and the god's name was Ahura Mazda. Later Persians worshiped the sun god Mithra. During the same time frame and the same region of the world the sun played the major/highest role in the religions of Egypt, Sumeria, and Akkadia. In ancient Buddhism the sun god was Suryaprabha, however with rebirth there was no omnipresence. The Aztecs worshiped the sun god—Tonatiuh. Today many people all over the world celebrate Lithra, June 20-21, the summer solstice. While fire/sun pagan symbols are abundant in Wiccan. Therefore, the sun and the fire have been linked to superior gods throughout human history. And today, man's time machine is based upon the presence, movement, and absence of the sun."

"Science or logic is derived from nature or witchcraft. Today's science/logic is the child of nature/witchcraft. The medieval scientist was a prophet, logician, natural magician, proto-alchemist, cosmologist, and an alchemist."

"What is alchemy? Alchemy is an ancient branch of natural philosophical and proto-scientific tradition, originating in the last-first centuries (BCE-CE) of Egypt-Persia-Greco-Roman worlds, and practiced continuously throughout Europe, Africa, and Asia."

"Alchemists were the first to take ideas from witches/shamans and extract, purify, and perfect various substances: if experimenting/testing was positive, repeat and go; if experimenting/testing was negative, change-repeat and prepare to go. Examples: water—for drinking; fire—for cooking; sharp stick—for hunting; seeds—for plant food; herbs—for cure/prevent disease. Today, this is the basis of all laboratory experimental/research and molecular-biological /medical sciences."

"WITCHES WERE THE FIRST SCIENTISTS"

"So, what exactly is alchemy? Alchemy is the intermediary between ancient and modern knowledge. Medieval chemical science and speculative philosophy was aimed at the transformation of matter, and the discovery of useful/practical objects/ways for life. Earliest alchemy focused on conversion of base metals to gold, universal cures for diseases, and mechanisms for prolonging life. Most early scientists were alchemists. Let me now give you an idea of the vast/massive mankind effort necessary to convert us from ancient life to modern life.

"Egyptian Alchemy – One great Egyptian king was super wise in operating with various forms of nature. He was born near 2000BC and wrote many treatises. Three famous books are the 'Emerald Tablet', the 'Asclepius Dialogues', and 'Divine Pymander Index'. These books and many others were partly destroyed by the Roman Emperor Diocletian. The Greeks managed to salvage much of his work and gave him the name 'Hermes Trismegistus'. Hermes's book the 'Emerald Tablet' is today considered to be one of the primary documents of modern alchemy. He lived more than 100 years. Normal age was near 30 years."

"Chinese alchemy – Chang Tao-Ling, first Taoist Pope, born 35AD, lived in the mountains in West China. He studied with alchemist Lao Tzu using supernatural powers and founded the mystical treatise which was determined to be an Elixir of Life. Copies of originals are no longer available. With it he lived many healthy years beyond what was then normal, much longer than two hundred years."

"Arabic Alchemy – Abou Mossah Djfar-Al wrote more than 500 treatises of which most were destroyed again by the Emperor Diocletian. His major teachings involved the unity of all matter. He 'established' that all basic truths derived from one root. All things form from one! A tree is composed of many leaves which came from one seed."

"Are you following me in these ancient interpretations of the evolution of life forms? The basis is strong if you believe. But much hard rationale has been destroyed by other believers."

They each looked at each other and nodded back in the positive.

"European Alchemy – In the era of the Christian Crusades, the center of alchemy study moved to Spain via the Moors. There were several important alchemy scholars at this time: such as Artephius who wrote 'Art of Prolonging Life'. It is claimed that he lived over two hundred years. Average lifespan was near 40 years. Alphonso, King of Castile, wrote 'Remonstrance of Nature by the Wondering Alchemist' and 'Reply of the Alchemist to the World'. Arnold de Villeneuve of Villanova wrote 'Theatrum Chemicum' which described sicknesses with substances. Both were eliminated by the Inquisition. Robert Lully, with use of the Philosopher's Stone, trans-mutated metals into gold and lived more than two hundred years."

"English Alchemy – The first and perhaps the best-known alchemist was Roger Bacon. He studied medicine, mathematics, philosophy, and mastered three additional languages—Latin, Greek, Hebrew, using the three different alphabets. He made numerous scientific discoveries such as production of convex glass—reading glasses and telescopes, modes of crystallization and purification, designed vehicles that would go faster than horses, flying machines, under water machines, combustion of various combinations of gases, and the formulation of the Philosopher's Stone. The latter has been the basic book for the studies of chemistry and physics. Since then, the basic concepts for the foundations of what we now call science continued to evolve."

"It was with alchemy in the 18th and 19th centuries that the chemistries of the human body were elucidated and the concepts of diseases were accepted. Jean Baptista van Helmont played a major role. He wrote 'De Nature Vitae Aeternae'. Using knowledge from the Philosopher's Stone, he convinced the medical world to accept both body external and body internal roles in disease causes and cures."

"During the past few centuries there have been numerous 'experiments' and 'experimental series' which resulted in new knowledge that could be referred to as alchemy. Today, most people, certainly children, do not recognize the word, alchemy. Experiments today are referred to as science. But this does not change the knowledge so derived through extensive investigation, observation, and innovation."

Jonathan asked, "All my life I believed in science to lead the new changes in our social lives, good changes, bad changes, and mis-used good changes. Would these changes have been different if alchemy had remained a regular part of our vocabulary?"

"The answer is probably not, but we will never know. Alchemy was the word used for more than two thousand years. Science is the word used to describe life system change over the past two-three hundred years, and is still the dominant word."

"I believe that doctors will never go back to blood sucking leeches. Or will we live without heated or air-conditioned homes or work places. Nor will we ever grow our own food, sew our own clothes, use outdoor toilets, walk to work, or on and on. Our modern world is too good and too comfortable to even consider returning to the past world."

Dr. Mathuson continued, "And concerning your current problem. In the nineteenth century we only began to recognize a few atoms. Today we recognize that every cell in our body has some one hundred thousand genes, each gene has a few million atoms, and there are a few billion-billion cells in every organ in our bodies. No one seems to be able to say how many trillion-trillion-trillion atoms are present in our bodies. My understanding is that you are dealing with some kind of nanotech molecular system that has a few atoms. How can anyone even try to find a few atoms of some molecule that will kill someone in our bodies which are loaded with super billions of atoms? Now you tell me that you are at zero-knowledge level! Me too!"

Each well-educated gentleman could only chuckle at this level of naivete. The point of searching for a solution was not to deal with the nanotech group of atoms, but the people who are creating and using them—who are they?—how are they using them?—how can they stop them?

Dagda asked, "You said in the beginning of your talk that witchcraft consisted of two general types of witches, white witchcraft and black witchcraft. Could you explain the differences? Should we expect that the black witches use killing molecular substances such as herbs or natural poisons, but white witches do not?"

Dr. Mathuson answered, "Excellent question. Let us look for a satisfactory answer. And I will use examples from our western world."

"**Modern white witchcraft** practices magic for altruistic purposes. There are many types of white witchcraft which are usually associated with some kind of positive folklore and a component of **white magic.** There is always a highly trained witch who usually bends the rules of the natural world, frequently with powerful forces and multiple gods and goddesses. Examples:

- "Gardnerian witches first came from a form of witchcraft that began in England and was incorporated into the Wiccan witchcraft structure which followed the ancient ways.
- Hereditary witches require a genetic-hereditary connection to witchcraft. The family connections involve the 'Old Religion' training of carefully selected candidate witches.
- Caledonii witches are from traditional Scottish witchcraft of the pagan folk in pre-Christian Scotland. Today they are used to celebrate many ancient Scottish rituals and festivals.
- Strega witches are located in the USA and emphasize all elements and spirits of nature such as air, earth, fire, and water with pagan emphasis.
- Pow Wow witches have a form of east Germanic Magic that came with German immigration to Pennsylvania. It is mostly social and medical healing spells.
- Celtic Wicca witches use a combination of witchcraft and religion along with several mythical gods and goddess. These involve numerous magic spells and rituals for medical healing and assistance in family life problems.
- Dianic witches always involve a female orientation with a divine goddess and involves numerous spells and ceremonies.
- Druidic witches are an extension of the ancient Druidic religion and involves polytheistic spirits; all rituals and ceremonies take place with special altars for Mother Earth in heavily wooded or forested areas."

"Most of these forms of witchcraft, good or not, have been decimated or downsized by the three major monotheistic religions—Christianity, Judaism, Islam."

"Is that why there is less witchcraft in countries or regions where there are predominately one of these three religions?" asked Jackson.

"Yes. And you can include regions of Hinduism in that observation. Are there more questions? OK. Then let me turn to black witchcraft," responded Dr. Mathuson.

"Modern **black witchcraft** practices magic for evil or very selfish purposes. And **black magic** is very real today. Various forms of black magic can be incorporated into white or black witchcraft. In general black is considered a dark art because it is used to control someone, for good or bad intents. A white witch can use white or black magic. And a black witch can use white or black magic. Most of the rituals, energy usage, ceremonies, curses, and hexes can be used by all witches. It is the intent of the witch that determines the whiteness or greyness or darkness or blackness of the magic."

"Let me explain more clearly. If a witch casts a certain spell in trying to gain something from a person, it would probably be considered black magic. However, if the same witch casts a similar spell on a person with the intent of helping that person, it would probably be considered white magic. Again, it is the intent of the witch as to whether the spell casting would be considered black or white, not a black or white witch."

"Another example—The witchcraft or witches who are considered white is because they usually use helpful intent with white magic/spells, rarely do they use black magic/spells. They have reputations accordingly. While witchcraft or witches who are considered black is because they often/regularly use harmful intent with the black magic/spells. And they have reputations accordingly. Hence, white witches can do black magic, but rarely do; and black witches can do white magic, but usually do black magic."

Jonathan spoke up, "Are you saying if we are seeking a witch to assist us in taking something from a person, we need black magic. But either white or black witchcraft should be able to help us?"

"Maybe, but if you want a witch who will practice special black magic for you, I would seek out a black witch who has a strong reputation of black magic and black witchcraft. Lifetime reputations rarely drop out of the sky."

And the Irish family did not know how to respond to that suggestion—so they just sat there and looked at each other. What do they tell their 'boys'? Or do the boys already know such things?

Dr. Mathuson closed out his talk. "As many modern witches today say:

Suicide is OK. Homicide is not OK.

23

WHERE, WHAT, HOW THE BOYS DO?

THE FOUR MUSKETEERS JAMIE O'Reilly (Ey'tuka) in Boston, Li Jiang (Tsu'tye) in Nanking and Los Angeles, Kefentse Legoase (Na'via) in Cape Town, and Aykut Turan (Mo'ata) in Istanbul survived their teenage years and were each now in college focusing on a lifetime profession. They had the rare experiences of hunting and being hunted by a group of international killers. They lived but their fathers and several friends did not. They can never forget! Revenge? Maybe? Someday? Wishful thinking?

JAMIE O'REILLY—

Jamie was studying in the pre-law program at Harvard University.—Boston is the major city in the north east corner of the USA. It is the capital city of Massachusetts, has a population of nearly one million, covers 80 square miles, played a major role in the American War of Independence, and continues to make major contributions to the social mobility and economy of America. It is the major intellectual center of the USA as it has a higher percentage of advanced degree people—engineers, doctors, scientists, bankers, and lawyers—than any other American city. It has more than 50 universities and colleges including 15 with international ranking—highest in prestige in the USA.

Harvard University is the oldest institution of higher learning in the USA as it was established in 1636. It is a private school with several compact campuses linked on 5,000 acres, 150+ buildings, 7,000 students, 11 major program areas, while the annual tuition is $55,000 per student per year. Most buildings were named after private donors. Harvard University is the number one rated university in the USA and is devoted to excellence in teaching, learning, research, and leadership development in all disciplines which are global in character. It is America's world leader in advanced education, more than 20% of the advanced students are foreign. And it has supported the establishment of 50+ universities in 18 different countries.

Jamie was in the second year of the pre-law program. He was studying in the internal transfer mode to qualify to enter the three-year Juris Doctorate program at Harvard University Law School next year. He was on track as his grades were mostly A's and his entry exam scores were at the top level, plus the political influence of Grandpa, Father, and his Uncles who were graduates of the HULS would help. The School offered a greater variety of courses and seminars than any other law school in the world. There was a very wide range of subjects and approaches to all domestic and foreign legal fields, many creative hybrid approaches to international legal systems, while all professors were deep into their own specific research and book publishing. Students were required to work with them. Great! Because of the O'Reilly, O'Reilly, O'Reilly and Associates law firm, he already had a 'permanent job' waiting for him. And these international areas were of special interest for his future. He wanted to 're-align' several international laws currently 'protecting' modern high technology terrorism. Revenge was still in the back of his mind.

Finishing his second year he was still taking courses in social sciences and pre-law areas. Many of his classes were in buildings in the Harvard Yard, south central campus. With students from almost every country in the world, this campus was a perfect place to maximize his own socialization. During a typical day, after classes, he frequently strolled through the campus. This time he selected a group of foreign students sitting outside at a fast health food eatery, and stopped to ask if he could join them. He was here to learn about people as well as law.

Jamie interrupted the group of three fellows. He guessed they were African. He spoke, "May I ask if you guys are from South Africa?"

The student closest to him answered. "My name is Aminu. I am from Nigeria. This is Khaled from Libya. And over there is Kami from Tanzania. Do you have an interest in Africa?"

"Yes, I have a best friend in South Africa," replied Jamie. "My name is Jamie. I am studying sociology and pre-law, and I hope to enter law school next year. May I join you?"

Khaled said, "Of course. What is your friend studying?"

Jamie replied, "No, you misunderstood me. Kefentse Legoase, lives in Cape Town. We worked together on a project over the past several years. He is now going to school at the University of Johannesburg. He is studying Public Management. I miss him very much; I am afraid that after he finishes, he will probably remain in South Africa and I will be here in the States. We might not see each again."

Aminu pulled up another chair to the table. Jamie shook hands around, smiled, and sat down. He then said, "It is ironic that all of us are studying Social Systems and Public Management here at Harvard. And we can understand our problems. All of us will return home when we graduate. Management of all kinds are badly needed in our home countries. Plus, our families wish that we would return yesterday."

And all three boys laughed. Jamie cringed. He could drive one half hour to his home almost every weekend. He understood close family relationships. Maybe he could help these guys feel more at home by entertaining them and some of his college buddies, who were studying social systems and business, at his house on occasional weekends. Afterall, only his mother and two servants were now living there. In the summer the pool was functional, and the ski boat could be made ready anytime with which to play. More friends in Africa could be positive for any research project in international legal systems.

Jamie asked, "Please take a few minutes and teach me about your countries. I am very ignorant about Africa, and I do hope to go there and learn/work someday."

Aminu spoke first, "Nigeria is one of the largest countries in Africa and is the most populated with 200 million people—one thousand ethnic groups and over five hundred languages. Fortunately, many years of British occupation allowed this non-African language called English to prevail. Similar to India, English is the accepted official language. Nationally, this is the only agreed upon concept. Christianity, Islam, and Ogboni are the key religions. Numerous social problems such as harsh crimes, civil wars, kidnapping, terrorism, maritime crimes, and on and on. The five geographic regions, where there is petroleum, are well off and modernizing; but the oil money is not shared so other regions are still living under sticks and straw. Nigeria is a member of OPEC, and it still has numerous seemingly unsolvable problems. Certainly, public management, solid politics, and a decrease in crime at all levels would be a tremendous boast to positive modernization. My country needs more of my new expertise, modern workable public knowledge."

"Thank you," said Jamie.

Khaled waved his hand, smiled, and began, "Let me go next as I can make it short. Libya is a large country on the Mediterranean Sea with a major land mass of desert. It has a population near seven million, mostly Arab, people. The official language is Arabic. And life revolves around hydrocarbons and politics. In this century there has been continuous/regular social unrest/civil wars. 95% of government revenue is from NOC, National Oil Company. We have near 40% of the oil reserve of Africa; and 20% of the natural gas reserve of Africa. Unfortunately, the excess black hydrocarbons have created more social unrest. Yes, we desperately need public management, but we also need consistent steady politics, and peace."

"I think I understand," replied Jamie. "Do you want to go next, Kami?"

Kami answered, "I guess so. But we have no oil so we have no problems. Right? Obviously, oil causes all of the problems. HA."

And now he could smile, a little. Then he began, "You can sort of think of us as a mini-America. The Republic of Tanzania was established in 1965. It is located on the east coast of Africa within the Great Lakes Region, bordering eight African countries, Lake Victoria, and the Indian Ocean. It boasts the highest mountain at 20,000ft, Mt. Kilimanjaro and deepest lake at 5,000ft, Lake Tanganyika, in all of Africa. Most of the land is unlimited plateaus with many types of soils—cultivation is the rule for numerous agriculture exports from cash crops (coffee, cotton, cloves), and minerals (diamonds, gold).—no hydrocarbons—Swahili and English are official languages. There are 120 ethnic groups with about half being from Bantu tribes. Significant agriculture support was brought about with European, American, Japanese, and Indian immigration. Religion is Muslim, Christianity, and traditional believers. Politics is that of a republic, President and Congress regularly elected. There have been no major political or military problems. Our country is one of the most modern in Africa. See, as I said. No hydrocarbons—no problems! But it still needs good public management systems."

And as the four lads thought through the brief comparison of the three countries, no one could say very much. They each knew that when there were major social/religious/political/military problems, there would be killings of families and friends. It was difficult to claim the problem originated with the hydrocarbons.

While Jamie began to understand that changes in international legal systems were not based only on the existing laws and their enforcement, but involved local capacities and modes of proposed changes to those laws.

Jamie said, "So are each of you fellows certain that you must return home when you finish you studies here at Harvard, or would you rather look for a position here in the States?"

The three Africans looked at each other, smiled, but did not answer.

LI JIANG—

Li had just finished his last Wu Shu or Kung Fu match of the morning. He lost. Li was a 5th Dan Grade and was defeated by a 6th Dan Grade. To advance to a 6th Dan Grade he would have to defeat a 6th Dan Grade. Next time?

Li had been studying and practicing the Wu Xing or 5 animals for more than twelve years. He had begun first learning it when he lived in Nanking, China, and continued studying it every year, and even now here at the California Institute of Technology.

The five animals were the tiger, crane, leopard, snake, and dragon. One had to mimic and master the natural offensive and defensive moves of each of these animals, and defeat someone who was using similar Wu Xing techniques. This was necessary every time he advanced in rank.

There are many types of martial arts in the world: judo, kickboxing, aikido, karate, Ji-jitsu, Muay Thai, taekwondo, kendo, etc. World ranking is controlled by the Martial Arts International Federation (MAIF). Two types of certificates are used. Kyu or Brown Belt is the lower grade. Dan Grade or Black is advanced grade at levels 1st through 10th.

Li joined his student buddies, who had finished their matches and were relaxing on the mats, still in their martial arts clothes. Eleven boys and two girls, all of various levels of skill were noted by the color of their belts, white to black.

Jim, a senior friend of Li, spoke up, "Li, you need to increase your speed on the tiger leap."

Li responded, "And you need to decrease your speed on the tiger leap." And then Jim jumped on Li and turned the martial arts mats into wrestling mats. Two other students climbed on the two crazies? Soon there was a free-for-all of adult children. Suddenly the teacher/coach blasted his whistle and the group, laughingly, broke up and headed for the showers and dressing room. Some were happy with their efforts and some were not so happy. Li was in the latter category. Jim had beaten him three times in a row. He would get him next time.

The California Institute of Technology was in Pasadena, California, near Los Angeles. It was established in 1891, specialized in natural sciences and engineering, It is a small private university, very prestigious, ranked number 4 in the world, 100-acre campus, 800 undergraduate and 1,300 graduate students, awards BS, MS, and PhD, plus MD in association with the USC and UCLA, accepts about 5% of all applicants, and costs near $55,000 per student per year—very prestigious.

CIT has six program areas: Biology; Chemistry; Engineering; Geology; Humanities and Social Sciences; Physics, Math, and Astronomy. The University has several alumni faculty who have won Nobel Prizes. Music is accorded by a symphony orchestra, concert and jazz bands. Twenty sports are supported with scholarships.

If you ask Li why he came to CIT for study he would give you two reasons. His Father had been a Professor of Biology here for twelve years. Plus, the university offered more than 50 advanced biology courses such as:

Courses in the Biology Program

animal biology	plant biology	molecular biology
biochemistry	human genetics	physiology
atoms & molecules	cells & tissues	behavior control
neuroscience	neuropharmacology	stem cells
nanotechnology	control of gene expression	evolution of genes

In addition, all students are required to perform tutorials and research projects with a professor each summer. Super successful projects are to be published. One must publish a research paper before the PhD can be awarded. One must spend one year in clinical internship before the MD can be awarded.

After Li and his friends had showered, he went to a small organic high nutrient food café on campus. Several of his friends were waiting for him. His special friend, not yet lover, Susan Parker, saw him coming, jumped up and ran to give him a kiss and hug. He was always a bit shy, but he hugged in return. She took a second look at him and grimaced.

Susan spoke first, "Oh! Oh! Li. Did you lose again?"

Li nodded affirmatively.

"I could tell because your head was down. Jim is two years older, and quicker than you. You know that Five Animals is a contest of quick thinking and quick moving, not physical strength. I know you will defeat him. And if not, there are other 6th Grade Dans here in Los Angeles. You can go to one of these private clubs, and challenge one of their 6th Grade Dans. Cheer up and have some cranberry-pomegranate juice."

"Ok," said Li. "Anyway, I have thought up a new approach, a new sequence of animals to use."

Li was the type that could not live with losing. He was still trying to overcome the fact that his Father killed his two brothers and then committed suicide. His friends knew this, loved him, and tried to help him live with this tragic personal history. But he remembered back ten years ago when, in Jenching City, his execution of the tiger leap was perfect. In fact, if it had not been, he might not have survived that street brawl with those hoodlums. Keep trying.

Susan tried to perk him up. "We were just talking about going to the beach this weekend. So far, we have a group of eight and two cars. Can you let your studies rest for one day?"

"Where are you going?" he muttered.

Jack spoke up and said, "Malibu Beach, that is one of your favorites. Is it not?"

They could see that Li was hesitating. It was obvious to him that Susan organized this when she learned he had lost his match, and his friends agreed it would be a good way to cheer him up. Li was not only science brilliant, he could read eyes/faces, the Chinese way.

Li did not like being babied. He started to make an excuse of needing to study for an exam next week. Then he thought of another way. "I really do have to finish my term paper, due in one month. But I will make you a deal. If I get the first surfboard, the first water scooter, the first jet ski, the first parasail, the first water ski, the first water bike, the first…"

And then he got hit on the side of the head by a large wet napkin, and two his bigger fellow buddies picked him up under the arms and started to carry him away when he shouted, "OK, OK. I will let you have the first jet ski but not the…"

And as everyone laughed Susan knew they had broken through his shell—at least temporarily.

KEFENTSE LEGOASE

Kef was wondering when his mind would take command and make a decision for him. He was multi-physical talented and multi-people talented. He was physically tall and slim, plus quick, fast, and agile, hence an excellent soccer/football player. Yet he liked people. He grew up with seven brothers and sisters, and in a crowded neighborhood where most of the families had several children. So, whatever age you were, all your growing life there was always someone older and someone younger. Values and viewpoints were in constant flux. He did not need school to become socialized. He grew up daily confronted with human change—human variety.

Obviously, it was partially due to the advice from his teenage hero, Kerneels Ramla, who had scored two goals against Brazil in the World Cup. However, South Africa lost in the finals when Kerneels broke his knee. The broken knee destroyed his career/life and he so told a group of boys. Kef was one of those boys, listening intently. He was fifteen and trying to decide if he wanted to make soccer a career/life. He had been thinking long and hard about what to do with his life. His most recent Voodoo experience was great, but he could not make it a career/life. He could and would maintain contact with his African Voodoo friends. Also, the nanotech death of his Father and the interaction with his Musketeers had re-oriented his mind. And his mind had re-oriented his body. So, he now found himself in college majoring in Social and Public Administration at the University of Johannesburg in Johannesburg, South Africa.

Johannesburg is historically known as Joze or Joburg, one of the best developed metropolitan areas in the world. It is the wealthiest of capital cities with a population of 6 million inside 130 square miles—direct access to abundant minerals of magnesium, chromite, platinum, vanadium, and coal—abundant gems of gold, silver, and diamonds. Utilization of the underground wealth had allowed the city to literally blossom—more than one million trees were planted over a twenty-year period. And tourism was super. Within two hours of driving time from the city there were numerous animal wildlife preserves. One day ride in a caged motor wagon a person could view numerous large animals in the open tundra plateaus—government controlled—pictures galore.

The legal system in South Africa from 1948 to 1994 was apartheid/separation. Nelson Mandela, born in the Tembu royal family with a law degree from the University of London, founded the African National Party, fought racial segregation during the era of total white man control, was arrested and spent 27 years in prison, voted for President from 1994 to 1999, and won the Nobel Peace Prize. Black workers had rioted in Soweto June 16 to 18, 1976; thousands were killed which woke up the world. In 2032 Kef had visited the Soweto riot areas, Mandela's house, and other now national landmarks associated with those apartheid years. He studied the when, why, what, how, and could it happen again. This learning about the multi-year struggle against racial segregation probably helped his mind to take control of his body and go north to learn management.

The University of Johannesburg was founded as a public institution in 2005. It has over 60,000 South African students, 8,000 foreign students from 80 countries, on several campuses in the Johannesburg area—Johannesburg, Braamfontein, Hatfield, Pretoria, Soweto, Doornfontein, Hoof, Wits, and Aukland Park. Eighty percent of the students were undergraduates. Education programs include Art & Architecture, Business & Economics, Health Sciences, Engineering, Science, Law, and Education. On-line programs offered many courses. And the courses were taught in Isi Zulu, English, and Portuguese. Tuition ranged from 2,000 to $10,000 per student per year. Kef was in his second year in the Program of Public Management on the Johannesburg campus; instruction was in English. Even though Isi Zulu was the major Zulu spoken in South Africa

However, on this weekend Kef and two of his soccer buddies, Lubanzi and Bokamosa, were sitting in Soccer City in Nesrec, Soweto, on the second row, center field in the FNB stadium, waiting for the Kaizer Chiefs (Amokhosi in Zulu) to kick and start the match against the Cape Town Spurs.

Kef spoke up, "You guys know that I have to cheer for the Spurs because I am from Cape Town. The Chiefs are the big guys, while the Spurs are the little guys. The Chiefs have won 15 national championships. While the Spurs have won only 1. That is all right. The Spurs have imported an English center fielder and a German left defender. That will make the two teams even. With a little—luck I bet ten dollars on the Spurs. What do you say Luba? You are from their home, Johannesburg South."

Bok interrupted, "Kef, you know that Luba has no betting blood. I will take your bet and double it. How about for twenty dollars?"

"OK," Kef replied. But, because you are better at writing manuscripts, I add manuscript editing into the bet."

"That is easy. My math is not so good. Therefore, I include our take home math/statistics for correcting, in the bet" said Bok.

'Hummmm! How about adding a verbal analysis of private versus government regulation of mineral and gem exports? Just before final exams of course." Kef came back.

"Well, can you explain which government is better—Congress and President or Parliament and Prime Minister, and why?" asked Bok.

"Is it possible for a government to regulate and control scientific research?" asked Kef.

"Will you guys shut up? The match has started and the Spurs almost scored," shouted Luba.

Kef and Bok looked each other in the eye. Did a high five. Laughed and turned to watching the match! Kef would be returning to Cape Town and Bok would remain here in Johannesburg after graduation. It would be good to have such friends who understood soccer better than management.

AYKUT TURAN

Aykut was racing his four-legged brother, Amber II, down the sidewalk along the Bosphorus Waterway in the Yenikoy area of Istanbul. He was only 30 meters behind his beautiful 75 kilo dog. And he knew that Amber was just coasting along. When Aykut closed the gap, Amber would look back and reopen the gap. He outran Aykut 100% of the time. Afterall, Aykut was twenty-one and Amber was only three, and no head-starts nor cheating was allowed, so Aykut had no chance of ever winning. Four paws proved a reliable comrade. If suddenly Aykut was in street trouble, like a few nights ago in Bebek, Amber would be there before any breath was taken. And he would solve any problem before any breath was expelled. He solved certain types of problems very quickly; and usually those problems did not return.

When they reached the Bosphorus cruise boat pier, Amber and he jumped onto a boat with about 50 people. This tour company stopped at 10 locations on each side, European and Asian, every two hours. It took people from the Black Sea to the Marmara Sea and back. Aykut and Amber frequently took this boat route south to the old city, and then they took the underground metro north back to

Bosphorus University. He liked the blowing-splashing water of the more than 100 boats that were in constant motion in the waterway. So did Amber as he had his head over the side all the time, continuously catching splashing drops, from up and from below.

The Bosphorus Waterway was the main route for 2,000 years of the Byzantine and Ottoman Empires. Today there are roads along both sides of the waterway, plus there are 10 major palaces remaining, including the very large Sultans' palace (Dolmabache Sarayi) and the much older palace (Top Kapi Sarayi), 15 smaller palaces, more than 40 famous large old wooden mansions/yalis (for very important families), foreign summer embassies, and a dozen large mosques (cami). Three bridges cross the water which allows you to go from Europe to Asia and back.

The two of them debarked at the Spice Bazar, just inside the walls in the Old City, located on the edge of the Golden Horn Waterway. They strolled around the spice bazar park area for a while. The smells were great and everyone, especially the children, loved Amber, and he loved them. His tail was on automatic motion. Aykut purchased a packet of pistachio nuts, sat down on a park bench, de-shelled and fed them, one by one, to his favorite warm-hearted animal. After the nearby New Mosque (Yeni Camii) called out to come for prayers, the two of them went underground, found the metro to Bebek; Aykut paid for one ticket, as dogs were free, but they had to sit on the floor, Aykut got the seat. Amber did not know the difference. The ground had been accommodating his popo all along.

They got off at the Bebek metro stop and entered Roberts College. This famous Istanbul college was established by Christopher Roberts in 1863. It was funded as a private college by Mr. Roberts, an American. In 1971, it become public as Bosphorus (Bogazici) University and has since expanded onto six campuses—South (original location in Bebek); North-Hisar-Ucaksavar campuses are all near Bebek. Kandilli campus is on the Asian side. While Kilyos campus is up near the Black Sea. The university now has 12,000 undergraduate and 5,000 graduate students on a total of 100 acres. The South campus is heavily treed and has fantastic views of the Bosphorus Waterway from nearly 500 feet elevation.

All courses in all disciplines are in English. It is one of the most prestigious universities in Turkey. Faculties offer the undergraduate BS or BA include Arts and Sciences, Economics and Administration, Education, Engineering, Applied Disciplines, and Foreign Languages. Institutes which offer the graduate MA or MS, and PhD include Science and Engineering, Biomedical Engineering, Social Sciences, Kandilli Observatory and Earthquake Research. The University has >50 student clubs, >20 sports teams, and >30 notable alumni. Turkish students must score above 5-5% in the national exams to be admitted. Tuition is $12,000 to $15,000 per student per year. Aykut was studying in year two in Economics and Administration. In a couple of years, the O'Reilly Foundation promised him a fellowship for entering a university of his choice in the USA. So, he planned to go to an American university, probably Harvard University, for advanced studies in international banking.

And Amber would be right there beside him, helping any way necessary.

The four boys, now almost men, had lost their fathers, family members, and friends, to the nanotech killers. Now they had each grown up with a frame of mind to seek some vengeance by preparing themselves in potential collaborative professions for future battles. Just how, where, and when was not yet determined. But at least they would follow Sun Tzu's first edict in the 'Art of War'—

If you know the enemy and, also know yourself,
you need not fear the result of 100 battles.

They would be ready this time.

24

X-X-X-X – X –

THERE WERE FOUR MATURING college boys from one-decade of living together-separately. They had unanimously decided it was important to sit down, face to face, re-examine the past and create some projections for the future. So here they were back in Switzerland where it all began at the International Camp Suisseland. They sat at the new moon semi-circular tables on the balcony overlooking Lake Geneva. This type of dining arrangement simultaneously allowed four people to look at each other as well as view the beautiful navy-blue lake. However, they were concerned about being all together in the same place at the same time. Their recent witchcraft efforts had been successful. So, they were worried about a comeback.

Jamie spoke up, "These past ten years have been scary and unpredictable. When we were having no success at finding any of the nanotech killers, I felt rather safe. Now that we have had some success, I am more concerned. I admit that I do look over my shoulder more often now. How about you guys?"

"From me," said Li, "I continue to practice my Wu Xing. I am pleased that I know some means of self-defense."

Aykut added, "And I also have a little piece of mind because I have my four-legged brother who would kill if anyone attacked me on the street."

And Kef contributed, "I am fortunate to be an athlete who keeps up on his exercise and sports programs. I am confident that I do have a reasonable degree of security from a street type attack."

Jamie looked at the other three, then at himself and said, "I guess I had better buy and carry a gun, or some other type of equalizer. Oh! And I do need to learn how to shoot the darn thing."

And they all looked at each other, laughed, and realized just how paranoid they were becoming.

But Jamie added, "Look, they started all of this by killing our fathers, and a few hundred others. Some have been neutralized, in time the others will disappear from the scene. Just develop an alert status at all times, and do what you think you can to obtain your degree of family revenge. Do not take extra risks."

"Let us finish our education and training towards a functional professional status," said Aykut. "When we are armed and trained with more knowledge in our chosen fields, we can consider more intellectual battles."

Jamie said, 'My area will be international-terrorism law."

Kef said, "My area will be international management and economics."

Li said, "My area will be nanotechnology."

Aykut said, "My area will be international and electronic banking."

And they saluted a high five over the top of the table. When suddenly their food orders arrived, they settled back and prepared to enjoy a good lake fish dinner with their white wine. The first round of wine was gone. They ordered a second round. The double filet of perch and white fish, plus an order of green and red vegetables, little red potatoes, and a fresh hot baget, was just what the doctor ordered.

They did not notice but there was an ordinary looking, very tall businessman sitting on the second balcony. He was closely watching each young man. Apparently satisfied, he finished his wine. Smiled. He stood up and left the restaurant, but forgot his briefcase. His name on the briefcase was Mr. Korrectorizer.

As they began eating, suddenly Jamie straightened up, closed his eyes, opened them, blinked three times. He then nodded to each Musketeer in turn. With his eyes he pointed toward the front door. They each got up, slowly, one at a time, walked to the door, and went outside. Jamie was last.

There were four taxis waiting there. He motioned for each to take a taxi, go to the airport, leave Switzerland now, and go home. Jamie was the last to climb into a taxi and leave the restaurant area when a massive explosion went off inside the restaurant. Jamie had just received a message from the Great King Dagda which said:

OUTDOOR S – 4 TAXI AWAIT 4 PEOPLE

NANO TRILOGY

SYNOPSIS

NANO TRILOGY – II
ANCIENT WITCHOLOGY IN BATTLE

Establishment of an International/American Government Committee of Nanotechnology Control; special recruitment is made from the International Witches Conclave; musketeers train with various witch groups; boys develop their own nanotech molecular systems; their unique cyber hacking methods, information from the Committee, and the witch's magic, herbs and trained wild animals are simultaneously brought into action; boys win most battles.

Printed in the USA
CPSIA information can be obtained
at www.ICGtesting.com
LVHW051918210924
791652LV00019B/270